A Romantic Suspense Novel

Names: Sigfusson, Sandra, Ann

Title: Wild Orchids / Sandra A. Sigfusson

Description: Romance | Suspense

Identifiers: ISBN 978-1-989829-25-7

Subjects: Contemporary Romance – fiction | Suspense - fiction | Travel – fiction | Interpersonal Relationships – fiction | Contemporary Women – fiction | Erotic Romance – fiction |

2nd Edition – Formerly titled Mr. Magnificent (2019)

Book Cover Design: Sandra A. Sigfusson

Cover image iStock ID 2202338882 Credit: Lynn Lawrie

Interior Art iStock Illustration ID: 1377648616

Credit: Ольга Логвиненко

Editor: Michael Dolan - Brooklyn, New York

This novel is intended for mature audiences only.

Meanings of the characters' names:

Liv is a traditional Scandinavian name that comes from the Old Norse *Hlíf*, meaning *protection*. In modern Norwegian, Swedish and Danish it is a homophone with the word *liv*, which means life. The Scandinavian pronunciation of Liv is *leev.*

Cali is a Greek name meaning *most beautiful*; Cali is an Arcadian mythological who transformed into a she-bear, then into the Great Bear constellation.

Daniel is a Hebrew name meaning *God is my judge.*

Jason is also a Greek name, meaning *healing*.

Warning: ***Wild Orchids is a suspense romance which takes place in several destinations, including Central America, Tahiti, London, and Vancouver. Elements of the character's journey will include unlawful capture and confinement, weapons, gunfire, ransom, death, snakes, post-traumatic stress disorder, panic attacks, vehicle accident, graphic language, graphic sex, smoking, alcohol, and nudity. Some readers may find one or more of these elements disturbing.***

TABLE OF CONTENTS:

Contents

Other titles by Sandra A. Sigfusson

Available in Paperback, e-Book, and Audiobook:

The Irishman's Promise (SOVAS Nominated Audiobook)

The Companion

From Bridges to Breakdowns

The Art of Love

The Creative Director – The Heart Never Lies

The Voice From 808

The Playboy Next Door

Rain on a Tin Roof

Tempted – The Erotica Anthology

Paranormal Novelettes:

Keeper of the Dolls & The Bone Gardener

Chapter One | Shopping Therapy

Cali floats into my condo like the effervescent butterfly that she is and stands before me sporting a hot pink boucle miniskirt with a matching cropped blazer. Her heels are at least five inches high and the points on the toe boxes are so sharp she could kill cockroaches in the corners of the room. If I had cockroaches, that is. She takes one look at me and huffs.

"What the hell is the matter with you? It's like," she checks her gold Cartier watch and reports, "Like almost two o'clock in the afternoon. Why are you still in PJs?"

"I'm depressed," I mumble, curling my blanket up tighter to my chest on the couch.

"No, honey. You're not depressed. You're bummed, big difference. Get up and get dressed. I'm taking you out for a late lunch. Or early dinner. Whatever," she declares while gesticulating with her hands on either side of her head.

"I'm not up to it, Cali. Can't you just let me wallow for a day?"

Cali parks herself next to me on the couch, shifts the blanket away from around my feet and smacks my heels with her hands so I'll move them. "Babe, this is not like you. I know you're feeling weird about being divorced, but shit happens to the best of us. I've been through this twice. It sucks ass, but you need to find your vibe and move on."

I sit up straighter on the couch with my back against the armrest. I weave the blanket edge between my fingers as I try to articulate how I'm truly feeling. "Did I let go of the only man I've ever loved for my own selfish needs?" I look over to Cali, and she expresses a loud sigh, then nods.

"Yes." She pulls my feet up over the top of her lap, then rubs my toes between her fingers to massage them. "But hear me out. Wants are selfish. Needs aren't. Needs have to be met. That's why you two were quietly quitting your marriage for the last five years."

She's right. How did I not see this until now?

"What were your options? Cheat on him to get what you need, or divorce and try to find someone else to fulfill you? You did the right thing, Liv."

Cali's massaging of my toes got firmer and firmer until I had to retreat them from her death grip and sharp fingernails. She meant well, but holy hell, I thought she was going to break a few of my toes off. I nod again and resign to her common-sense rant being exactly what I needed to hear. "Okay, you're right. I'll get in the shower. Where do you want to eat?"

"Somewhere close. My fucking feet are killing me in these shoes." I smile and laugh at her. She'll wear anything that makes her look like she stepped off the pages of Vogue magazine, even if it means sacrificing a few toes…like she did mine.

The following morning's sun nearly blinded me through my open deck doors as it popped out past the adjacent condo tower. It would be a shame to draw the curtains when sunlight is so welcome in a city renowned for its rain. And the sun felt cathartic.

I close my eyes, standing before the sliding doors, basking in the warmth, but the ringing of my cell phone abruptly interrupts my contentment. Brushing my hair away from my eyes, I reluctantly attend to the incessant ringing sound coming from my kitchen.

"Hello."

"Liv Beckinsale? This is Alyssa from Clarkson, Davis, and Wright."

"Hi, Alyssa."

"I'm calling to let you know your divorce is finalized," Alyssa says in her typical bright, youthful tone.

I pause briefly, wondering whether sharing this information with such a happy tone in her voice wasn't something the young legal assistant should reconsider. It's nice that she has such a pleasant phone manner, but she couldn't possibly know if this was happy or sad news being shared. In the grand scheme of things, though, I had resigned myself to admitting that it was good news. Cali helped me understand that. I'm the one who instigated the divorce proceedings, and thus I should be happy to hear the process is complete.

"Thank you for letting me know, Alyssa. Have a nice day." As I end the call, a hint of sadness envelops me again. I chide myself for letting my lingering doubts seep in every time I think of Carter. You never imagine a marriage you thought would last a lifetime ends with a phone call from a stranger. When we say our I do's, we don't mean just for now. We are hopeful. Blissfully hopeful that the person we are marrying is *the one*. But times had changed for us over twenty years. And as of today, Carter Beckinsale is no longer my husband.

I put the kettle on the stovetop and sort through the cupboard next to the stove to decide which flavour of tea I desire. And while the water boils, I can make my daily check-in phone call with Cali. Tucking my cellphone between my chin and my right shoulder, I grab a coffee mug and wait for the high-pitched sound of the kettle whistle.

Cali has been my true soulmate since we met in high school. She moved here from California with her family in ninth grade, and we've been inseparable ever since. Her name is Catalina, but we all called her Cali from day one. "Cali?"

"Yes, Liv, good morning… You're not bummed again, are you?"

"No. I got a call from my lawyer's office. The divorce is final."

"Ooh – that's awesome!" Cali says. "The hard part is over and the great beyond beckons you."

"Yes, well, I have just one question before I enter the great beyond," I say, now feeling slightly confused.

"What's that, Liv?"

"Hold on a second. The kettle is boiling, and I can't hear you over the whistling." I pull the kettle off the stove and turn the burner dial to the off position. "Okay. So, now that I'm no longer Mrs. Liv Beckinsale, who the hell am I?"

Cali laughs harder at my question than she probably should have but having been in my shoes a year earlier when she divorced husband number two, she likely understood my minor moment of confusion.

"Well, my artistic side wants to tell you that you can be whomever you want to be, but I don't think that actually answers your question."

"No, it most certainly does not. You're no help there, *buddy*," I reply.

"Sorry, I was trying to lighten your mood. But in case you've forgotten, your maiden name was Nelson, so I'm guessing your new title, same as your old title, is Ms. Liv Nelson," Cali confirms. "Well, if you officially change it back, that is."

"I guess you're right. Why didn't I think of that?"

In her cheeky smug undertone she says, "You always knew I was the smarter one, so I won't tease you about it. I got drunk the first day of being a single woman again. I highly recommend it."

"That's it? That is your sage advice for me? Get drunk? I think I need a new best friend."

"Well, the other option is shopping therapy, but in all honesty, two bottles of wine are cheaper than a bunch of slutty new clothes you'll regret buying four hours after you bring them home."

"Okay, wine it is," I say and sigh. "Am I supposed to drink it all by myself or are you going to join me?" I ask while I tend to the three beautiful Trichophilia orchids in the centre of my kitchen table.

"Oh, I'll be there, Hun. I'll even buy the wine and bring Chinese food!"

"You're the best," I say, smiling to myself. "I take back the comment about needing a new best friend."

"All is forgiven. I'll see you about five-thirty."

I end our call and look out the kitchen window of my fourteenth-floor downtown condo. The sun is still shining, and despite Cali's negative take on shopping therapy, I am very much up for buying some new clothes – slutty or otherwise.

Chapter Two | The Big Four-Oh

Since our daughter Grace has recently graduated from high school and has taken on a position in Carter's landscape supply company as his secretary, she is now well on her way into the real world. Our divorce would be easier for her to understand and deal with after graduation. Grace has always been close to Carter, so I don't need to worry about her if I spend extended time away. I need to set some time aside to talk with Grace so I can understand how our divorce has affected her. This can't have been easy for her either.

I take a deep breath as I reaffirm my decision in my head and my heart. I wasn't his *wife* for so long that I started to refer to him as my roommate, not my husband, and most certainly not my lover. That should have been my first red flag.

With three fully operational branches of Carter Landscape Supplies in full swing, and Carter's dad retired, Carter is busier than a dung beetle in a pigsty. Carter lives and breathes his oversight of a large-scale operation. For many years, it has been his dream to expand beyond what he and his father built. I begrudge his success only because it impacted our relationship, yet in all fairness, I could have tried harder to make him see how his absence was affecting me.

While trying to reassure myself as I trace my fingertips gently over my cheeks, analyzing my reflection in the bathroom mirror, I say, "Forty isn't old anymore." My 'talk out loud to myself' statement was important. I need to stay positive, now more than ever.

I pull myself together, shower, get dressed and apply my makeup, then I sit down at the kitchen table to review my finances with another cup of tea and a box of my favourite chocolates within arm's reach. With my alimony payments from Carter, my half share of the landscape company in a payout, and the agreement to take over sole ownership of the lake house instead of a share of our downtown penthouse, I'll be comfortable financially. Having worked with Carter for twelve years as his stock agent and sales manager, I'm confident in my ability to find work elsewhere if unemployment bores me. But that kind of work isn't what interests me. In my heart, I'm an artist. Although painting watercolours is for pleasure rather than a business endeavour, the thought of one of my paintings hanging in someone else's home appeals to my ego. "Dreams, dreams, and more dreams," I mutter.

For now, I'll use some of my money to enjoy a few holidays to places I'd always wanted to see. I'll take that time away to review the long-term plans for my new future. I'm free now, but once I speak these words aloud to myself, I become nervous about what exactly "free" means to me.

Cali arrives just slightly later than I had expected, but she was rarely on time. She likes to say she invented the phrase "fashionably late" when given the gears over her lack of punctuality. Her hands were full of bags of Chinese food and two bottles of red wine, as promised, when she buzzed my suite from the main entrance.

I admire Cali. She still works in real estate, even though her ex-husband, Garret's settlement with her after their lengthy and bitter divorce was a handsome sum. She loves finding the perfect property for people and is damned good at it. In contrast, my career was given to me – sales and purchasing – not my true calling.

"So, how the hell are you?" Cali asks with sincere concern while unloading her bags onto the kitchen table next to the orchids and leaning into my face to peck on my cheek.

"I'm fine, Cali. Really, I'm fine."

"And what about this condo?" Cali asks. Do you plan to stay here forever or find something else down the road?"

I open one of Cali's bottles of wine and pull out two wine glasses from the glass cabinet. "Carter and I are joint owners on this property. We bought it for our out-of-town guests to use—and as an investment. When I decide to sell, we'll split the profits. As for our other assets, we agreed that he'd sign over the lake house to me instead of me taking money for half the value of the penthouse, which is perfect because I was the only one who ever went there." I pour the red wine into the glasses and hand one to Cali. "And I plan on spending my summers there every year to relax and paint and drink copious amounts of wine on the dock. Speaking of the lake house, it's been too long since you joined me up there."

"I know, Liv. I would love to take next summer off and bum around with you up in lake country. I haven't been on a good wine tour in ages." She sips her wine and then looks through her purse to find her cellphone. "I'm going to put a note in my calendar now to remind me."

I lean my hip against the edge of the countertop. "Perfect. I'm going to the lake for the last two weeks of August next summer to decide how I want to redecorate and then close it down for the fall and winter. This will give me time to devise my makeover plans for the spring." I move to the kitchen table to sit next to Cali and gaze out the window, appreciating the intermittent glow of the late afternoon sun between wafts of clouds reflecting on the other downtown buildings.

I pose a question I've had in the back of my mind for a few days now. "I wanted to talk to you about going on vacation with me, Cali. Not just the lake house. My first trip is going to be to Tahiti. For years, I've yearned to stay in one of those over-water bungalows, and now nothing is holding me back. I'm booking the trip this week, and hopefully by the first week of September, I'll be on a flight there for a two-week getaway." I hold the last of my glass of wine up in the air to decide if I want a refill before we unwrap dinner.

"Seriously? Tahiti? How exotic!" Cali says. "I'm totally in. Find out what dates are available and let me know. I just need to give the office a week's notice. There are enough crew on the team to take over for anything I have in the works. This is going to be amazing, Liv," she says, punctuating the word amazing in a sing-song way. She raises her wine glass to clink hers with mine.

"Yay! I'm so excited. Best divorce present ever!" I say.

Chapter Three | Indulgence

Just after lunch, Cali calls me on her cell asking to take me out on the town for some girl fun at her favourite dance club. It has been several years since she and I partied at a club, and I am hesitant to agree.

"Aren't we a little too old to be clubbing?" I ask.

"We are not too old, Liv. Okay, maybe you're too old, but I sure as shit ain't! Have you looked at yourself in the mirror lately? You look amazing. Put on your sluttiest dress and meet me out front of your place at eight o'clock."

"Eight o'clock is my bedtime," I tease.

"Not anymore, Liv."

At 7:55 pm, I'm standing outside in a low-cut form-fitting red cocktail dress that makes me feel more naked than dressed. I couldn't feel more uncomfortable or awkward. This isn't my jam, but Cali has a way of dragging me out of my comfort zone, and so here I am. All that I can think about is that I haven't chosen the right shoes to go with this dress. And Cali is fashionably late as expected. One of these days I'm going to purposely be ten minutes late and then I won't have to chide her for her tardiness. I glance at my cellphone to check the time: fifteen minutes after eight. I head back inside to the lobby as I feel like I could be mistaken for someone waiting for a downtown drive-by date on a street corner in Vancouver.

Finally, Cali arrives in an Uber—twenty minutes late, and I am none too happy about it. "Why bother telling me you're coming at a specific time when you know you're going to be late, Cali," I say climbing into the back seat.

"Baby, I'm sorry. It wasn't my fault this time, I promise I actually tried to be on time just for you. My Uber driver got a flat tire, so I had to wait to be rescued by a second driver."

"You have the most creative excuses," I huff. "I could have walked to your place twice over in the time it took you to get here."

"Okay, okay, I'm sorry. This isn't how I wanted our night out to start, Liv. Please believe me," Cali pleads. "It isn't my fault."

"Fine. But you're buying the drinks tonight."

"Yes Liv. Now can we *please* forget about the rough start and get into a party mood?"

"Where are you taking me tonight?"

"We'll start at the Sin-Bar on Sinclair Street and if it's a bore, we'll move on."

Cali manages to make wherever she lands the happiest place on earth. Even if a club or restaurant is boring, she'll find some way to make the experience worthwhile. She can turn a boring conversation with anyone into something lively. It is what I like to call the Cali effect, and it never ceases to amaze me and anyone else who knows her.

The music at the Sin-Bar is much better than I anticipated. As we dance to a few songs and drink a few rounds, a couple of guys sitting at the booth behind us are eyeing us up.

I steal a glance over at Cali and see her doing her thing, analyzing the room and the possible male options for a tease session while she wiggles her hips to the beat of the music on her bar stool.

"So?" I ask between sips of my red wine. "What are your thoughts, Cali? Is there anyone here you think worthy of our attention?"

"Yup. Those two," she says, elbowing me and pointing just behind her.

"Are you sure? They look like they haven't been laid in months."

"I've taught you well Grasshopper," Cali says, laughing at me.

"I think they're coming over," I whisper into Cali's ear.

"I know, Liv. I can hear their heavy breathing from forty paces," she says dryly. Cali continues to enjoy the beat of the music, sipping her martini, pretending she doesn't know the booth boys were ready to pounce.

"Excuse me," the blond one says, addressing Cali. He leans on his elbow over the edge of the bar beside her, waiting for her response. "Are you two waiting for someone or can we buy you a drink?"

Cali turns her head just enough to see his face out of the corner of her eye. It is the "I can't believe you interrupted me" face she is also famous for. "Sure, why not," Cali says without looking at him square in the eyes.

I smack Cali on the arm, reminding her that the booth boys were being polite and offering to buy us drinks. "Isn't that what we're here for?" I ask under my breath.

Cali smiles like she is the cat that swallowed the canary. "Easy, girl. Watch and learn," she purrs.

I roll my eyes back into my head and spin myself around on the bar stool to smile at the booth boys. "Ignore her. She's had a rough day and hasn't had enough martinis yet to make up for it."

"Ah, seems legit," the blonde one says and grins. "I'm Paul, and you are?"

"Liv," I say.

"Leave?" he asks. "But I just ordered another beer."

"No, Liv. L-I-V. Pronounced Leev. Everyone has trouble with it. This is Cali," I say, while I reach to shake his hand.

"Nice," he smiles and nods in understanding. "This is Brendan," he says, pointing at his bar mate standing next to me.

"Would you be interested in dancing before buying us drinks?" Cali asks.

"After you," Brendan says and nods.

While Cali and Brendan danced, I took a moment to get to know Paul. He seems sweet. "What kind of work do you do Paul," I ask.

"I'm a heavy-duty mechanic specializing in helicopter maintenance."

I can't hold back my surprise at his unique job. "Wow. That sounds interesting. Did you plan to work in that field, or did you follow in your father's footsteps?"

Paul's smile widens slowly as he leans closer toward me to answer my question. "My father was a mechanic, but he worked on farm machinery for most of his career. You are the first person to say more than 'okay' when I've told a woman what I do for a living."

I nod and raise my glass to clink with his beer bottle. "I'm a woman of many questions," I say and force a one-eyed wink since I'm not good at doing the sexy wink like Cali is. Paul laughs and sips his beer. I think my genuine interest helped him relax, and now we are at ease with each other.

"What do you do?" he asks.

"I am between jobs. It is a long and boring story, but I plan on focusing on my art, painting that is, for the time being."

"Do you sell your paintings? What kind of paintings?"

"Watercolour landscapes, mostly. I don't have a website yet."

"Hmm," he says, then nods approvingly at me. I'm not sure what that means, mind you, having a proper conversation in this loud environment isn't ideal, so we decide to join Cali and Brendan on the dance floor.

We continued to dance, chat and drink with the booth boys for the balance of the night. I never asked how old they were, but they didn't seem to mind hanging with us, even though the age difference was obvious. I thought Cali might take Brendan home with her, but at the last minute, she turned cold, leaving the poor boy wondering what he'd done wrong. I wasn't interested in taking anybody home with me.

This was Cali's idea of a night out to burn off the week of stress. I made that decision long before Cali picked me up in the Uber at eight twenty, and I tried my best not to lead Paul on, including insisting that I pay for my drinks to ensure he didn't get the wrong impression. I was happy to have someone to dance and talk with without worrying about any possible strings attached.

I get an a-ha moment on the way home from the club when I realize that Cali wasn't interested in getting laid by some random guy at a club. She likes to pretend that it's her game, but I know there were only a handful of guys Cali would let slip off her panties to over the years that weren't Jason.

Cali and Jason seem to have the strangest relationship – twenty-year on and off fuck buddies who'd never agreed to be anything more than that, even though they should have been. The only time they stopped was when Cali was married.

I kiss Cali on the cheek as she leaves the cab in front of her condo. "Thanks for the night out, Cali. I can always count on you to put the word party back into my vocabulary," I say, giggling at her.

Cali smiles with one eye struggling to stay open or focused, then waves sloppily back at me. "Goodnight, my lovely Livvy," she says. And then the cab driver whisks me down four blocks back to my condo. Now, all I can think about is how quickly I can get these damned shoes off.

It is the twelfth of August, and I have my bags packed for both the two-week trip up to the lake house and the upcoming vacation in Tahiti with Cali.

Before I head out the door to load my lake house suitcases into my car, I give the orchids on the kitchen table a fresh spritz of water on their leaves and a drink of water in their containers knowing I'll be away for two full weeks. When I reach the lobby, I check my mailbox one last time and find a greeting card without a return address on the envelope.

Opening the envelope, I see that the front of the card has a picture of a bulldog with its tongue hanging out as if to be giving the receiver a raspberry. Inside the words "Good Riddance" are written boldly, followed by the name Josephine. I burst out in a fit of laughter. The card is from my ex-mother-in-law, who has hated me since the day we met.

"Well, good riddance to you too, you insufferable cow!" I blurt out while still laughing. "Oh, if Josephine only knew how much her card had made my day," I say smiling while locking the mailbox and heading to the parking garage.

The drive to the lake house is roughly four hours long, but the scenery is spectacular. I always look forward to the journey. I pick up some groceries and two decorating magazines to peruse for ideas while I enjoy the last days of summer.

My neighbours Karl and June up in lake country are full-time residents and graciously keep an eye out for my property when I'm away. In the back of my mind, it seems such a waste that the house sits unused for three-quarters of the year, but snow and inclement weather isn't my thing.

I'm in my happy place having arrived at the lake in time to enjoy a quick swim in the teal-blue lake water before making lunch. The house is all mine now. Nobody can ever take away my favourite getaway, and I'm excited to make it my own, clear out all the old furniture and buy new pieces, replace the flooring, update the kitchen and bathrooms, and hire a painter to brighten the place up. It has been the same, tired old vacation house for the last fifteen years since me and Carter decided to buy it. The only upgrade we made over that time was adding a garage to store the boat, excess water-skiing equipment, and garden supplies. The house is long overdue for a face lift, and I'm eager to get started.

After my enjoyable swim in the inviting waters off my dock, I quickly dry off and head upstairs to the kitchen to make myself a canned salmon sandwich on rye and pour a nice refreshing cocktail. I settle myself on the spacious deck in the bright warm sun and start flipping through the pages of the decorating magazines, as speedboats zip past in the distance. "If only the weather here was like this all year, I'd never leave," I say aloud and sigh.

Within an hour of my arrival, my neighbours Karl and June wave at me from the front deck of their home. "Hi Liv! So glad to see you. When did you get in?" June inquires excitedly.

"About an hour ago," I reply as I rise from my chair to lean over the deck railing. "I'm here for two weeks, so we'll have to make sure to share a few meals together while I'm here."

"Yes, yes. Are you busy for dinner tonight?" June asks. "We can make an extra plate for you. Are you here alone, or is Grace here too?"

"It's only me here. Grace is working for Carter now at the landscape supply main branch and, well, there's lots of other news I will share with you. What time are you serving dinner?"

"Five-thirty. Karl is going to barbecue steaks. You like your steak medium rare, if I recall?"

"Yes, that's perfect. Can I contribute anything?"

"No, no. Just bring yourself."

"See you then." I raise my drink glass towards June as we part ways.

I've finished my lunch and cocktail and decide to take a quick nap in the lawn chair before dinner with the neighbours, relaxed and dreaming of my upcoming trip to Tahiti.

It is well past four-thirty when I wake from my deck nap. The sky has clouded over a bit, and the sun is dancing between puffs of clouds looking for a spot to highlight the lake in various on-again, off-again intervals. I remove my sunglasses as a warm breeze flows across the deck, gently flipping the pages of one of the decorating magazines one page at a time, as if a ghost were reviewing the articles. I stretch before heading inside to take a quick shower and change my clothes. Not wanting to show up to June and Karl's empty-handed, I grab two bottles of red wine from the cabinet and tuck them into a canvas beach bag along with my cellphone and keys.

June and Karl greet me with big hugs. "So nice to see you both again. How is everyone?" I ask, bursting into a joyful smile.

"We're doing great. You look so trim—have you lost a bit of weight?"

"I'll take the compliment and pretend you don't need new glasses, June," I joke. "No, I haven't lost any weight."

Karl glances over his shoulder toward us. "So, what have you three been up to since last summer?"

"Hmm, where to begin?" I say and smile forcibly. "Well, Grace graduated high school at the end of June – wonderful ceremony. She did very well in her last year with almost straight A's across the board. We are quite proud of her."

"She's a bright one. Tell her we said congratulations," June says.

"I will, thank you. There's some other news that I think I should share with you guys," I add.

"Oh? What's that, Liv?"

"Carter and I are divorced," I say sombrely.

June seems confused. "Oh, I'm so sorry to hear that. What happened between you two? You always seemed so happy."

"We, well we, I don't know what to say, June. We drifted apart and couldn't find our way back."

"How did Grace take the news?"

"Surprisingly well. Maybe she knew what was going on before we did. Carter and I are not bitter with each other, which I'm sure, for Grace, is helpful. Anyway, in the settlement, I got the lake house, and he and Grace will stay in the downtown penthouse. I didn't want to uproot Grace from the only home she's ever known. None of this is her fault."

"Do you plan to remarry, or are you going to wing it for the next while?" Karl asks while flipping the steaks over the flickering flames of the barbecue. I hear the sizzle of the steaks as they are flipped, and my mouth begins to water in anticipation.

"I'm going to travel to far-flung places that Carter never had time to visit with me. I'm going to drink brightly coloured cocktails on white sand beaches, take cruises through the tropics. You know, live the life I want to live while I have the time and the funds to pull it off," I confess.

June pitches her eyebrows high. "Alone?"

"Yes, mostly. Cali is going to join me on a two-week vacation to Tahiti the first week of September, then I'll figure out what my travel plans and timeline are like after that trip. I'm splurging for one of those overwater bungalows. I can't wait!" My excitement can't be contained while I reach for a taco chip from the centre of the deck table.

"Aren't you the least bit nervous about travelling alone?"

"Maybe a little. What's an adventure without a little uncertainty? But," I say while trying to finish chewing the taco chip before replying, "if I stick with tour groups and book my excursions with reputable places, I should be quite safe."

"You're a braver soul than I," June replies.

"I'll be fine, June. You worry too much." I reach for my bag on the floor next to my chair. "Listen, I brought two bottles of red wine to drink with dinner. Let me crack one open and we can sip a glass before

Karl finishes up with the steaks."

Chapter Four | Tahiti

I manage to paint one watercolour on canvas while sitting on the dock and decide I will hang it up over the fireplace once the spring renovations are completed. It feels good to clock back into my creative side, and it only took me a few minutes to get my mojo back. I set my cleaned brushes and paints back inside my paint kit, then stand to view my painting from a few steps back. June yells from her deck, "That's beautiful, Liv!"

I turn and smile at June. "Thank you!" I call back.

The afternoon sun is too hot, so I settle into my living room to read a book. While I find the page where I'd left off, I realize I've had several solid nights' sleep in a row. This place is magical. I feel grounded here like an endemic plant to the region. The peace and quiet, (and the wine) help.

Sadly, my time at the lake has gone by too quickly. I wave goodbye to Karl and June before I crank over the engine of my Jeep and back out of my driveway. As swift as this visit seemed, nothing is stopping me from coming up again in early fall. I'll have to chat with Grace about that, as I'm sure Carter will give her a few days off to spend with me after the busier summer garden season has passed.

Upon returning to my condo in Vancouver, I texted Cali to confirm our flight times for Tahiti. It is all set. In last-minute preparations, I also text Grace a reminder not to forget to go to my condo once a week to check on my plants.

Me: *"Hey, Grace. The blooms are starting to fade now, so give them half a cup of water each and remove the spent blooms as you see them dry out. Thanks, Sweetie."*

I rummage through my refrigerator to see if there is anything I need to eat before it turns mouldy to make sure I don't have any gross surprises in the fridge when I return. I have to laugh at how empty my fridge is. As a newly single person, I find I'm eating out for most meals or having food delivered in cardboard boxes, rather than cooking nearly every night as I have done for twenty years as a mother and wife.

The journey to Tahiti is a long one with two stops—one in San Francisco and a second in Hawaii—before reaching the capital Papeete. Once Cali and I have been guided to our overwater bungalow, the stress of getting here melts away. The scene before us is almost too beautiful to believe. The photographs I'd seen of French Polynesia were dazzling, but to finally see it with my own eyes, I am almost brought to tears. "That's it," I report to Cali. "I'm not leaving until I'm dead."

"Me neither. This is too ridiculous to believe," Cali agreed.

"What do we do now?" I ask, completely dumbfounded.

"Whatever you want, Liv."

"Whatever *you* want," Cali says, dropping her bags at her feet. "This is your glory moment. Don't bother to take off your clothes. Just jump right into the ocean and enjoy."

"That is the best suggestion I've heard all year!" I state, unceremoniously dropping everything in my hands and diving into the translucent teal waters at the edge of the bungalow. Cali smiles and laughs, watching me enjoy this lifelong dream moment.

I yell from the depths of my turquoise paradise, "What the hell are you still doing on the dock, Cali? Get your beautiful ass into this water right this minute!"

"I was admiring how amazing you look in that water, Liv. I'm right behind you, just as soon as I take a picture of that unbelievable smile on your face," Cali calls back. "Okay, picture taken. Move out of the way, my friend, because I'm going in via cannonball!" And with that, Cali takes a running jump off the dock and lands ass first with her hands wrapped firmly around her knees in the crystalline water right next to me. Once she surfaces, she looks at me and the two of us laugh at each other like we were back in ninth grade.

"I love that you decided to come with me, Cali. I don't know what I'd do without you sometimes."

"I'm as happy as you are to be here," Cali says and smiles as she splashes her palm into the surface of the water towards me.

"I'm hankering for a cocktail. Something totally tropical and colourful. You in?"

"You don't have to ask me once!" Cali confirms with a broad smile.

Our first full day in paradise was exactly how I dreamt it would be. In the following days, Cali and I signed up for anything we could. We went parasailing, snorkelling, shopping, hiking, sampled all the local foods, relaxed in the hammocks with cocktails and rode bicycles around the island. After our first full week in paradise, we were exhausted. We decided to trim down our activities and do more relaxing things, like morning walks and photographing the various surreal beaches our toes had the pleasure of touching. At first, Cali found it harder to do nothing than I did, but eventually she resigned herself to just being there, as that was the reason for her agreeing to accompany me on this dream vacation.

"You know, Liv," Cali says over seafood dinner at the edge of the beach. "I think we need to talk more about your divorce. This was a major step for you, and I'm not sure you've come to fully absorb how different being single is going to be."

"Why do you say that?"

"Well, as much as Carter was the easiest guy in the world to divorce, I'm sure there are some things floating around in the back of your mind that you haven't said out loud to me yet," Cali says, staring me eye to eye. "I think you need to let it *all* out, and I'll just sit here and listen."

"Honey, I appreciate your concern, but there is literally nothing to say that hasn't already been said." I set my fork down and dab at the corner of my mouth with my napkin. I lean back into my woven bamboo chair and glance up at her. I shrug, then say, "We lost interest in each other a long time ago—you know that. And it took us way too long to realize we didn't need each other anymore. Now that I've pulled the plug and freed myself from that loveless relationship, I've never felt happier. I should have done this years ago, but I didn't want to upset Grace. And in all truth, I was scared of the consequences of divorce. So, I waited either for our relationship to magically rekindle or for Grace to graduate. She graduated, and I stayed true to my decision. It's not as scary as I first thought it would be."

I lean forward and lay my forearms on the edge of the table. A strong but warm gust of wind whistles through the open-air restaurant and the draped ends of our white tablecloth flutter around our legs. I take a long sip of my tropical cocktail and continue.

"The only challenge now is to figure out what I want to do with myself now that I have no obligations to even cook dinner, let alone show up for work, or pretend I like my mother-in-law." I break out into laughter. "Oh, and you're going to love this!" I say, smiling while setting my cocktail back down on the tabletop. "Josephine sent me a greeting card by snail mail. It said 'Good Riddance' inside, written in huge letters. I laughed so hard at it. That insufferable cow thinks she got the last word," I say, pausing a bit before adding, "But fuck it." I hastily grab my drink and drain it of its contents before my honest feelings are exposed. "She did get the last word, and I hate her even more for that."

I am suddenly overwhelmed with emotions. What's wrong with me? I abruptly stand from the table and run down to the shoreline, while Cali sits speechless across from my empty chair. She chases after me, wrapping her arms around my shoulders from behind and says, "I'm so sorry, honey. I didn't mean to make you cry. Please forgive me."

I fold my arms over hers and force myself to gain control. "Truth be told, I hated Josephine as much as she hated me, and every time we had to share the same air in a room, I dreaded the thought that I was breathing in her exhaled fire breath," I say and sniffle as I wipe the tears off my cheeks. Suddenly, I go from sobbing to uncontrollable laughter. "Fucking dragon lady. I don't know how I kept my mouth shut for twenty years!" I turn to look Cali in the eyes, wiping more tears from my cheeks, and then offer Cali a quick smile. "Do you know what that bitch said to me at our first family Christmas after Carter and I married?"

"No, what?"

"She pulled me aside in the kitchen and said, and I quote, "*I didn't get you a Christmas present. I think allowing you to marry my son is gift enough to last a lifetime.*"

"Oh… my… God!" Cali says as her jaw hangs open, and her eyes grow as large as grapefruits. "That is horrible! How did you not ever tell me this story before?"

"You were gallivanting all over the planet with Jason back then. Oh, it gets better than that. You must remember, Cali, I spent twenty years having that hag try to muscle her way into every nook and cranny of our lives. I finally reciprocated the gift a year later, after Grace was born. Josephine's birthday was two months after Grace's birth, and I didn't buy her a gift. I pulled her aside and said, *I didn't buy you a birthday present because I'm allowing you to spend time with your granddaughter. That is gift enough for a lifetime, don't you think? Also, I named her Grace because you don't have any. You know, power of suggestion and all that.*"

Cali blinks her eyes twice slowly and then covers her gaping mouth with her left hand. "Ha! That my dearest friend, is why you and I are inseparable. I'll bet that every time that hag has to speak Grace's name, she has to recall your comment. You are truly brilliant. Best bitch story ever!" Cali bends over laughing and then high-fives me. "Stay right here, honey. I'm going to go grab some fresh drinks. I'll be right back."

We sit on the sand listening to the water lap up between our toes and the leaves of the palm trees rustle in the breeze, chatting about the good and the bad things in our respective marriages.

"I don't know what I expected, if anything, about my future when we married. We were so young. Delusions of grandeur?" I say, stirring my straw around the bottom of my drink glass.

"Starry-eyed newlyweds," Cali says.

I smile and nod. "Ain't that the truth." As the sun begins its slow sink into the horizon line, we remove our bathing suit cover-up dresses and stroll into the depths of the warm water for one more swim. Our conversation resolved many unanswered questions for me. The answers were there inside of me. Cali helped bring them to the surface.

With just one week left of our dream vacation destination, I decide to shift things up and spend today shooting images of the interiors of whichever buildings we can get inside to view. I plan to use them as inspiration to redecorate the lake house. Cali and I went shopping for artwork and trinkets, then I had the hotel package up my larger purchases into a shipping box to be sent home. My landscape photographs of the island will be an inspiration for a new collection of watercolour paintings. For the rest of the week, we will enjoy seaside massages and the other amenities of the resort.

Tonight is the last evening of our holiday, so Cali and I are attending the nightclub at the resort. We dance with a few guys, but don't flirt intentionally. We know tomorrow is departure day, and we are not sleeping with strangers or getting drunk. In fact, the mocktails from our bartender are equally as delicious as the alcoholic ones.

On the morning of our departure, I enjoy one last swim, floating freely on my back in the soothing waters, letting the warm sun and soft breezes caress my skin. Nothing in my life has ever been as revitalizing as this vacation. I figured out who I am and what I need to do while here. A bucket list item checked off that was worth every expensive penny.

"I'll have to come back again someday," I tell myself. "Someday soon."

Chapter Five | Purging and Parties

As the weeks pass, the West Coast weather becomes quite unpredictable. A mix of rain, sunshine and blasts of cold wind bandy their way through a ten-day stretch, and on some days all three weather patterns floated in and out at random. Typical late fall weather for Vancouver. To bide my time, I find myself doing a lot of cleaning and sorting. I weed out the clothes and shoes I no longer like to wear, box the knick-knacks I no longer find pleasure in, and prepare the lot to be donated to a local charity.

This purging feels good. So much clutter for no reason, and with the weather being so random I'm not interested in going outside unless I have to. As I'm trying on numerous outfits to decide what to donate, I realize that June is right. I had lost a bit of weight recently. I look at my thinner but still shapely body in the bedroom mirror and notice I am losing a bit of muscle tone as well. "I should get back into cycling and swimming," I mutter to myself as I discover my riding gear and swimsuit in the middle drawer of my dresser. I quickly undress and step into my swimsuit and then turn from side to side to inspect myself in the wall mirror. "Well, Liv. Your legs aren't so bad, but your butt is looking a bit saggy." I frown at my ass then take off the suit and redress.

My condo has a gym, even a good-sized pool, so I have no excuse for letting my physical appearance slide. And if I'm going to attempt to date a few men here and there, I may as well give them an ass worth ogling at. I sigh loudly and shake my head. Jesus. Me dating at 40? This is going to be a disaster.

If I'm honest, dating isn't a priority. Instead, I've been considering the upcoming Christmas season and decide to go shopping to get my mind off my saggy ass. Also, my roomier space in my closet isn't going to fill itself!

When I return from shopping, I ponder what Carter, Grace and I are going to do for Christmas Day. Am I going to have Grace at my condo for dinner, or is Carter going to have Grace on Christmas Day? I decided to call Carter and get that conversation out of the way. I'm nervous to hear his voice. Will he rush me because I don't matter anymore, or be the same Carter I was married to a few months ago? I have to stop overthinking how he feels and suck up whatever attitude he throws at me.

My voice is a bit shaky when he answers. "Hi, Carter, how are you?"

"I'm doing okay, Liv. How have you been?"

"I'm okay. A little lonely here in the condo, but that's my own doing, so I guess I shouldn't complain," I say lightheartedly.

A soft chuckle, not intended to insult me, comes from Carter, and then his honesty follows. "I have to admit, Liv, I'm feeling the pinch of your absence as well." There is a small pause before he continues. "I should have made a bigger effort to attend to your needs. I should have spent more time with you, but work is just so demanding."

I nod and look up to the ceiling to quell the tears I know are coming.

"I miss seeing you in the penthouse, even though those moments were fleeting," he says softly.

My heart sinks deep inside my chest. I know it wasn't a loss of love between us, but Carter had become a friend in place of a husband. I yearned for a lover, one who would touch me, kiss me, make unabashed love to me like he used to. I wanted to know where the man I married went. Attempting to redirect this moment of reflection, I go direct to the question I need answered. "Carter, I'm calling to discuss what we should do about Christmas Day. Should we decide whom Grace visits? I mean, do you want Grace on Christmas Day, and I'll have her here for dinner on Christmas Eve?"

"I haven't really thought about it, Liv. I…I don't know. Do we need to separate our Christmas celebrations with Grace? Why can't we just do Christmas together at the penthouse like we've done every year?"

My eyes popped in surprise at his response. I never expected him to be so congenial. "Oh, well, I just assumed you'd want to celebrate without me. But I guess if you aren't worried about us celebrating together, then I suppose that would be fine." I feel a warmth over the phone with Carter that I haven't felt in years from him.

"I think Grace would be happy to have us all together for Christmas Day and dinner, Liv," he says.

"You know I don't hate you, Carter. We are just very different people now than we were twenty years ago. If you want me to come to the penthouse for Christmas celebrations, I'd be delighted to take you up on that offer. Problem solved, then?"

"Yes, problem solved," he agrees.

"Okay, well, that was all I had to ask of you. Enjoy the rest of your day," I say, trying to be upbeat and casual.

"You too, Liv." And with that, my first conversation with my ex-husband is over.

It was only a few short weeks after the divorce before word got out in our chain of friends about Carter and I officially parting ways. A few of our friends have also divorced in recent years as well. When I start to get calls from men well known to me from our mutual acquaintances and friends, it shocks me. Do they think that I'd date a friend's ex-husband? Awkward much? Some calls were just to say they were surprised that Carter and I had called it quits, and others were more forthright, asking if I would be interested in going out for cocktails or dinner. I don't know what to make of their interest. I've been single for all of five minutes. Can a girl not get a minute to breathe?

Of our friends and business connections, there were only two men I would consider dating, and only one of those men are divorced and available. "Would it be too forward to contact him?" I wonder aloud. If I bump into him in a natural way, then I'd feel him out for any possible reciprocated interest.

I am not in a hurry to get full-time involved with another man. A one-night stand wouldn't be out of the question right about now, though. My libido is strong, and self-pleasuring is no longer cutting it for me. There has to be somebody out there that I can trust to be safe whom I can use to get my urges quelled. But who? I pour myself a tall glass of red wine and sit down on the edge of my bed contemplating my future dating scenarios.

No matter what I imagine, likely none of it will ever come to fruition. It's odd what a mind can imagine versus what falls true. I remember my first job interview was over the phone. The man on the other end of the line had a mature, confident voice. I envisioned him wearing a pinstriped suit, vest and all, dark tie, middle aged, and that he had dark hair and a beard. After the phone interview he suggested I come to the office and talk further about the position. Low and behold, the man I thought I was talking to on the phone was nothing like I had envisioned him in my head. He was tall, slender, with blond curly hair, no beard, about mid-thirties in age, and the only thing I had right was the pinstriped vest. I'll never forget how wrong I was about his appearance, and even today I am surprised at the appearance of those I meet whom I've only ever talked to on the phone.

I stand to refill my wine glass and put on some music. I'm more motivated when music is playing. And this mess shouldn't take that long to sort out.

As my Christmas party invitations pour into my email inbox in early November, I gladly accepted all of them. It will be a good time for me to socialize with my friends and business connections, and I'm feeling rather hopeful now that I'm getting into the rhythm of being a single woman. I've spent the past month focusing on my new version of myself, working out every other day in the pool and exercise room in my condo's facilities. The muscle tone in my arms is returning. I'm beginning to see the new me. That's just the physical side. I'm still sorting out who the new me is mentally.

Chapter Six | 'Tis the Season

On December fifteenth, the second of my four Christmas party invitation dates, I dress in a sleek, black, form-fitting sleeveless dress. I added my Tahitian pearl necklace and bracelet along with a white shrug to cover my shoulders. The final touch is a pair of black mule-styled three-inch-high pumps which display a splash of tiny white pearls across the toe boxes. I'll let my hair cascade over her back, which makes me feel like I look more approachable.

Just as I'm slipping on my shoes, my cellphone dings, indicating that my ride has arrived. "Shit. They came quicker than I thought. The app said ten minutes." I hurry to grab my coat and purse, check that I've not forgotten anything else, then rush down to the lobby.

A bitter chill whistles between the buildings on my street. My hair flips in response to the gusts of wind as frosty air exhaled from my mouth at every breath. The air smells of a classic downtown winter evening, complete with the distinct scent of car pollution, as if a truck running on diesel had just driven by. I wave at my driver then slip into the back seat. My legs are still chilled by the brisk wind, but they will warm up soon enough.

Jason is standing in the foyer of his massive penthouse and spots me when his private elevator door opens. Holding his cocktail elegantly in his right hand, he opens his arms to greet me with a gentle embrace, so as not to spill his drink, and a warm kiss on my cheek. Jason is still the fabulous party host he has always been. He's never looked better, even with the grey touches that adorn his deep brown hair and expertly trimmed mustache and goatee.

"How is it that you get more gorgeous with every passing day, Liv?" Jason asks.

"Just lucky I guess," I reply while flipping my hair off my shoulder with a hint of exaggeration. "Are you going to offer me a cocktail, or shall I go into the kitchen and mix it myself?" I give Jason a cheeky grin.

Jason chuckles. "No, no, darling. You, of all people, know that mixing *cock*tails is one of my many hidden talents." He offers me an exaggerated wink, and I laugh. After I hang up my coat Jason grabs my hand to lead me deeper into the mingling crowd of his friends. "I'll be back in two shakes with your drink, Liv."

Jason always surrounds himself with a mix of interesting business people and I recognize a handful of them. I'm happy to know I won't have difficulty entertaining myself. As usual, Cali is fashionably late, leaving me to drink two martinis before she eventually glides into the room like a puff of smoke from a Cuban cigar.

"You're late," I remind her.

"I'm always late, Liv—it's my thing and you can't take it away from me," Cali replies in a cheeky dismissive, I-don't-care kind of way to tease me. She takes the cocktail from my hand to sip it and returns it to me.

"You can get your own drink, you know. They're free," I say as I adjust Cali's pendant earring, which had gotten tangled up in her hair while removing her coat.

"Really? So, this is a fancy shindig? Not one of those cheap ones where you buy your own?" she counters, giggling.

"Well, well. Aren't *you* in a silly mood," I say. "I don't think Jason has spotted you yet. He's over by the sliding doors with Jenni."

Cali heads toward the bar to fetch herself a chilled glass of champagne, then wanders off to mingle with Jason's guests.

As I glance around the room, I straighten my posture slightly and meander past the bar to find Cali chatting up a handsome man whom I've never seen before at one of Jason's parties.

As I move toward them, the stranger takes a quick look at me and smiles beautifully. His smile has a genuine warmth, as if he already knew me and was pleased to see me again.

Cali turns her head to see who her gentleman friend is smiling at and isn't surprised to see it's me.

Cali grabs my arm, drawing me closer. "This is Daniel Wesley," Cali says brightly. "Daniel, this is my dearest friend Liv Nelson."

"Hello," Daniel says as he continues to smile, lowering his head a bit then looking back up at me. That is it. I'm smitten. The look he just gave me melted my heart.

"Hello," I say, offering my hand to shake while my eyes drink in the handsome man before me. Holy *Gentleman's Quarterly*, I think to myself.

Cali giggles. "Ooh, look at my empty glass. That won't do at all." She winks at me then slips herself over to the bar for a refill.

There is a tension between Daniel and I now that we are left alone together. Mine is sexual, but his is not as abundantly clear. "And how do you know Jason?" I ask, finally, breaking the momentary silence.

"Oh, well, Jason and I have known each other for several years. I've worked with him on international banking transactions, and I've recently moved here to Vancouver from London."

My body tingles with delight at the subtle ruggedness of Daniel's features. His eyes are an incredible shade of blue and when I notice them, I can't look away. He has olive toned skin and rich dark hair which reminds me of Ethan Baker—the captain of our high school rugby team that every girl wanted to date. But the clincher for me is his voice. If melted dark chocolate had a voice, his would be it—rich, velvety and sensual.

I chase myself out of my reverie and say, "London. I've always wanted to see London." I smile, showing interest. But my interest isn't on the topic of visiting London. I give my brain an imaginary shake and shift the dirty martini in my left hand over to my right. His English accent is delicious, and I feel like I'm in an alternate version of *Bridget Jones's Diary* just waiting for myself to do or say something stupid. In a nervous reaction I shift my weight from my left hip to my right hip and sip from my glass.

"The photographs don't do it justice. It is much dirtier than it looks in photos." Daniel chuckles lightly, and then that beautiful warm smile of his reappears.

"Most big cities are dirty, I find." My responses to these early stages of introduction are polite and mechanical, in an attempt to hide the fact that I'm dying to know much more about Daniel. "And why did you move from London to Vancouver? Is it a work move or a personal choice?" The word *dirty* made my stomach flip – especially the way he said it. I've already consumed three *dirty* martinis and now this beautiful stranger was unceremoniously making me think dirty things.

"Work, with Jason," he says, while his dark blue eyes stayed transfixed on mine. Or maybe I'm imagining him being transfixed on me. I try not to be too obvious as I study his features, painting a watercolour portrait of him in my mind. It would be a glorious challenge to paint his eyes. How could I replicate such warmth and depth? I ask myself. They are large and almond-shaped, holding an appeal that is soulful, kind and that he knows something about me that I have not yet discovered. I internally chide myself for staring and shift my weight over to the other hip again.

Cali pops back to check on us. She looks at me, then at Daniel and back at me again and says, "Apparently, you two don't need a third wheel. I'll check in on you both later." She moves back a few steps and turns to look out at the view of the city lights through the large living room windows, slowly wandering off to let me and Daniel get better acquainted without her interrupting the flow. My eyes follow her as she leaves us. This feels suspiciously like a setup. From the corner of my eye, I can see her watching our reflections in the massive window as the two of us continue to make idle chit-chat about where we lived and what we do with our time.

It is two hours later when Cali has finished making her loop through the guests at the party. The Cali Effect is in full swing as she mingles, being highly social, intelligent, and accommodating—perfectly suited for sales in real estate, which explains why she is so successful. As she circles back to me and Daniel on the couch, she quietly sits down next to me and places her wine glass on the table.

"I see you two are getting along famously. I'm so happy you've made a new friend, Liv," Cali laughs, flashing her beautiful smile at us.

I knew she was setting us up.

Daniel smiles at me and then at Cali. "Your friend is quite entertaining, Cali. If she'll stay sat here and chat with me, I'll not move from this spot."

"Liv, is it okay if I steal you away from Daniel for a minute? I need your help with something." Cali looks at Daniel and says, "I promise to bring her back in a few minutes."

I follow Cali into the powder room and close the door behind us. "Is something wrong?" I'm looking at Cali worriedly.

Cali lets out a little giggle. "I want to know how it's going between you two," she whispers.

"How many drinks have you had? Maybe you should slow it down a little," I suggest.

She waves her hand in front of her face as if to erase that comment then sits on the toilet lid and crosses her legs. "No, I'm fine. What do you think of Daniel?"

"He's amazing. He's gorgeous. Do guys like him actually exist or am I only imagining it? Is that what you want to hear, my sex-crazed chum?" I punch Cali lightly below her shoulder then turn to look at myself in the mirror.

"Okay, well then, carry on!" Cali says as she rises to pull down her undergarments and decides to relieve herself since she's in a bathroom.

"Wait, wait, wait. Is this an intentional hookup, Cali?" I ask, while her tinkling is making me want to relieve myself as well.

"Yes, it is." She reaches to unravel a wad of toilet paper and giggles again. "My powers of connection are still strong. I knew you and Daniel would be fast friends the moment I met him a few years ago."

"You know Daniel well enough to trust him?"

"Yeah. Of course."

"How much do you know about him?"

Cali redresses and flushes the toilet. "Look. You trust me, right? Just enjoy his company. I'll fill you in about him later."

I agree but wonder if there's a bigger story surrounding his move here. Regardless, Cali has sixth sense about people that defies explanation. I trust her without question.

I return to Daniel's side on the couch. Another two hours pass like it were mere minutes as we are wrapped up in our own little world of conversation and laughs. I'm so taken with him, and we cannot keep our eyes off each other.

Cali returns to check on us once again, a little tipsier than she was earlier, and Daniel says to her. "I was just offering to give Liv a lift home when she's ready. Do you need a lift home as well?"

Cali looks at him with a funny grin on her face. "Oh, it is entirely too early for this party girl to go home. No, no, you two decide when you want to head out, and I will find my own way home," she says, as she tucks her hair behind her shoulder. "I'm only a few blocks from here anyway. I'll get Jason to walk me home after his last guests are gone." Cali grins at us as she readies to sip the last of the cocktail in her hand, then slips out of our conversation and heads back to see where Jason has wandered off to.

I've lost count of how many cocktails I've sipped, having been enthralled with Daniel's accounts of his life and business dealings in London and Madrid. But now the only thing going through my mind was how to artfully suggest that Daniel come up to my condo for a nightcap after he's driven me home.

I've never asked a man to come home with me before. This is brand new territory for me as a woman who's been married since before my twentieth birthday. I'm terrified of the concept of being so forward with a man, least of all one I'd known for only four hours. Weird and random thoughts race through my head. Would he even want to have sex with me? Would he have a condom in his wallet? What would happen if we did have sex? Would he leave or spend the night? I started to feel a flush of dewy sweat bead along my spine at the prospect of taking this deliciously perfect stranger to my bedroom. This desire was overpowering my logical mind – the one that kept telling my I'm crazy and probably more drunk than I should have let myself get.

"Did you hear what I just said, Liv?" Daniel asks.

"No, sorry. I must have zoned out there for a moment, my apologies," I say, touching the top of his hand. It was in that moment that I felt a warmth course through me. His hand was strong and his skin soft and warm to the touch. He placed his other hand over mine and a sexy grin tugged at his lips. My face flushed at his touch.

"That's okay. What I said was, it's getting late, and I wondered if you were ready to go home for the night?" He looks contentedly into my eyes, like he is waiting for me to somehow confirm I am also feeling as attracted to him as he appears to be with me.

"Yes, I'm ready to go home if you are." Slipping my hand slowly away from his, I reach for my shrug draped over the edge of the couch behind me and slip it loosely over my shoulders. When I turn my back to him, he carefully adjusts my shrug, causing me to look over my shoulder and thank him.

"And where am I taking you?"

Daniel let me lead the way out into the foyer before I wave goodbye to a few people and Daniel retrieves our coats.

"It's not that far from here. Cali and I both have condos downtown, just a few blocks from Jason's."

"I'll text my driver and have him meet us out front," Daniel replies as he pulls his phone from his breast pocket.

I am flush with nervousness. Moments earlier I was desperate to jump on Daniel's lap and start kissing him feverishly while we sat on the couch. Then when he suggested taking me home, I wasn't sure that once I got into a car with him, I'd be able to contain my ever-increasing sexual desires. I also knew that the alcohol coursing through my veins was not helping me to make the most logical decisions. I'm way past logic. I'm as aroused as a hormonal teenager.

Chapter Seven | This Kiss

Once we enter his vehicle, I muster up the courage to ask Daniel if he is interested in coming upstairs with me for a little while to continue our conversation. I'm gazing out the window when I pose the question, hoping that my expression won't give away how desperate I've become to have mad, feverish, unadulterated sex with this delicious man.

When I turn away from the window to look at him, side by side in the back of his chauffeured car, his lips are mere inches from mine. He is patient as he waits for my eyes to say it is okay to kiss me. Daniel smiles warmly. He reaches for my hand and says, "I'd be happy to keep you company for as long as you'd like."

I'm so close to him I can hear his breathing, smell his subtle cologne and feel the light squeeze of his hand wrapped around mine. I close my eyes and lean in for his kiss without hesitation, and I savour every second of his lips on mine.

I'm not the type of person who hooks up with the first guy that shows me some attention. As much as I'm stepping out of my comfort zone, I also know I'm bolder by way of alcohol. I had questioned this moment while looking out the window moments before. Is this the pickup trick I've fallen for? Get the girl drunk, tell her she's pretty or interesting and then hope like hell she'll let you fuck her? I don't care. I need someone to make me feel special. Even if it's just for tonight.

Our lips touch in a soft and gentle, exploratory way, and for a moment I forget who I am—where I am. This was the first time in many years that I'd passionately kissed a man, and it is proving to be well worth the wait. His kiss is glorious, a tease, a taste that left me wanting more. Much more. I want to know what his lips would feel like on the edge of my shoulder or teasing my nipples or pressing against any other part of my hungry body. I await another kiss immediately, but he hesitates.

Daniel's eyes dart to his left, snapping a glimpse to the front seat, where his driver can see every private moment between us reflected in the rear-view mirror. I sense that this is not what Daniel wants—an observer. I understand now. He is hesitant to continue kissing me while we ride in the car because he yearns for privacy. As do I. Another layer of his personality unveils itself in the silence of this intimate space. I tip my head down, touch my lips with my fingertips, then adjust my white shrug under my coat around my shoulder and gaze out into the traffic on the street.

As he tenderly squeezes my hand again, a smile grows larger on my face with the hope that his incredible kiss is an introduction to other things he is just as amazing at.

As he continues to clasp my hand in his, thoughts of what could happen when we reach my condo fumble precariously into my mind like tumbleweeds on an open western plain. Would I make the first move, or would Daniel take the lead like he had a moment earlier by intentionally tempting me into that beautiful kiss? God, how I wanted another kiss. My body aches for his touch while my internal temperature rises. His desire to give me what I so desperately need—genuine affection—was the undeniable emotion I felt in our kiss.

Chapter Eight | Feast After Famine

Our car reaches the front of my building within five minutes of our lips tenderly meeting for the first time. Daniel's driver opens my door for me to exit, extending his hand to be sure I am steady on my feet, and Daniel slides across the seat to exit behind me.

He tells his driver to go home for the night. "I'll take a cab home from here," he says, and his driver replies, "Sure, Mr. Wesley."

As we ride up in the elevator to my fourteenth-floor condo, I stand quietly holding my handbag with both hands in front of me, glancing briefly over at Daniel. What am I doing? I ask myself as my nerves begin to shake my confidence.

He adjusts his hold on the overcoat on his arm and reaches to touch my hand. I can't contain my smile then laugh lightly, nervously. Daniel reciprocates the laugh, then we both relax when the elevator door opens at my floor. I fumble inside my purse for my keys at my suite door as Daniel stands behind me, resting his hand upon my shoulder. He traces his fingers across my back to move my long hair away from the nape of my neck. Leaning down, he presses the skin just behind my ear with his warm lips in the gentlest of kisses. And there it is again. The scent of his subtle cologne teasing my senses and sending shivers of yearning down my spine. The door lock makes its distinctive click as it releases and the sound echoes down the empty corridor.

A flush of goosebumps run down my arms as the door opens. I promptly drop my coat, shrug and handbag to the floor, turn around and dive straight into kissing Daniel as he closes the door behind him. Nothing else matters to me in this moment. The only thing I want is to take this beautiful man into my bedroom and let him have all of me in any way he wants.

There are no more prying eyes now. The rush of excitement, the fear of making a mistake or saying something stupid in the heat of the moment clouds my mind while I sink every ounce of my sexual energy into his lips. I fear I'm behaving desperate.

Daniel stands with me for several minutes in the foyer of my suite, holding me and kissing me with a gentleness I'd never experienced before. It is so incredibly romantic and arousing to have this tenderness and passion bestowed upon me in a mature way. A sensation of light throbbing between my legs reminds me how incredibly turned on I am. He presses my body harder against his as the kissing becomes more intense, and I can feel his erection pressing into my abdomen. It thrills me to know I am wanted like this.

I pause to gather a deep breath. I touch around the edge of his chin with my fingers and gaze into his eyes before reaching for his hand, leading him through my suite towards my bedroom. We'd not exchanged a single word in the last ten minutes. Entering my building, waiting for the elevator, the ride up sharing only a light laugh, the walk down the corridor to my suite, and the kissing in my foyer were all done without words. But we didn't need words to understand what we want from each other—what I need from him. Words would only have muddied the anticipation and the thrill of not knowing how far either of us are willing to go tonight.

Without a second thought I lead him through my bedroom door, where the light from my kitchen offers a subtle glow that is the perfect amount of illumination. Not to bright, and not too dark to see each other.

He asks, "Are you sure this is what you want?"

"Yes. Oh, right. We have to ask permission now."

He chuckles. "Yes. My God, you have been out of the dating world for a long time."

"Shut up and kiss me."

The following moments of touching and teasing are measured and purposeful. The slow undressing of each other, the audible breaths we each exhale, the gentle trace of his fingers over my skin after another piece of clothing falls to the floor at our feet, are the beginnings of something truly beautiful to follow. My trust level is undeniable as we search longingly into each other's eyes, letting the experience unfold between us with such ease and grace.

I delight in this beautiful tenderness. My ears tune in on his deep masculine breaths, a moan of anticipated pleasure, the light clicking sound of his lips leaving mine for brief seconds before another kiss arrives at my waiting mouth, neck and shoulders. And once we were standing in front of each other completely disrobed, ready to engage more deeply with each other, Daniel traces the tips of his fingers down the length of my arms as he absorbs my naked form in the soft light with his eyes. Another rush of shivers rides the length of my spine and bring my nipples to full attention.

He caresses my breasts, teases my nipples with his fingers and cups his hands around the fullness of them, kneading gently while his tongue searches for mine inside my mouth again. My hand drifts downward from around his back, reaching for his cock. I feel the hot fullness of him within the palm of my hand, stroking his length and teasing his crown. I'm amazed at his size. Have I forgotten what an average sized cock feels like, or is he a remarkably endowed man? For a moment I worry he'll be too big for me to handle.

"You have skilled hands," he says, finally breaking the silence with his velvety-timbred voice. "Talk to me," he urges. "Tell me what I need to do to make you happy."

His words echo back to me inside my head as if I needed to repeat them before I'd believe he asked *me* what I wanted. I step backward slowly to sit on the edge of my bed, and he follows. I ease myself back deeper into the centre of the bed, reaffirming my surprise by how impressive his cock is. I shift my eyes up to meet his and we lock on to each other's gaze.

"I'm ready for anything," I manage to say in a quieter breathy voice. "I haven't made love to anyone in almost five years. I'm certain whatever you have in mind will be perfect."

It is obvious from the expression on his face that those were not the words he'd ever expected me to say. I could be lying for effect, but I think my honesty is perhaps a bit disarming. Daniel's eyes widen.

"How could someone as divine as you be celibate for so long?"

"It doesn't matter now," I whisper, trying not to break the moment with my back story.

Daniel moves forward, crawling over my body and I lean back into the mattress. He grasps both of my wrists to stretch out my arms on either side of my head. I've given him a dare to make his pleasuring of me something that I'll never forget. He stares directly into my eyes and smiles before dropping yet another tender kiss on my lips.

"Your words challenge me. I promise to treat you with the utmost respect." He lowers his face to suckle my right nipple to make it more erect. "I'm going to make you come for me, and I want it to be so spectacular that you'll be begging me to do it again," he says in a deeper affirmative tone.

I'm regretting drinking so much now. I want to be as sober as possible to appreciate where I am in this moment. But I'll take him, all of him, regardless of my state of mind. "Yes," I say, and then let my eyelids close slowly as he reaches between my legs with his fingertips.

Gently, he slips his thumb inside of me to tease and explore me. I'm wet, ready, and he is anxious to make good on his promise. He traces the length of my body with the tip of his nose, breathing in the scent of my skin from my breastbone down to my lower abdomen, kissing me just above my pubic bone while his right hand continues to bring me mounting gratification from within.

Daniel now has his tongue flicking rapidly over my clit while slipping his hands under my hips to lift me up higher. His movements continue to be slow and meaningful, and the anticipation brings me to an elevated arousal. I reach for the top of Daniel's head, threading my fingers through his soft hair as he continues flicking gently and rapidly, bringing this indulgence to a level I'd hadn't reached in many years. He's now sucking on my clit. It makes my eyes roll back inside my head. "Yes," I say just loud enough for him to hear. "That feels too good to be real," I say, my voice now pitched higher and louder.

What is this magic? I ask myself. What is it that Daniel instinctively knows about my body that I had never discovered myself? In the moment before I climax from his talented tongue and lips, I hold my breath as I squeeze my thighs tight and then come for him.

He smiles as he lowers my bent knees and crawls back up to stare into my eyes. I reach for him, wanting to hold his massive firmness in my hands now more than ever before. "I want you inside of me. Now," I beg while I stroke the length of him within my right hand. "Now, Daniel, please." I'm impatiently guiding him near my entrance as I try to catch my breath, letting him slide in deep with his first thrust.

I relish how he fills me, moving so beautifully, slowly, and repeatedly rocking my body with each press. He watches me as I moan, and I love that he wants to see me in my erotic state. This is all for my sake. My confession of how long I'd been untouched moved him. I feel his compassion for my need in his eyes, and he understands this is more to me than a drunken one-night stand.

I matter.

Why, I can't say, but *my* pleasure matters to this beautiful stranger. I close my eyes when he starts to pulse deeper and firmer. I should have told him I wanted him to press in hard, slowly retract and slam back inside of me but the opportunity escaped me in my feverish desire.

Five years, I told him. Point stated and taken. He has erased the last five years in a single tryst. My audible breaths, moans and mews seem to have heightened his pleasure within me, and he arrives just moments later.

Daniel laid his weight upon me, briefly resting his head next to mine, exhaling his warm breaths like a series of pulsed whispers into my ear. I sweep my left hand up and down the ripples of his spine as we both relax. He has such a strong impressive body. He feels unbreakable. Invincible even.

After a minute, Daniel rolls onto his side, and I do the same to face him, to touch his face and continue to enjoy the nurturing look in his eyes. The kisses with which he adorns my eager mouth unequivocally cement that compassion. He didn't come here to fuck me. We made love.

A subtle smile emerges upon Daniel's face as he gazes at me now. "Do you prefer to close your eyes when you make love?" he asks.

"Do you always keep yours open?" I counter, smiling.

"I enjoyed watching you experience pleasure. It turns me on," he adds, and he flashes his eyes wide for me.

I laugh. "Are you saying I have a bad poker face?" "Yes. It's the best bad poker face I've ever seen. I love it!" He leans back and laughs with me.

Daniel settles back on his side and places his face nose-to-nose with mine. I touch the pad of my thumb to the centre of Daniel's lower lip. "You were right. I *am* going to beg you. Please do that to me again."

"Mm, I see. How badly do you want it?" he asks as he weaves his fingers into mine.

"So badly." I smile and then climb atop his body. He threads his fingers behind his head, curious to what I have planned.

"I'll admit to enjoying your playfulness and cheeky thoughts. Tell me," He says before clearing his throat, "Where precisely have you been all my life?"

"Is that a rhetorical question or do you want to butter up my heart before you disappear into the wild?"

"Not rhetorical at all, I promise," he says in a more serious tone.

"I'm sorry. I'm skeptical of this connection between us. You are the first man I've had in forever."

"I know. No need to dwell on the past. Be here and now, Liv." His eyes search mine for an answer to his question.

I flip my hair away from my eyes and look up at the ceiling before answering. "Lost. Until today when I found you. But I'll bet you ask that from all the girls who share the pleasure of your company," I tease and smile.

"No," he whispers. "Only you." Daniel releases his hands from behind his head and cups his palms around the back of mine to draw me in to kiss him.

I believe he is telling me the truth, and if he has lied to appease me, he was damned good at that too.

I'm in awe of him, his toned stature, his tongue, his lips, his cock, his everything. I drink in the man I have in my sight in this soft glow of light.

With my knees bent and thighs straddled over his torso I let out a long breath then whisper, "I'm going to be so incredibly pissed if I wake up and discover this was a dream."

I slide my legs down to his thighs and lean down to place my lips over the crown of his cock. Just as he had done for me, I want to explore all of him, starting with his most impressive appendage. He watches wide-eyed as I close my eyes, taking as much of him in my mouth as I can. Perhaps it's too soon for me to expect him to get hard again but I'm willing to give it a try. Having never experienced a man as well-endowed as Daniel, this is a challenge I am willing to attempt.

"That's fucking brilliant," he says.

I open my eyes to witness how much he's enjoying this and I'm not disappointed by the expression on his face. His half-hooded eyes and parted lips encourage me.

"That's it, Liv. Christ, that feels good."

I continue to make the most of what I'm doing with my hands and lips and tongue. I try to recall what I'd seen in the silly porn movies that Cali and I rented for laughs from time to time when we couldn't agree on what mainstream film to watch on TV. Hell, we even watched lesbian porn on my laptop out of sheer curiosity since most porn movies focus on the guy getting off instead of the girl. I try not to laugh at those memories and stay focused on satisfying Daniel.

As his cock slowly grows firmer with my teasing, I hear him state firmly, "I want to come inside of you again, Liv." And with that his hands grip my hips moving my body up to straddle his cock. He needs to watch me ride him, and I oblige without hesitation.

"You are a brave woman," he jests to me as I try to take the full length of him inside me from this position.

I'm moving slowly over him, adjusting myself as I go, feeling the deep penetration. He's so far inside me, I'm hitting a pleasure center I thought I'd never feel. I believe I've found the elusive A-spot it in this position, back near my cervix and as much as it's gratifying, I don't think it will be the reason I come. Still, I don't know that I've ever been so aroused as I am now.

Daniel's soothing voice breaks my thoughts. "No other has tried as skillfully as you to take in all of me."

"Your magnificence has its price, I suppose," I say and quirk a grin.

I realize now that my laboured mouth breathing is louder than I imagined in the otherwise quiet space of my condo. "I thought I'd give it my best effort," I say being cheeky. The truth is I'm fascinated by this whole experience. Am I out of my comfort zone? Yes. And it is exhilarating.

I can't break my rhythm now. We are a wave that has been slowly building over the vastness of the ocean. Daniel's warm broad hands squeeze tighter over my thighs. He's about to give in. I close my eyes and increase my rhythm over him in the hope that we reach our orgasms in unison. Pace, timing, connection—all these things make lovemaking beautiful. Coming together would be like the riotous foam display after the wave breaks. Tension and glorious release.

It happens. We both reach our climax within seconds of each other. I know it is uncommon, but *everything* aligned with us tonight. Our intellectual connection, unbridled spontaneous passion, and our desire to give our all to each other in a loving way.

Once we'd calmed from our second round Daniel says, "How was that for you?"

I hesitate to answer because I'vc never been asked that before. Is this a Brit thing, or does he really care if I am satisfied? I nod instead of answering verbally. He pulls me down to his chest, kissing me hard and passionately. When we stop to take a deep breath and relax before he says, "Again, I *must* ask where you've been hiding."

I laugh at him and can't help but blush now. "It probably wouldn't surprise you to know that Cali is an expert at fellatio, and she's filled me in on a few tricks over the years."

"God bless," Daniel says and laughs. "I must remember to thank her."

"Don't you dare, Daniel! I'll never hear the end of it from her," I warn with eyes wide. "This moment feels like a déjà vu or something," I say, "I'm so comfortable with you and I don't know how to explain it."

I wanted to ask him so many questions now, but I doubt if talking seriously so quickly after drunk lovemaking twice would be appropriate. I knew just enough about Daniel to know I wanted him to make love to me, again and again and again – but not enough to know if he is relationship material.

Is this a booty call to him as well, or could he be interested in me for much more than this? And dammit all to hell if Daniel didn't feel like the man I'd want in my bed every night for the rest of my life.

The deeper question is will I still feel this way about him in the morning when I am completely sober? Is what we shared this amazing because I'm still a little drunk, or is sex supposed to be this fulfilling? And how the hell did his monster cock fit inside me? I try to rest my internal inquisitive mind and focus on what is right in front of me now. Out of seemingly nowhere, I open up to Daniel in a way I hadn't intended.

"When Carter and I were young, our lovemaking was fantastic. We were feverish, playful, and the world around us ceased to exist for that slice of time. And those memories stick with me because I desperately want them back. I want what I had just now with you in *this* slice of time to be with Carter, not a random stranger I picked up at a Christmas party. I mean," shit, that was rude." I sigh after that harsh last comment and try to quickly make amends. "I, I didn't mean that the way it came out."

I want to cry, but those tears will be wasted on a past I'll never get back. I'm nervous. Did I insult him?

"I'm sorry, Daniel. Forgive me, please." I try to rise from within our rumpled sheets but Daniel's hand on my shoulder stops me.

"Your honesty, albeit a tad brutal, is refreshing. Don't ever feel like you need to hide your thoughts from me, Liv."

I nod then lean over to kiss him. "Thank you. And thank you for this." My gaze lands softly on his eyes. He has no idea how attractive I find him on so many levels. It's not simply a matter of appearance that makes him so special. He's smart, kind, gentle, interesting, funny, and I'm still losing myself in his eyes when I look at him.

I wrap the edges of my duvet cover over my hips, and he follows suit, pulling the sheet from the other side of the bed to cover us. As we rest, spooned together within the covers, his kisses upon my shoulder gently fade, my eyes close, and we fall blissfully asleep.

Chapter Nine | Showered with Love

As the sun begins to rise at seven-twenty in the morning, I awaken to the sound of my shower running from within my ensuite. Daniel has risen before me and taken this quiet time to shower. I wonder if he intended to dress and leave while I sleep, or if he will linger until I get up. Instead of lying there questioning his possible motives, I get up and slip on my silk housecoat, then quietly pad my way into my bathroom to let Daniel know I'm awake.

"Did you sleep well?" I ask after I enter the ensuite.

Daniel turns his body to see me standing next to my glass shower, leaning my hip against the vanity counter with my hands nested deep inside my silk housecoat pockets. He smiles as he draws his palms over his face to remove the water away from his eyes. "Are you interested in joining me in the shower, or would you rather gaze upon my magnificence from the edge of the vanity?" he asks, then chuckles.

I grin at his comment, knowing full well that he did not think of himself as magnificent, although I did use that word to describe him last night.

"I would very much like to join you," I say, as I slowly untie my housecoat, letting it slip off my shoulders and fall to the tile floor. Daniel's eyes widen at the sight of my body revealed in the brighter light of the bathroom. I open the glass shower door and step inside next to Mr. Magnificent. He smiles broadly and opens his arms to hold me next to his warm wet chest. He adjusts the shower head to make the water cascade over my back and then draws his fingers across my forehead to push away my hair from my eyes. Such a gentle touch. I'm immediately aroused.

This is a man who understands how to touch a woman, and it baffles me as to how he could possibly be single. Or is he single? I never asked Daniel if he was married, divorced, never married, bisexual or an outright playboy like Jason had become in the last few years. Again, the questions I have unanswered from last night fill my mind, and I have to bite my tongue to prevent myself from speaking words that would dampen this wonderful shower experience.

Waiting in anticipation, I hope Daniel will take my advance into his shower time as a signal that I want him to make love to me again. He tucks his forefinger under my chin and guides my face up to meet his. "Are we agreeing to an extension of last night?" he asks softly with a cautious smile.

I nod my head and then rise up on my toes to kiss him.

Daniel places his palms around my neck with his thumbs at the edges of my jaw, caressing my face, continuing to kiss me tenderly while pressing his firm body against mine. He lifts me up into his arms and I wrap my legs around his hips. He presses my back snug into the corner of the shower walls, then guides himself into me, slowly driving himself deeper and deeper inside of me. He tries not to press too far for fear of hurting me, but I have no complaints. My kisses are near ravenous in nature, and he reciprocates with fervor. His pleasure of moving in and out of me lasts much longer this time, and he seems even fuller and firmer than he did when we made love last night in my bed. Perhaps it is the position, or that neither of us is drunk that I notice this.

When he reaches his climax, he squeezes me tighter within his arms and tips his head back in reaction to his gratifying orgasm. There is a strange power in knowing I have satisfied his need to have me yet again. I imagine it is my fragile ego that is being stroked by this mini power trip. I rest my head on Daniel's shoulder and shudder, realizing that even though I didn't reach an orgasm, I loved every second he was inside of me.

He continues to hold me strong, and I close my eyes to fully absorb this pleasure-filled moment of incredible intimacy. I lift my head and look him square in the eyes. We stare in wonder at each other as our laboured breathing slowly subsides. I release my legs from around his hips and slip down to reach the floor with my toes. Resting my head upon his chest, stroking my hands over his shoulders and around his neck I notice he is tight, fit, but not overtly muscular like a bodybuilder. We stand together for a few minutes, showering in the warmth of our bodies while the water cascades across my shoulders.

I reach for the bar of soap and start to wash his chest, circling the soap over his pectoral muscles while I fully explore his form with my eyes in the daylight. I know he's already washed himself, but I need to touch him for a bit longer. I need my curiosity sated in a way I did not attempt last night. Is there a scar somewhere that has a story behind it? A birthmark on his butt cheek? My curiosity gets the best of me, but I don't ask him to reveal his secrets. This is my treasure hunt.

He is everything I imagined he'd be under that expensive suit he was wearing at the party. God he is glorious.

A subtle grin forms across Daniel's lips as he takes the soap bar from my hand and reciprocates by washing my body. He guides his soap-covered fingers slowly over my breasts and up around my neck and shoulders, then moves his hands down and around to the small of my back. His smooth touch gliding over my body feels heavenly. The tender connection – the sensation of being loved – washes over me like the steamy water spilling over our bodies.

I think he senses that the touching, the embraces and the tender kisses are what I want most from him. I openly traded my body for his tenderness last night and this morning and wonder if he knows I am more fragile emotionally than I let on publicly.

Daniel moves his right hand around the shape of my hip and slips his fingers into the edge of my vagina to pleasure me. I inhale deeply at his move, waiting in anticipation for his fingers to bring the same magic his tongue had just hours before. He does not disappoint. I feel so safe in his hands, feeling as though I've known him for eternity.

I did not wake to him being a dream. He's real.

Daniel's obvious experience at pleasuring a woman is as welcome now as it was last night. His history before me is irrelevant; I only care that he is with me.

I am quickly and easily satisfied by his fingering. He loves watching my face while I react to what he is doing for me, and it turns him on to know I am enjoying this. I reach a deep and exhilarating orgasm, and he is as pleased as I am to know I have been so splendidly satisfied. I shudder again and he asks, "Are you cold?"

"No," I say as my arms encircle his waist. "I couldn't be more comfortable."

He places a kiss on my forehead and gives me another long warm embrace before he says, "I'm going to step out and dry off. Are you going to shower for a bit longer, or can I get you a towel as well?"

I fumble for words inside my crowded mind but eventually say, "I want to wash my hair, and then I'll be ready for your towel-down service. You are welcome to watch," I add cheekily while my blissful release fades to form a new memory.

"Oh, I'll be watching," he says smiling back at me with a light chuckle.

As I wash my hair, I glance over to Daniel to see if he is watching me. He has wrapped his towel around his waist and is leaning against the glass shower panel with his shoulder, holding another towel in his hands for me when am done.

I turn the shower tap off and step out of the glass enclosure. He clears his throat before he speaks his next thought.

"Can I ask you something, Liv?"

"Sure. What's on your mind?"

"Why me? If you've waited so long before making love again, what made you choose me?" he asks with a subtle furrow to his brow.

"I felt like I could trust you to be kind and gentle. You seemed to want this as much as I did when you kissed me in your car. I swear that kiss was charged with electricity." His smile turns bashful. "And you? Why me?"

"I sensed you needed something, but I wasn't certain what it was. I thought that our connection was immediate and quite wonderful. I was compelled to know you better, and now I do," he says, laughing lightly at his innuendo. "A little better than I'd hoped for, I might add." He kisses me tenderly again.

"I don't know what it is about you," he says as he drapes a towel around my shoulders. "I just can't keep my lower regions from misbehaving in your presence." He wriggles his eyebrows at me and continues, "I may have to take you back into the shower with me again."

My entire body blushed at his words.

Chapter Ten | Keepsake

The questions in my mind about Daniel's marital status continued to interrupt me as I searched in my fridge for eggs, milk, and bread to rustle up a French toast breakfast for us. As the kettle on the stovetop whistled, Daniel entered the kitchen with his cellphone in hand. He looked as amazing as he did when I first laid eyes on him.

"Is there anything I can do to help?" he asks.

"It's all good, Daniel. I have almost no groceries in my fridge, but I thought a few pieces of French toast would tide us over. Are you a coffee or a tea drinker?" I reach into the upper cupboard for two mugs and look back at him for his answer.

"Whichever you are making is grand," he says, then smiles. I love that smile. It has a calming effect on me and is so honest and beautiful.

"Tea it is," I say while quietly mulling over my concerns and filling the mugs with the boiled water. I wondered why making love to this man twice last night and again this morning had not made me feel less awkward about our breakfast conversation.

As I sit down beside him, he says, "I imagine there are a few things we didn't talk about last night that might be worth discussing over breakfast." Daniel's expression is serious although his demeanor always appears quite calm.

"Oh, like what," I reply cautiously. I hand Daniel his cup of tea and the sugar bowl, then reach to the edge of her counter to bring over a half-litre carton of milk.

In a serious tone Daniel confesses, "I think it is important that you know I am married, but amid a divorce. We've been separated for over a year. And to be clear, I'm not a man who sleeps around with beautiful women I meet at parties as a general rule. I'm not like Jason."

I get up from the table and start to remove the pan cooking the French toast from the burner, keeping my head down to focus on his words. “To be fair, Jason has really only been the playboy you know him as since Cali married Garret. I think he missed her more than he thought he would, and it was his way of coping with it.”

“Oh, I see. I didn’t know they had that kind of history together.” He reflexes into a quick smile then continues, “I haven’t been with anyone else for several months. I felt an immediate connection to you.”

I think he paused just then waiting for me to express how I’ll react to his confession. I didn’t look up as I arranged the French toast on our two plates on the counter. I had to think for a minute before opening my mouth to say something – anything.

“I see,” I reply, as a stopgap to my next train of thought while my eyes stay focused on the task at hand.

“You seem upset by what I’ve told you, and I’d understand if you were.”

“I’m not upset…but I am surprised to know you’re married.” I look back over my shoulder toward him and make my own confession. “These past twelve hours have been unusual for me. You’re the only man I’ve slept with in —well you know the story.” I raise my eyes from the plates in my hands to meet Daniel’s gaze as I hand him his French toast. I sit down at the table beside him. “Carter and I met when we were very young, and so for me this experience with you is completely out of left field.” I smile nervously as I hand Daniel cutlery and a napkin. He takes my hand and gently holds it as his eyes lock on mine.

“I sensed that about you when we were at the party,” Daniel states with sincerity. He releases my hand and continues. “When you divulged your celibacy of five years, I was quite honestly knocked for a loop.”

“As shocked as when I asked you up to my condo?”

"No. The five-year thing was much more shocking," he admits. "I hate to prod, but why so long?"

"The world around us just kind of got in the way of our physical connection and neither of us seemed to know how to address it, or even if we should. I was afraid to call him out on it, if I'm honest."

Daniel leans back into the chair and focuses on me intently. "I think the odder scenario is that any man would purposely go that long without sex."

"Cali called it quietly quitting the marriage and I can't think of a better way to describe it. When I realized that part of our lives was never going to change, I filed for divorce."

"My apologies for asking such personal questions, but I'm glad I now understand." Daniel takes another bite of his breakfast and a sip of tea before he continues. "I felt your attraction to me, and I thought you felt my attraction to you. You flirt quite subtly, but the signals were definitely there," he says. He tried not to laugh a little while taking another bite of toast but failed.

I nod and turn my head to look out of the window. I understand Daniel's perspective and know what he is saying. "I don't disagree, but it was more likely a catalyst than a cause," I say. My eyes wander over to seek his gaze, and my heart melts into the deep pools of blue in his eyes staring back at me.

"Interesting thought. And you didn't regret asking me up to your suite for a booty call?" he asks, then wipes the corner of his lip with a napkin.

"No, I don't regret it," I reply and laugh. I try to sip my tea and taste a piece of my French toast before they both grow cold. "In fact, I have never been made love to like that by any man before, and so if you walk out the door and never see me again, you can take that compliment with you as a keepsake of our *booty call*," I say, laughing more robustly at him now.

"A keepsake, is it? That's a new one," he replies, looking a bit surprised but just as amused as I am. He pours a bit of pancake syrup over his breakfast plate, then continues. "If it is any consolation, you are a very passionate lover, Liv. And if you say it has been that long since you've made love with anyone, I'd have to say that I don't think you've lost your touch." He glances back up at me. "I so enjoyed your touch," he adds grinning.

I try not to laugh at his comment. Even more amusing is that this conversation is so cordial that it smacks of what I'd imagine a date with a proper Londoner would be like. *High tea after an evening of snogging and shagging? Why, yes. Don't mind if we do.*

I keep my giggles to myself. "That is sweet of you to say, Daniel. I don't know that I've ever had a 'touch' per se, but I do enjoy the process of lovemaking. And truth be told, the alcohol did help me feel relaxed with you. You seem to know my body better than I and found ways to make me feel like I've never felt before sexually." I pause for a minute to look Daniel in the eyes again. "Plus, that accent of yours is *incredibly* sexy. Five stars, my friend." The corner of my lip tips up as I wonder if it was possible to embarrass a strong, confident man with my glowing review.

Daniel seems a bit flustered. "You really must not talk that way. I have a mind to take you again this minute." He appears embarrassed to know that I am complimenting him on his lovemaking moves, and a boyish grin erupts on his lips.

I laugh at Daniel's words and almost choke on my last bite of French toast, wondering if it was an offer I shouldn't refuse.

"No woman has ever told me I was an exceptional lover, not even my wife of ten years. You have rendered me nearly speechless, Liv," he responds, looking wantonly into my eyes.

"Well, don't stay quiet for too long." I try not to let the gleeful smile in my heart display too obviously on my lips. "I have many other questions for you." I am having a hard time trying not to let him know that I'd have taken him up on his offer for another round of lovemaking if he made the advance.

"I'll come whenever you call, Liv. I mean that. I'm taken with you, and happy that I've moved here, now that I've met you … and made love with you." The boyish grin reappears on his face again.

I valiantly attempt not to blush, but the heat fills my cheeks without warning. "I'm glad you didn't slip out on me in the middle of the night. I'd have felt very dirty this morning if you had. Although, I'd not blame you if you had."

He chuckles at me. "Now, why would I leave after such an enjoyable evening?"

In my mind, the words "Don't leave, and please make love to me again now" may as well have been carved into my forehead. I have the worst poker face.

I continue to stare at him, resting my chin upon my hand and placing my elbow on the table. "I want to know more about you. I want to see if there is more to us than great sex and interesting conversations. Is that being too forward, or are we both on the same page here?"

Daniel's eyes widen and he nods in agreement. "I'd love that." He smiles confidently at me as I pour myself a second cup of tea.

"So, we're agreed then? This was not a one-night stand *or* a booty call. We feel a solid connection, and we are going to explore it." I lean back into my chair and hold my warm teacup in the palms of my hands.

"Yes."

"I do have one more question for you," I say with a hint of a grin on my face.

"What would that be?" Daniel replies, wondering why I was trying to hold back a smile.

"I turned forty a few weeks back, and so I was wondering how old you are."

"Forty-three."

"I was just curious." I say as I lean forward. "Okay, last question, I promise. Lake or ocean?"

"Lake," he says assuredly.

"That *is* the correct answer. Ding-ding-ding! You, my friend, go home with a prize," I say, trying to make Daniel laugh. And he does.

Daniel raises one eyebrow and his deep blue eyes sparkle. "What did I win, out of curiosity?"

"Dinner here with me on Thursday night. Tell me your favourite meal and I'll make it for you."

"I like spicy food, so whatever you cook, make sure it has some heat," he confirms.

"You got it," I say, saluting him with my right hand.

As Daniel reluctantly gathers his coat and shoes at the front door, he turns to me and leans forward for a long, heated kiss. "'Til Thursday, love."

Gently closing the door behind him, I couldn't help but blush, even though I know a new love interest always seems to create a euphoric world that can never be lived up to for the long term. This feeling of eternal hope inside of me generating a perpetual grin on my face is addictive, as if a drug I had taken twenty years ago is suddenly giving me a flashback effect. "Oh, to be twenty again," I mutter to myself.

Breaking my thoughts, my cellphone rings out from my kitchen table. It's Cali calling to check in on me. Avoiding the typical pleasantries, Cali jumps right in and asks me, in a school-girl-kiss-and-tell kind of way, "So, how did it go last night? Did he *rise to the occasion,* or did he drop you off and head home?"

"I don't like to kiss and tell, but yes, if you *must* know, he did come up to my condo to talk … and do a few other things," I say, bashfully laughing.

"Don't keep me hanging, Hun. What other things? Do I need to use my imagination or are you going to spell it out for me?" Cali urges.

"Okay, I'll be honest. Best sex ever. Period."

"*Oh, myyy!* I knew you two would get it on," Cali says, then begins laughing heartily.

"Well, my intention was just to use him for sex, assuming I could get him to go there, but *ho-ly crap* – that man is really something. I have goosebumps on my arms when I think about the things he made my body do last night."

"Tell me more, don't leave me hanging. Details, Liv. Cali wants details!"

I take a deep breath and squeeze my eyes tight before blurting out, "Hard nipples, tongue-induced orgasm, intercourse, another unbelievable orgasm, sleep, amazing morning shower sex, breakfast, see-you-later kiss, and a date for Thursday night." I'm blushing again and laughing after I give the itinerary in sequence like I'm ordering a specialty coffee at Starbucks.

"That's my girl! I knew you could break out of your shell. He's a real catch, Liv. I know he's still technically married, and I guess I should have told you that, but Jason told me Daniel was getting divorced, so I wasn't worried about introducing him to you."

"Yeah, he did admit to being married this morning. The married thing really wouldn't have mattered if I was just interested in him for an occasional bump and grind," I say, "But now that I know him a little better, I'm really hot for him. I was a little pissed about his admission, but then I thought it was good of him to be honest about it."

"He doesn't come across as the cheating kind—that much I figured out pretty quick about Daniel. In fact, it surprises me that he's so chummy with Jason, considering Jason's history for being a player and not being shy about it either."

"I'll have to see how dinner on Thursday goes with him, Cali. Maybe I'm feeling so euphoric because the sex was so amazing—tamed my frustrated libido, so to speak."

"Okay. Just keep me posted. I want *all* the dirty details, so I can add them to my diary," Cali states excitedly and laughs hard at me again.

"Not funny, Cali," I chide, and follow that with a groan.

Chapter Eleven | Truths

I am panicking over the thought of cooking dinner for Daniel tomorrow night. I decide to attempt a Thai chicken dish, hoping it will satisfy his request for a spicy meal. I put together a grocery list based on a recipe I found online and set out to pick up the ingredients. Upon returning home I do a sweep of my condo looking for anything that looks out of place, dusty, or in need of a cleaning, then put in a load of laundry. All this fussing seems to be unnecessary since Daniel has already seen my condo in a mild state of disarray, but whenever I become stressed, I find cleaning a good distraction.

It's Thursday evening, and I manage to get my dinner going as planned and place a bottle of my favourite white wine in an ornate container with ice.

"White wine goes with chicken, right?" I ask myself aloud. I'm so nervous. I glance around my kitchen looking for something worthy of adjusting or rearranging to calm myself down. Just then the building's door buzzer sounds off. Daniel is here. I quickly run to my foyer intercom to buzz him in, then run to my bathroom to double-check my makeup and hair. "You are not eighteen anymore, Liv," I mutter. "Get over yourself."

Within minutes, a quick double knock tells me he is here at my door. I race to the foyer, sliding a little on the hardwood floor in my stocking feet, then take a deep breath before I open the door.

"Hi," I say nervously, smiling like an idiot.

"Hiya back," Daniel replies with a reciprocating silly grin. "I've been waiting four long days to kiss your lovely face again," he says, moving forward to hold me in his arms and plant his lips firmly onto mine.

I melt into his frame within his embrace, savouring the kiss like it is going to be the last one I will ever get from him.

"I can't believe how much I missed you. It was almost impossible to get any work done this week, thinking about you nearly every second. Tell me I'm not completely mad," he asks, looking deep into my eyes.

"You're not. I've been consumed by thoughts of you too," I say, laughing at us both. "I hope you like Thai chicken, because that's what I made for us for dinner." I reluctantly release myself from his embrace.

"Sounds delicious." He removes his jacket and shoes and follows me into the kitchen. I love that he's wearing jeans instead of a suit. Casual Daniel is equally as delicious as business Daniel.

"And does white wine suit your taste buds?" I call out, not realizing he is right behind me.

"Yes, white wine is brilliant. Is dinner ready now or do I have a little more time to hold and kiss you before we eat?" he whispered over my ear after he slid up behind me to wrap his arms around my waist as I pour two glasses of wine.

"Dinner first, dessert later," I answer, smiling to myself.

Daniel seemed impressed by my Thai chicken dinner and eagerly complimented me on it. While we are sipping wine and completing our meals, my mind is once again filled with questions to ask Daniel about his past, his present and his future. He must be sensing how much I have to discuss, so he leads the conversation somewhere more intimate than idle talk about food. "What are your plans for the rest of your life?" he slips in casually.

"Oh," I say. "Loaded question. To be honest I'm not sure. Do you have your entire future mapped out in your head?"

"No. I'm sorry I phrased the question that way. What I meant to ask is if you had a vision of how you plan to spend your time in the future. Is it to find another man to marry, is it to stay single, or have you not had time to figure that one out yet?"

"Travel," I say. "The only thing on my mind at this moment is travelling to places I've been wanting to see for years. My ex-husband Carter and I didn't travel much because it was difficult for him to leave his business for any great length of time. I took a dream trip to Tahiti with Cali in September, and so that was the beginning of my travel bug being satisfied. Do you travel much for pleasure, or are all your trips business-related?"

"I did travel quite a bit with my wife and her son in the early years of our marriage, but in the last couple of years we didn't travel together much. She went off on trips with friends here and there and I was happy to let her do so, since we differ in what appeals to us for vacation destinations. I like to go to warm and sunny climes – the south of France, Greece, Spain – and she preferred skiing in Switzerland. We alternated between sun and snow to keep each other happy," Daniel says.

"You have a son?"

"He's not my son, he's Jane's. She was pregnant at seventeen and never married the father. When I stepped into the picture, Ian was fourteen and really didn't have any interest in me being his father. We got along fine, but he never resolved to calling me Dad."

"So, Ian is an adult now and on his own?"

"Yes, he's a brilliant tech wiz and I invested in a tech start-up he and a few buddies put together last summer," Daniel replies. "I have a thirty-percent interest in whatever applications they develop, and I inject twenty thousand monthly for a two-year term into their company for my interests. They seem very promising, and so I hope they do well. Not strictly for investment reasons, but because he has worked very hard at this project, and I think he really has what it takes to make good on it."

"That is very generous. I hope he does well too. I have a daughter named Grace. She's just nineteen and working with her father in his landscape supply chain. I think she'll do well, and Carter is a patient man," I say. "So, you don't have any children of your own?"

"No. I've been in three relationships with single mothers and so technically I could say I've helped raise four children, but none are my own." He smiles briefly, but there is a tell of a regret behind that smile. "Do you mind me asking why you and your husband divorced?"

"No, not at all. We married young as I told you, and we were good until about five years ago when we just stopped being intimate with each other. I still love Carter, but our relationship went from lovers to roommates. Do you know what I mean?"

"Intimacy is important to you, yeah?" Daniel asks softly.

"Yes," I admit. "I need to be touched and made love to. My libido is strong, and I can't ignore it. The only other option was to cheat on Carter, and I didn't want to go that route. I don't believe that resolves anything. If Carter couldn't be the man I needed him to be, then I needed to move on without him."

"My wife cheated on me with a manager in my London office," Daniel says dryly.

"Oh, so sorry to hear that. Is that why you moved here to Vancouver?"

"Yes. Partly. I filed for divorce months ago and the lawyers are dragging their arses hoping they can con me into giving her more than I agreed to in the first round of negotiations. I just want the damned thing to be done with. I've given her my London estate, the apartment in Switzerland, and a rather large alimony. I'm not sure what else those leeches can bilk out of me before she signs off on the documents, considering *she* slept with someone else. I had a prenup which outlined the value of what I was willing to give her should we end up divorced, but she wants more." Daniel seems quite agitated over the subject of his divorce details, and I decide to change the subject.

"Can I interest you in going for a walk around the neighbourhood to work off the dinner calories, and maybe a few of your anger issues?" I offer, gently teasing him.

"You're on, love. I'm sorry I got riled up. Bring a scarf—it's cold outside," he says, slowly returning my smile.

Chapter Twelve | The Trouble with Bubbly

Daniel and I spent every night enjoying each other's company over the Christmas holidays. Instead of going alone to the remaining two parties of which I'd been invited, I brought Daniel along as my plus one. I also joined him at events he had been invited to attend. I am meeting so many new people it is becoming hard to keep track.

In light of the newness of our relationship, we agreed to not gift each other anything for Christmas. Despite that agreement, two days after Christmas, Daniel gifted me a pair of ruby earrings encircled by tiny diamonds. "They are stunning, Daniel. Thank you, but you shouldn't have."

"We never agreed to not give gifts after Christmas," he says.

"That's just semantics," I chide, "but I'm in love with the earrings already and can't wait to wear them at the upcoming New Year's Eve party."

"I'm glad to have pleased you, Liv."

"Don't get so smug. I'm mad at you for breaking our rule."

"Just call me a semantic romantic and be done with it, yeah?"

"I forgive you, but just this once," I say holding up my pointer finger before I kissed him.

As our relationship continues to bloom, we find the dinners out and the party events are all we need from each other. And the sex, of course. The glorious sex between us is a gift unto itself. Daniel is kind-hearted, constantly willing to offer affection and he's content to be by my side regardless of where we are.

Still, among all these feel-good emotions, a niggle of negativity seeps through. I briefly consider if I should attempt to slow things down between us, despite having such an incredible time. Yet, the idea of trimming off my dates with Daniel also feels pointless at this juncture. The truth is, I'm already in too deep.

I guess what I'm waiting to see is if there is some big flaw in Daniel that hasn't come to light. Why would any woman want to cheat on this man or leave him? Either those women have to be crazy or somewhere along the way I'll discover where he is at odds with me or my values. Something irreconcilable. But other than his minor blast about his divorce settlement issues, he's not raised his voice or shown any sign of aggression or a short temper.

This whirlwind relationship has my head spinning. How did I jump from the frying pan into the fire so fast? How did I get so quickly tangled up in love with someone so soon after my divorce? This wasn't the plan.

As the end of December drew nearer, Daniel, me, Jason and Cali decide to party it up in high style for New Year's Eve. Jason has booked us into a highly coveted party in the hottest club in downtown Vancouver to bring in the New Year. As we enter the club, I see the Champagne flowing like water over a pyramid fountain of crystal glasses in the centre of the room, and every fashionable multi-millionaire in town appears to be in attendance. It is a perfect opportunity for Jason and Daniel to schmooze with the elites in hopes of acquiring a few more clients for their new venture capital company.

I knew this was a part business, part party situation ahead of time, thus I'm fine to see him mingle without me. I don't follow the markets or finance as a general rule. The venture capital project that the two of them have been discussing for over six months (before Daniel decided to move to Vancouver) culminated in the necessary funding to officially launch, including setting aside some of their sizable fortunes for philanthropic purposes under their new company name.

On a business level, Jason and Daniel suit each other well. Jason has a law degree, and Daniel is a financial whiz kid, having invested in markets and new ideas fresh out of high school, eventually becoming a very wealthy self-made man due to his dedication and a sharp mind for finding companies which show potential for growth to invest in. When I witness the two men connecting with the elite guests at the club tonight, I recognize what Daniel's flaw is—he's a workaholic like Carter. The thought of having to deal with another man who spends the bulk of his time working, rather than being a devoted mate, put me off kilter. I swallow hard at that thought.

I sit down at the nearest table with my glass of champagne to compartmentalize this situation. I have to decide if continuing to date Daniel is going to be worth my time if it is going to lead to me being alone most nights, just like I was in the last five years of my marriage to Carter. During these holidays we have been inseparable, but when the holiday break is over, what will become of our time together?

I'm shaken by this discovery. I continue to watch him in an attempt to quell my fears, hoping that I'm overreacting. But the truth is there, dressed in an expensive black and white tuxedo holding a manner akin to James Bond like it were second nature. It's New Year's Eve, and he's… working. I hold back the urge to shatter my composure with a defeated heartbroken demeaner by emptying the contents of my Champagne in one gulp before escaping to the restrooms.

"Get your shit together, Liv," I chide myself under my breath as I grasp the lower length of my gown in my hands to prevent myself from tripping on it in my haste to retreat.

Cali is quite oblivious to the inner-circle workings of Jason, or so she pretends. She parties like she is still twenty-one, mingling and dancing with anyone who will pay her any attention. I rarely let myself go so easily, and I admire Cali for her free spirit. But as I steady my thoughts and compose myself in front of the gilded gold framed mirror of the rest room tonight, I decide it is day and event are all about being relaxed, positive and celebratory.

"'Tis the season," I hear another woman state into her cellphone as she exits one of the bathroom stalls. With a deep cleansing breath, I repeat her words to myself and return to the party to follow Cali around the club. What I need right this moment is to enjoy the fervour of the night, and Cali's infectious energy. My possible Daniel problem is a tomorrow problem.

When the giant New Year's clock above the massive marble fireplace feature wall nears the stroke of midnight, the music stops, and an unexpected hush comes over the room as several people point to the clock's ticking second hand. At ten seconds before midnight, Daniel and Jason appear out of nowhere to hold us in their arms, citing the countdown in unison with the crowd.

"10-9-8-7-6-5-4-3-2-1! Happy New Year!"

The room nearly bursts its walls when the crowd erupts into a loud chorus of cheers. Glasses clink around us while the crowd sing out the words of Auld Lang Syne. Just then, a raft of gold and black balloons release from the ceiling of the club. I love this moment. It feels magical. Daniel dips me backward in his strong arms to kiss me on this momentous night. He appears giddy, having no doubt had too many glasses of Champagne in the three hours we've been inside the club. At least he's a happy drunk, I think to myself.

His New Year's kiss is a bit firmer and sloppier than a sober Daniel would have given me, but the pure joy emanating from him made up for its lack of perfection. I should be feeling the same level of excitement as everyone else, and I try to keep my mood festive, but my newly developed concern over my future together with Daniel manages to slip past my earlier defence and dampen the moment. I'm going to drink more Champagne and get that devil on my shoulder drunk.

In the morning, this first day of January, I awake with a whopping hangover, almost feeling ill enough to throw up. A quick warm shower before Daniel rises will be worth my effort, I decide, as I look like and feel like hell warmed over. And a quick bite to eat— preferably toast— would help settle my queasy stomach.

When Daniel crawls his way out of my bed an hour later, he saunters into the kitchen looking dishevelled and tired. I can't help myself and start laughing at him. He looks nearly as bad as I did when I woke up, but I'm feeling much better after my shower, some toast, and a soothing cup of honey laced dandelion tea.

"Good morning, sleepyhead," I say as he glances up at me. "You look like I felt an hour ago."

"I cannot confess to knowing how you felt an hour ago, my love, but I will confess to never wanting to drink Champagne again in this lifetime."

"You of all people should know not to count your chickens before they hatch, Daniel."

"Eggs, have you got eggs? I could devour eggs."

"Yes, eggs I have. Boiled, scrambled or fried?"

"Fried, please. I'll cook if you'll hand me the eggs and butter," he says, forcing a smile amid his discomfort.

"I'm glad I was up before you, because I woke up to raccoon eyes and Axl Rose's hairdo!"

"Aw, too bad I missed it, Liv. I could use a good laugh right 'bout now."

While Daniel cooked and sat down to eat his fried eggs, I took the opportunity to discuss a few things with him. I set my teacup down on the kitchen table and clear my throat to be sure I've got his attention. "I have a trip planned for a Panama Canal cruise with an extended landed jungle stay afterward. I leave on the twelfth and I'll be gone for fifteen days."

Daniel's expression is of confusion. The inner corners of his brows tip down toward the bridge of his nose as though something smells distasteful. "Why didn't you tell me about this before now?" he asks, gently wiping his lips with his napkin and squaring a look into my eyes.

I tuck the loose strands of my hair over my eyes behind my right ear and nervously tap my fingernails on the edge of my teacup. "We were so busy making googly eyes at each other that I had all but forgotten about it. It wasn't until this morning when I checked the emails I'd ignored for the past few days that I was reminded by my travel agent about the trip."

Daniel leans back into his chair and places his fork on the top of his empty plate. "I can't go with you, Liv. I can't leave Jason for fifteen days."

I subtly wave my left hand across my chest and reply, "No, I wasn't asking or expecting that you'd come with me. I hadn't planned on anyone to come with me. I booked this trip before I met you and I'm not going to change my plans, just as you can't change yours. This trip is important to me, and I have to do this my way. On my own," I state firmly.

He doesn't appear to have much fight in him as he's swift to respond. "Alright, alright," he says, holding his palms up in the air at me as if to signal defeat. "You're right. If you had these plans before we met, I can't step in your way. You just have to know how much I'll miss you when you're away." He smiles softly at me, not wanting to make a fight over it. I'm grateful for the ease with which he took my surprising news. "What is it that you plan to achieve on this solo journey?"

"I'm interested in finding wild and rare orchid varieties within their natural habitat. As you're well aware, orchids are my favourite plant, and a trip like this has been in the back of my mind for several years."

An accommodating nod and smile are offered, and I breathe a sigh of relief that he's okay with my plans.

Daniel showers and dresses as he waits for the painkillers to quell his hangover, then settles down in the living room with a fresh cup of tea next to me on the couch.

Now that we've returned to our relatively normal selves, I broach another subject filling my mind from last night. "Will this new business with Jason take up a lot of your time?" I ask casually.

Daniel reaches for a coaster and sets his teacup atop it on the coffee table before leaning back comfortably into the couch cushions. "It is still early days, Liv. I will be quite busy," he admits. "We need to acquire a few more high-end clients and get on with finding the right investment opportunities for the existing clients to attach themselves to. My hope is that by the end of summer this year, I can semi-retire and spend only two or three days in the office overseeing the progress of the investments, and the cash flowing in and out of their portfolios. Why do you ask?"

I adjust my position on the couch, feeling a bit anxious. "I watched you both last night mingling and schmoozing, and it dawned on me that you were enjoying that aspect of your business. I also realized that you would be busy with this new venture, and I wonder how that would affect the time we spend together moving forward.

I pause for a minute as I don't want to rush this conversation. "We've been side by side since November and if I have to sit at home for the next eight months waiting for you to finish work, then … then I'd like to know now," I say.

Since my discovery of Daniel's dedication to his work, and hearing his affirmation now over his obligations, I am getting cold feet over our relationship. I find myself confused over what I want for myself and this seemingly perfect man who fell so quickly into my life and heart, but I continue to press the point to Daniel.

"I gave up on my twenty-year marriage because Carter was a workaholic and didn't have time for me. I'm not interested in going right back into that same kind of relationship, no matter how much I feel for you. Can you understand how this concerns me?"

Daniel stares at me in bewilderment. He swallows hard while he tries to comprehend my words and the consequences they could bring. Had it crossed his mind that his work obligations would be an issue for me? But there it is. This is the cold truth about where I stand on what I want for my future. I refuse to be left abandoned by a man who valued work over love.

Daniel is revered for his talent of keeping calm under pressure, but I'm not so sure relationship issues are as easily dealt with for him. His lengthy pause after my last words tempts me to say more, but I have nothing to add.

"Liv, I enjoy my work, and I've put myself and Jason into a position where we will be quite swamped with details of our new business and clients. I can't tell you how much time I'll be away from you day to day. Sometimes I'll be gone for a week travelling, in addition to doing loads of evening entertaining while I'm home. But as I've said, by the fall, the business will be up and running. I'll be able to take a step back and have more free time. Even more time to spend with you."

I already knew that his work commitments with their business venture would take up the bulk of his time, including evenings and travel away. That is a given with any new venture. With Carter I'd been witness to the amount of energy operating a thriving company can absorb from a dedicated owner, and how much more time his expansions took of what little time he'd had left in a day. It is too much for me to go through again.

"I don't want to be waiting in the wings for your time. I know your work is important to you, and I would never ask you to choose me over your business. Again. I'm not sure this is going to work for us," I say, purposely avoiding having to look him in the eyes.

Daniel appears taken aback by my perspective. This is a blow he clearly wasn't expecting, and I can see he is having a tough time grappling with my words.

I began to choke up at the thought of saying goodbye to a man who fulfills me in so many ways. I struggle to decide if I'm being stubborn or smart. I have to trust my gut. This is pure emotional torture, but I've made up my mind. It is obvious now that Daniel wants a long-term relationship with me, but he won't have any more time for my needs than Carter did. The only difference between Daniel and Carter is the affection, but that alone isn't enough to bridge the distance between our relationship being a priority or not.

I've only been single for a few weeks. Maybe this was all too soon? How do I know I'm not repeating my mistakes? How can I look myself in the mirror every day knowing that I'd faulted on my own deal—to be independent. Initially I'd thought that Daniel and I would become the same people that Cali and Jason are to each other—free to love each other, but also free to do whatever we want, whenever we want, without strings attached. But after nearly six weeks of constant togetherness, I knew Daniel didn't see our relationship unfolding that way, and neither did I. We are in love.

Daniel moves closer to me on the couch, wraps his arm around my shoulder and kisses the top of my head, almost making light of what I'm trying to tell him. "I think you need to think about what you're saying here, love. Either that or I'm misunderstanding what it is that you want from me."

"Daniel, I think you understand perfectly what I'm saying, but you aren't appreciating what I sacrificed by leaving Carter."

I'm angry as much as I am heartbroken. He releases me from his hug and leans back to see me eye to eye. "You can't be serious!" He stares hard at me now. "You are *absolutely* killing me here," he says, raising his voice to a level I'd not experienced before. Daniel stands from his seat next to me on the couch, towering above me and massages his face with his hands to keep his cool. He shoves both of his hands into his jean pockets before looking back down at my blank face. He begins to pace the floor in front of the couch in his bare feet while he searches his mind for the words that will offer the most compelling argument to change my mind.

His tone is softer now. Compassionate. "I cannot lose you, Liv. Not now. Not after who we've become to each other. I'm mad for you. Surely you know this." His eyes begin searching mine for the punchline, as if this is a joke that has gone terribly wrong. "I beg of you. What can I do to change your mind?"

I may have fallen deeply in love with him in only six weeks' time but there is nothing more to say on the subject. I can't answer his question. There is no punchline to a cruel joke. This is very real.

Daniel is torn by his emotions and trying not to let me see him be weak. "You are quite serious? You'd give up on us simply because I am a busy entrepreneur?" he asks. "What I don't understand is, why do we have to break up this brilliant thing we have together because of my work? We haven't even started yet. Why can't we try? We can manage this. I promise you."

He takes his hands out of his pockets and approaches me where I had settled into the corner of the couch. He kneels before me and takes in a deep breath.

"What happens now, Liv? I go home to my condo, and I'm supposed to forget about you?"

My face remains blank because I'm lost to answer his question. He searches my eyes then stands to his feet again. He turns his back to me, attempting to walk towards the kitchen, and then stops to turn around to look at me. "I don't think—no, wait—I *know* you'll find the concept of us being apart just as difficult as I will." Daniel's brows furrow deeply as he tries to maintain composure, and I can see this is proving to be difficult.

I hope my next words don't get stuck in my throat as I curl up tighter on the couch, tucking my knees under my chin, and wrapping my arms around them. I realize I'm losing control of the conversation, that I've disappointed him on a level I'd not completely anticipated but I have to cut the cord.

"Daniel let's be honest," I say in a calm but affirmative tone. "Neither you nor I were intending to get involved in a relationship. You are still married, for Christ's sake, and I'm on my own for the first time in my life. You and I had plans that didn't include each other no less than six weeks ago!"

I'm not getting through to him as easily as I'd hoped. The truth is I've had much more time to analyze this than he has. I have to be respectful of how jarring my position is to him.

"I wasn't supposed to fall for you. I was looking for someone who would be interested in a few dates, some casual sex and a couple of good laughs. I had plans to be comfortable on my own, travel at whim and do the things I've always wanted to do. I can't do that if I'm deeply involved with someone – even if that person is as incredible as you. This … this you-and-me long-term thing wasn't the plan!"

I'm desperately holding back a wall of tears, and the task is proving impossible.

"Dammit!" I yell. I raise my hand to cover my mouth, jump up from the couch and run to my bedroom, closing the door abruptly behind me. My body heaves as I try to breathe, questioning myself for what I'd done. Is leaving Daniel the biggest mistake of my life, or is this the right decision? I lean my back heavy against the door, standing inside the very room where this beautiful romance had sparked, and I call out to him in a strained voice. "Daniel, you should leave now." My voice cracks again. "I can't see you anymore."

I can hear his heavy footsteps approach my bedroom door. I hear a thud sound, and the door vibrates a little against my body. He quietly says, “Not from behind a closed door, Liv. Please.”

I don’t know how long he is willing to stand there with this door between us. It is a metaphor for what I’d done to him and myself emotionally. Was he going to get angry with me now or let me be?

“We can find a common ground, Liv. Surely there is some way for us to stay together while you get yourself what you need, and I get my workload settled. This is madness,” he says as I hear his hand attempt to open the door. “Let me into your room. We can talk this through.”

I remain silent, staring up at the ceiling and willing myself to be stronger and to stop crying.

Taking as deep a breath as he can manage, he adds, “If I leave now, I can’t guarantee I’ll be strong enough to let you back into my life. Do you understand this?”

My continued silence from the other side of the bedroom door is all Daniel needs to know. He has not won this battle. “Please reconsider us, Liv,” he mutters while I use the sleeve of my shirt to wipe the tears from my eyes.

I wait for him to retreat so I can throw myself onto my bed and have the hard cry I need to release. I know letting him go may be the biggest regret of my life. I have to trust myself, believe in my vision of the future. I listen to him collecting his belongings, and as he leaves my condo, I hear the spare keys I gave him drop onto the entry table, then he lets the door slam shut behind him.

Chapter Thirteen | Setting Sail

A week has passed since our breakup. Neither I nor Daniel tried to contact the other. I couldn't bear to hear his voice for fear of giving in to his pleas for me to reconsider even if he did call me. This is much more difficult to deal with than I anticipated, and Daniel was right when he said as much.

Cali is upset about the two of us calling it quits over what appeared to be something that could have been rectified had we tried a little harder. Her words, not mine. But Cali also knows that when I put my mind to something, when I've firmly made a decision, I stick to it even when it makes no sense to those around me. I've talked to Cali only briefly about the breakup because I didn't want to make a huge fuss over it. What is done is done. I'm standing firm, but at the same time I'm dying inside. I finally halt Cali in her tracks by saying that I was glad I found out early in the relationship that it wouldn't work out for us.

I can well imagine that regardless of me throwing up a brick wall on Cali about discussing it further, Cali will in all likelihood try to get any information she can out of Daniel. But I'm fairly certain he isn't the kind to talk openly about affairs of the heart. He's a private man. The strong silent type. Meddling into our relationship to fix it is not going to go as well as Cali hopes. Maybe that's a good thing. Maybe Daniel's brick wall will finally put a stop to her meddling. But I get it. The reason she's good at her job is because she solves other people's problems. She gets inside of people and finds the perfect home or solution to their living situation easily.

All that being said, on the following Sunday, Daniel calls me to see if I'd changed my mind now that he'd given me some space to think it over. His heartfelt request that I reconsider went to voice mail. A few hours later, I broke down and texted him.

I'm sorry, Daniel. I am so conflicted and never would have thought I'd miss you this much. Maybe when I return from Panama, we can find a way to spend some time together and figure us out? Missing you, Liv.

His reply allowed me to breathe a little easier:

I'll wait for you for however long it takes. My devotion to you has no time limit. Love, Daniel.

I began to soften after having been so firm with him, because deep down I know he's too special to let go.

Feeling hopeful again, I began organizing my paperwork for the Panama trip and filling my luggage with the things I'd need most. I'm notorious for over packing for holidays and so being mindful of that helps me stay focused on surviving with limited extravagances. I don't need perfume or hairspray, or evening clothes. I need to be practical. Baseball caps, a light sweater and a hoodie, t-shirts and sport pants that can convert to shorts, two semi-casual dresses for the cruise, a raincoat, waterproof shoes for hiking, a backpack, swimwear and hair ties. I can't forget my DSLR camera and mini laptop. My goal is to find and photograph as many species as possible of wild orchids in Central America. If I need anything else during my travels, I can buy it on board the ship of from my hotel. As I zip up my mid-sized suitcase, I affirm to myself, "I'm ready for a journey I hope to never forget. You can do this, Liv."

The excitement in my heart upon boarding the sailing ship I'd chosen for my travels through the Panama Canal via Windstar Cruises on the *MS Windstar* was palpable. I'll be sailing from Puerto Caldera in Costa Rica to Colón, Panama with a guest list of up to one hundred and forty-eight, and a staff of eighty-eight. The staff appear to be friendly and accommodating, and although the ship is small, it seems like a beautiful place to call home for the next few days.

The queen-sized bed in my surprisingly large stateroom feels firm, and my window's view to the ocean outside gives me the impression that I've been thrown back in time to an era when sailing the seas was the only way to travel from continent to continent. This is what intrigued me about the sailing ship cruise over the massive cruise liners that also offer a similar itinerary. There is a sense of adventure to a smaller vessel—a feeling of intimacy that one cannot get from a larger ship. Additionally, the smaller ships can port in places the larger ships can't, giving me a more unique travel experience. At least that's the objective. At long-last I'm where I need to be. Free as the breeze that will fill this ship's sails.

I unpack my suitcase to place my clothes in the two drawer Birdseye maple dresser beside the narrow, yet ample sized closet for my needs. The finishes on the furnishings in my stateroom are adorned with polished brass hardware, and as the sun begins to beam through my portal window the room glows golden like the sun itself.

I see from the itinerary that dinner will be served an hour after we launch from port, so I don a simple white t-shirt, a light jean jacket and my favourite olive-green hiking shorts. This is not a formalwear dinner—that one is on Tuesday evening. I noticed that most of the guests were wearing comfortable clothes. I'll follow suit unless otherwise suggested. Sporting a pair of new white deck shoes and a pair of high-end sunglasses specifically for this trip, I exit my stateroom and head up to the top deck to catch what is left of the afternoon sun. Feeling a bit like a kid in a candy store, my grin and excitement cannot be contained. Time to familiarize myself with the rest of the ship.

The temperatures are in the mid-seventies, and a light breeze sweeps over the upper deck as I look out over the port in Costa Rica before we set sail. Having spent some time researching my journey prior to this adventure, I am prepared to be rained on and to be doing some hiking in muddy locations, as the jungle is a consistently damp environment. The evening temperatures could drop to around sixty degrees, which is why I packed two sweaters for walking the ship's deck at night.

At the first dinner sitting, me and my new cruise mates toasted to adventure and to fresh starts, which is exactly what I'm there for. Many of the travellers I speak with are surprised to know I'm travelling alone. I am asked twice if I wanted to join other couples or groups on excursions from the ship at the various ports of call. Graciously, I turn them down as I've arranged tours for every location well in advance through my travel agent.

The dining room is equally as polished and detailed as my stateroom. The chandeliers inset into the ceiling in plaster clamshell like coves glisten like diamonds over our grouping of tables. Even our cutlery is gold coloured, and our plates have a wide gold trim encircling the edge. Now I'm feeling underdressed regardless that everyone else is wearing casual clothing similar to mine.

It appears my table mates are younger than me, traveling in a group of four. To my right are Andrew and David who are newlyweds from San Diego, and on my left are Krissy and Pete, who are on their fourth anniversary holiday. The two couples know each other from Andrew and Pete's architectural firm, which they started ten years ago. They must be doing well as this cruise is quite pricey, even by my standards.

The food is amazing; however, having never cruised before, by day four I am feeling like I was ready to leave the ship permanently. As lovely as the ship is, the confined spaces within the ship's layout begin to feel claustrophobic to me. This isn't something I anticipated about cruising on a smaller ship, but overall, this experience has been top notch.

The best part, aside from the amazing ports of call, were the food and being lulled to sleep each night by the gentle rocking of our ship, as well as the fast friendships I made. Within a short time, I'd met many interesting people on the ship, held some fascinating conversations with perfect strangers in all age ranges, shared heartfelt belly laughs with a retired comedian, and drank far more wine than I should have.

During this first phase of my journey, at every port of call I had made a point of texting Grace and Cali to let them know where I am. I knew they both were worried about me travelling alone, and it is a simple and effective way to get them off my back about it. Cali was also texting Daniel to advise him, because he'd asked for updates from her after I flew down to Costa Rica. I don't think Cali can keep a secret if you duct taped her mouth shut. But in this case, I don't mind. Knowing Daniel cared enough to keep track of my journey warmed my heart.

Our ship has reached the Panama Canal. Me, and most of the guests are wide-eyed and fascinated by the lock system that takes ships along the forty-eight-mile canal leading into my last port of call in Colón. My landed portion of my stay in the Republic of Panama is booked at the Radisson Summit Resort and Golf hotel, in a jungle setting just outside of Panama City. I can't wait to rid myself of my sea legs and be on land for the balance of this trip.

The well-appointed hotel and the lush jungle foliage outside the balcony of my suite are lovely. It has recently rained leaving the foliage with teardrops of water hanging from their tips, and the thickness of the tropical air fills my lungs in a way I'm not used to. I leave my sliding door to my balcony open as I unpack my suitcase so I can listen to the chorus' of various birds bringing my heart and mind a kind of calm that spurs me to take a quick nap once I'm unpacked. I had forgotten how exhausting lugging around a suitcase, and the rigors of entering a new country can be when you are unfamiliar with the location and their customs.

I am quick to sign up for a jungle tour excursion offered by the hotel that was not on the list my travel agent arranged for me. This house-offered tour sounds like it is right up my alley, whereas the other tours appear to be less tactile to the environment that I yearn for. I am interested in the wildlife, the deep tropical forest trails, and the exquisite array of orchid species for which Panama is known to have in abundance. With my new camera I'm anxious to photograph as many orchid species I can find to use as inspiration for some of my watercolour painting projects when I arrive back home. And I might find a reliable supplier from local growers to ship some of the more unique orchids to Carter's landscape supply company back home. I remind myself that I'm retired but why waste a perfectly good opportunity to make a face-to-face deal on behalf of Carter while I'm here. I send Carter a quick text to ask if he's interested in my help. He replies within minutes.

"Send me pictures of the available stocks. I agree it would be beneficial to offer plants that other local plant stores don't. Thanks for the gesture, Liv."

Chapter Fourteen | It's a Jungle Out There

Back at home in Vancouver, Cali got wind via a conversation with Jason that Daniel was interested to see if they could add a third party to manage the investment portfolios he and Jason were working on. Jason was skeptical at first, but after meeting two perfectly suited candidates, he agreed that a third partner in their venture would be of benefit. The new name of their venture capital enterprise became JDM Investments, representing Jason, Daniel and their new partner Michael. She also told me that Daniel had arrived at a final settlement agreement with his wife Jane.

As usual, Cali has her nose stuck in places it really shouldn't be, but Jason's lips are as loose as Cali's, so I'd have heard all about it sooner than later. A sigh of relief flowed through me with her news. Not that I was spending every minute of my time worrying about either of those things. Regardless, I am delighted to know everything at home is going smoothly. The following afternoon, Cali told me she had forwarded a text to Daniel from me with images of the hotel and the jungle around the hotel grounds. Daniel replied to both of us that he was jealous of my travels and wished me well in my search for my wild orchids.

I take a selfie from my hotel room balcony, holding one of the orchid plants that decorated every room of the hotel and posted it on my social media accounts before taking a stroll around the hotel grounds. Tomorrow will be my first full day to explore.

The first jungle tour I try is a two-hour trip around the local forested area with a botanist as our guide. I have a quick bite at one of the poolside restaurants before joining the group at the front of the hotel. Our guide speaks English well enough for the group of interested guests to understand and is very enthusiastic about sharing his knowledge of the flora native to the Republic of Panama.

This tour is a perfect opportunity for me to practice using my new camera and getting the settings right for the variable lighting situations common in a jungle environment. We came across glass-winged butterflies, a resident toucan and a few smaller monkeys who seemed to be very interested in the new arrivals traipsing through their home. And not far from the hotel is a small natural waterfall and a beautiful stream leading away from it. Ferns and palms draped themselves artfully over the edges of the stream, and to my absolute delight a few blooms I'd never seen before nested among the foliage, adding a dash of tropical colour to the varied shades of deep green in the forest. A perfect image for me to recreate in watercolour.

My second tour is a deeper trek into the jungle. The trip will include a guided motorboat ride up a river, some kayaking and a three-mile hike round trip. It had rained heavily the night before and so the naturally damp ground of the trails will be quite muddy and difficult to navigate without proper footwear, but I'm ready for the worst it has to offer. Donning my long pants and long-sleeved shirt to protect me from bug bites, waterproof hiking boots and a lightweight rain jacket, I was prepared for whatever weather conditions came of the day. There is also plenty of room in my waterproof backpack to store the raincoat if it wasn't needed.

One of the things I quickly found frustrating about this tour was the tight schedule the guide was on. There was little time set aside for naturalists to truly absorb their surroundings or photography buffs like me to linger and dabble with exposures or angles in the forest and along the river we traversed. Twice within the first half hour I had to run to catch up with the group after I got lost in my photography efforts. A poison dart frog appeared along the trail, and an interesting butterfly landed on the tree next to me, vying for the photo op.

There is only one other person in my tour group who had an interest in photography. Before long he was hanging back with me, dawdling behind the others to snap pics of bugs and foliage he found interesting. Eventually we struck up a conversation.

"I'm Brad," he says, smiling at me when our eyes finally met. "Do you have a lot of experience with photography or are you a newbie like me?"

"I've had a few years of photo experience," I reply politely.

"Maybe you can show me a few tips?" he asks.

"I'm no professional. I take photos to use as inspiration for watercolour paintings."

"I guess we look at photography in different terms," he says. "I think we've lost track of the group. We'd better hurry to catch them."

"Yes, okay. It's pissing me off that the guide seems to be in this giant rush. I wonder if they do a few of these tours a day or something, because I'm having a hard time enjoying the trek with him speeding past everything that's of interest." Brad and I quicken our pace to find the tour group, which is now well ahead of us.

"I can still hear them, so they can't be that far ahead," he says, looking back at me as I follow closely behind.

As the tour continued, I find myself constantly trying to play catch-up with the group but am glad that this young stranger is with me to keep me company and remind me to move faster.

"Have you seen any orchids on this tour?" I ask. "You'll likely find them attached to trees, not necessarily rooted in the soil. They are epiphytic plants in their natural setting."

"No, not yet. Is that something you're looking to photograph?"

"Yes. It's the primary purpose of my trip. But there doesn't seem to be any in this section of the tour. We might find some further down. If you don't mind, keep an eye out for me, will you?" I ask.

Just then I spot a toucan in the tree above me and stop for what seems like a brief amount of time to take multiple captures of it. Just inside the edge of the trail I spot a Cischweinfia pusilla; it's a smaller bloom with five duotone yellow and orange pointed petals, and one broad white lip to attract pollinators. I'm delighted and lean forward to capture its beauty in its natural setting. Finally, I've found what I've been searching for on this tour.

When I stop shooting pictures, I realize that I can no longer hear the group's voices in the jungle and I'm worried that I'd lost them completely.

Angry with myself and this joke for a tour guide, I start walking as fast as I can, stopping from time to time to listen for voices. Eventually, Brad pops out in front of me and asks if I know where they all went.

"Nope," I say sharply while shaking my head. "We've been abandoned, I think. I'm going to have some serious complaints about this tour when I get back to the hotel. This is bullshit!"

"If we run along this trail for a few minutes, I'm sure we'll find them," he says encouragingly. I'm glad one of us is thinking positively.

The two of us pick up our pace and try fruitlessly to locate the tour group along the trail. When we return to the place where the kayaks we had paddled in on had landed along the river, we noted that the kayaks were no longer there.

"Is this where we landed?" I ask, now quite confused and somewhat disoriented. "This was a loop trail, right? How could they just take our kayaks and not realize we're not with them anymore?" I ask in sheer disbelief.

"That's fucked up," Brad says, sighing loudly as he shakes his head. "We're fucked now. Are you a good swimmer? I think we're going to have to swim the river to get back to the tour boat launch place." Brad steps into the edge of the river before looking back at me.

"Do you want to swim in that muddy river?" I ask.

"No, not really. The trail ends here. What other choice do we have?"

"None, I guess. Fine. Let me put my camera back into my pack before we start swimming. Are you sure that's the direction we came from? At this point I'm kind of disoriented directionally."

"I'm sure it's this direction," Brad says, pointing downriver. "We'll be swimming with the flow, so it won't be that much effort to get back to the boat launch."

Once my backpack and camera equipment are stored securely, I slowly wade into the murky water. It isn't that deep, and for the most part I didn't need to make much of an effort to move through the water toward the initial drop-off location. I'm thankful for all my years of swimming experience. If I couldn't swim, this situation would have been disastrous. And surprisingly, the abundance of flies and mosquitos that hounded us along the trail were no longer a bother while we are in the water.

It took me and Brad nearly a half-hour of wading and swimming to reach the place where our tour group had been dropped off by the river boat to use the kayaks. It didn't surprise me that the boat was nowhere to be found. "Just another insult to injury," I say, throwing my soaking wet arms up in the air, exasperated. I begin laughing hysterically now at the ridiculousness of the situation we are in. "Truly, I do not know whether to laugh or cry right now, Brad."

Brad climbs out of the river and tries to squeeze as much water out of his clothes as possible. "I think we're going to have to hike for a bit, until we can find somebody driving by who'd be willing to pick us up to take us back to town. Are you okay to walk for a bit or do you want to take a break here for a while?"

"I don't know what to do. I'm so pissed off that I can't think straight." I bend forward, pressing my palms against my thighs, to catch my breath and have a look around me. "I'm getting tired, and I have no idea where the fuck I am. Do you remember which direction we came in on with the tour boat? And where in the hell does this dirt road lead us to? I'm kicking myself for not paying more attention to how we got here. Fuck!" I yell. "Sorry for all the bad language. I don't swear very often, but right now I've got a whole arsenal of foul in my head, and I don't think I've ever been this pissed off before."

Brad laughs at me. "My ears aren't virgin, so swear all you want. My parents were porn stars, so bad words are music to my ears."

"Very funny, Brad. I highly doubt that, but I appreciate you trying to lighten the mood."

"Okay, so we're walking that way," he says, pointing to our left.

We walk for as long as we can and have no idea how much further we need to go to see some semblance of civilization or a person with a car or a horse. I observe Brad as we walk. He was only slightly taller than me with a thin frame. He appeared relatively fit, but because of his youthful face it was hard for me to rightfully guess his age. I assumed he was in his late twenties. His positive outlook and sense of humour are welcome. It helps me feel more at ease than if I'd been stranded alone, or with someone who had a bad disposition. I sit down on a rock at the side of the dirt road and try my best to stay positive. Brad sits down next to me on the dirt and wipes his hands on his wet pants, which had no effect on the amount of dirt covering his palms.

"Did you check your phone recently?" I ask. "Do we have any cell reception yet?"

Brad digs out his waterproof cellphone lanyard from inside his shirt and turns on his iPhone. "No reception yet. And my power is getting low too. What about your phone? Do you have power left?"

I pull my backpack off my shoulders and stick my fingers inside one of the pockets for my phone. I turn it on and say, "I have about half power, but I have a charger pack in another pocket. Turn your phone off and we'll use mine until it's dead and then we'll have your phone as a backup."

"Good idea."

It is just past sunset, and I have no idea how well I'll deal with being lost in the jungle in Panama in the depths of night with a perfect stranger. As much as I do feel safe around Brad, we know nothing of each other, and I'm not sure yet if trusting him wholeheartedly to get us out of this situation is wise. The only source of light we have is our cellphones, but saving power is more important than light, so we'll have to find a place to rest and wait for sunrise.

We continue walking along the dirt road until it's too dark to make the route worth following. I'm spent, emotionally and physically. I'm scared for my life, my clothes are still damp from swimming in the river, and I'm absolutely starving. I take my backpack off my shoulders again to see if I still have a granola bar in the bottom of the bag somewhere, but I come up empty handed. I have never felt so unprepared in my life.

"I'm beginning to think we should have turned right instead of left, Brad," I say, sounding defeated. I've lost my ability to be positive.

"Are you blaming me for this situation now?"

"No, no, sorry. I just can't believe we haven't seen or heard any other human on this road since we started walking. How long do you think we've been at this?"

"I don't fucking know, Liv. I don't fucking know anything at this point!" he says as he wipes his brow to rid it of an insect and drops his backpack on the dirt with a thud.

"Okay, okay. Let's just sit down here against this tree and close our eyes. We can't do anything in the pitch dark. Obviously neither of us considered this would happen, we don't smoke so there is no lighter or matchbook to start a small fire. And all the wood in this area is too damp to light up if we did."

I nod and say, "I sleep light. If I hear anything, I'll wake you."

As we sit under the tree next to the road, I lean up against Brad's body and rest my head upon his shoulder. "I hope you don't mind me leaning on you," I say, and yawn.

"No, it's okay," he replies in a near whisper and nods.

As I rest my body against this young man, who rightly smells as bad as I do at this point, I decide that trusting Brad is important. I'm sure he trusts me now too. We've got each other, which is better than nothing.

"Are you cold?" he asks. "Do you want me to wrap my arm around you to help you stay warm?"

"Yes, if you don't mind. My clothes are still damp and I'm getting a chill. Aren't you cold?"

"No, but if we sit close together, you might get warmer. It won't get any colder than this."

As I close my eyes, I try to rest my mind as well. Still, the randomness of the tour guide leaving us behind like that is incredibly irresponsible. And what the hell was going on in his mind when he left us without kayaks?

It is unfathomably dark inside the forest. The jungle sounds have softened a bit now that the animal kingdom that rules this place has nested in for the night, but there are still sounds – and it disturbs me not knowing what creatures are making them. Add in the flies and mosquitos that are relentless during daylight hours, and I begin to wonder if I'll be going to go home with a deadly case of malaria or a botfly having laid eggs inside one of my numerous mosquito bites around my neck, head and hands.

"Maybe we should have stayed where we were, Brad. They could have picked us up with the next tour group," I mention, with hindsight.

"That never crossed my mind, Liv, but we've come this far now," he says and sighs. "We may as well just keep going."

An hour after I close my eyes I'm awakened by the sound of a vehicle. Brad quickly scrambles to his feet, slipping briefly in the softer gravel at the road's edge in his rush to see the vehicle approaching. It has only one headlight functioning and didn't sound like it was in good running condition. Brad stands in the middle of the road and waves his hands back and forth above his head, yelling out to catch the driver's attention.

As the truck limps its way down the dirt road, it slows and stops in front of Brad. Brad runs over to the driver's side to address the driver, who has a gun pointed at him when he nears the window. We can only hope that the driver is willing to help two lost tourists. My heart pounds. I can see more clearly now past the headlight's beam. I approach near Brad and smile as sweetly as I can.

"No need for the gun, *senor*. We're lost. *¿Entiende?* Can you help us?" Brad asks.

The driver stares at Brad for a minute then puts his gun down on his lap, his hand still within his grip.

"Estamos perdidos," Brad continues. *"Nuestro grupo nos dejó atrás. Puede hacernos llegar a la ciudad?"*

"What are you saying to him?" I ask.

"Just a minute, Liv."

"Sí," replies the driver. *"Meterse en la parte trasera de la carretilla."*

"What did he say?" I ask again impatiently.

"He told us to get into the back of the truck. He's going to take us into town!"

Brad grabs my hand and leads me to the back to help me lift myself into the bed of the old beat-up single-headlight farm truck. *"Gracias,"* Brad calls out to the driver as he bangs his palm on the side of the cab.

As the farmer starts to drive, I feel the heavy jerk of the manual transmission lurching the old beast forward from first gear and once again when he shifted into second. The bumpy ride was uncomfortable, but a far better solution than sitting in the mud shivering all night, not knowing where in the world we are. It took me a minute to realize I am sitting on top of a chicken cage. I grab the well-worn two-by-six wood slat at the edge of the truck bed to keep herself from flopping back and forth as the truck limped its way along. Hopefully, by morning everything will be back to normal. A meal and a hot shower are all I want now. And a comfy bed. God, I'm so tired, and by the looks of Brad, he's done with this bullshit too. I lean forward to ask Brad, "You speak Spanish fluently?"

"I'm a little rusty, but I lived in Mexico for a few years with my brother, so I picked up the language quickly. It's very helpful to be able to speak Spanish when you live there. They can't con you when you know what they're saying behind your back," he says, laughing then gives me a relieved smile.

"I can't speak a lick of Spanish," I tell him, "So I'm going to have to rely on you to get us the hell out of here."

The farmer's truck turns down a narrower road leading to a farm. I wonder what the farmer is doing. When he brings the old truck to a full stop, Brad jumps out of the truck bed to find out where we are. *"¿Dónde estamos?"*

"Puede dormir aquí esta noche y volver a la casa mañana."

"Sí, gracias."

"What did he say?" I ask.

"He wants us to stay here tonight and can take us into town tomorrow morning. He thinks it's too late to drive into town and return to his farm after." Brad checks his watch and reports that it is nearing ten-thirty. He shrugs then offers to help me get out of the truck bed.

"This just keeps getting better and better!" I mutter with deep frustration. "Where the hell are we supposed to sleep? In the back of this truck with the fucking chickens?"

"No, he's pointing at his barn, Liv. We can sleep in there. It will be warmer and drier in there, hopefully."

Brad reaches into the bed of the truck to retrieve my backpack. We follow the farmer, who told Brad his name is Manuel, into the barn, where coffee-bean sacks were piled five high against the aging boards of the interior structure. Next to the coffee sacks there is a loose pile of hay near to the horse stalls. "It looks like he's a coffee farmer," I say.

"Yeah. The smell of coffee is strong, eh? I think we can lay down over there in that hay pile. The hay will act as an insulator and maybe our clothes will be dry by morning." Brad looks over to Manuel and asks, *"Tienes algo para comer o beber?"*

"Sí," Manuel replies.

"What now?" I ask.

"I asked him for something to drink and eat. He said yes."

"Oh, thank Christ! Finally, some food! I'm starved."

Less than ten minutes later, Manuel's wife brings us hot coffee and warm pita bread. Brad hands Manuel's wife a US twenty-dollar bill to thank her for her generosity. She nods and smiles brightly, popping the bill deep in her apron pocket. We devour the bread and sip the coffee eagerly.

According to my cellphone it is just past eleven at night, and now that we'd had a bite to eat and a coffee, we were more relaxed and find ourselves fighting to keep our eyes open. There is no cell service on the farm, so I turn off my phone and tuck it inside my backpack. I move the hay around my body in a cocoon shape to warm myself, and Brad follows suit just a few feet away from me. "You can sleep closer to me if you want, Brad. I promise I don't bite."

"Sure. If we're spooning, are you big spoon or little spoon?" he teases and winks at me.

"Big spoon," I reply. The last thing I want is his morning wood pressed up against my ass and his hands cupping my breasts when we wake, but I'd rather not mention it if I don't have to.

Just before sunrise, a rooster crowing at the side of the barn brings our sleepy selves to full attention. I am desperate to find somewhere to go to the bathroom and decide to have a quick squat pee in the corner of the barn opposite where we'd slept. With any luck,

Brad won't see me peeing from his position in the barn, but at this point I'm not as bashful about it as I normally would have been.

"I promise I'm not looking," he says with his back turned to me.

"Well, if your mother truly was a porn star, I'm sure this isn't anything you haven't witnessed or heard her doing before," I say dryly. "If you have to pee, do it over here, but if you have to do the other thing, I suggest you do it outside behind the barn."

"Nah, I'm good," he says and chuckles.

"Do you think they're awake now? Should we try to see where we are?"

"Just tell me when it's okay for me to open my non-virgin eyes."

"You're in very good spirits considering the situation we're in. I'm not feeling as amused as you."

Brad turns his head back toward the wall of the barn. "I can hear voices outside. We should go check it out," he suggests.

Brad jumps to his feet to open the barn door but hesitates. Outside there were three male voices talking to Manuel and the conversation seemed quite aggressive.

I whisper, "What are they saying?"

"Something about the farm. I'm guessing these guys are drug smugglers that go around harassing the local farmers. Quiet, Liv. Let me listen," he urges in a hushed voice.

The conversation is short-lived, but Brad got the gist of it. The farm is being used to grow coffee beans, and coca for cocaine. Brad knows this is going to be a bad scene for us if these thugs know he and I are hiding in the barn. He turns around and pushes me back deeper inside, putting his finger up to his lips to quiet me. He points over to the haystack we'd slept in and grabs my hand to take me over to it. He pulls piles of the hay back and whispers for me to hide inside the hay pile and stay perfectly still.

I quickly take Brad's advice and climb inside the hay for cover. I am shaking uncontrollably with the fear of something truly horrible happening to us if we are discovered. The horses in the barn start to make rustling sounds like they know something is about to happen.

We can hear the squish of footsteps in the mud next to the barn wall, then suddenly the barn doors burst open. I peer through the straw pieces and see Manuel being pushed inside. The horses are startled and making a fair amount of unsettled movement within their stalls.

"¿Cuándo se cosecha el cacao?" one of the men demanded.

"Pronto, la cosecha de la próxima semana," Manuel replies, sounding upset.

The man put his gun up to Manuel's temple. *"La semana próxima, la semana próxima,"* Manuel confirms with urgency.

Satisfied that he had made his point, the man put his gun back inside the waistband of his pants. He slaps Manuel across the face firmly with the back of his hand then marches out of the barn, slamming the door behind him. *"Largarse, largarse,"* he yells out to the other men in his group. The engine of their truck starts, and then we hear all of them slam their doors and hightail it away by spinning their tires in the damp soil of Manuel's driveway.

Brad and I pop our heads out of the haystack and look at Manuel. He is on his knees, rubbing the side of his face where he had been struck before standing to his feet. He looks over toward where Brad is emerging from the haystack and signals for him to stay put. Brad nods his head and lays back into the hay next to me. Brad reaches to nudge my arm and whispers, "Stay quiet for a bit longer. We need to make sure those assholes are long gone before we exit the barn. And I gotta tell ya, if I didn't need to take a crap earlier, I sure as shit need to take one now."

Chapter Fifteen | Stowaways

At eight o'clock in the morning, Manuel returns to the barn to bring us hard-boiled eggs and more coffee. I'm so grateful for him and his wife's generosity and I wish I had something to give them in thanks. Brad used his last twenty-dollar bill to give Manuel's wife, and I only have my credit cards, which are useless to repay this lovely family for their kindness.

He tells Brad he will take us into town, but we will have to hide under a cover in the back of his truck in case the guys who were harassing him earlier are watching him leave the farm. Manuel backs his truck up to the door of the barn and then signals for us to climb into the bed and cover ourselves with the loose jute coffee bags. We do as he tells us as quietly as possible.

Brad and I are face to face under the coffee bags, holding our backpacks to our chests and assuming the fetal position, up tight to the top end of the truck bed. Manuel climbs inside the cab of his truck and cranks the starter over twice before the engine sparks to life. He then drives off towards the city with us, his stowaways, while I reach for Brad's hand to hold. "Do you believe in God, Brad?" I whisper.

"Not as a general rule, but I'm thinking now is a good time to start praying just in case."

I nod. "Same."

Just a few minutes down the dirt road towards the city, Manuel's truck is stopped in the road by who are likely the same crew that had harassed him earlier this morning. Brad translates that they wanted to know where he was going. Manuel told them he has seven dozen eggs and a large bag of coffee beans he will sell in town with him in the cab of the truck, but that wasn't good enough information for them. We can hear their footsteps as they walk around his truck, one man on either side of it. They poke their rifles at the chicken cage and the jute coffee bags that were covering us. I am petrified of being discovered—my eyes wide and ears on high alert. The bag over Brad is flipped up, and then without warning the bag covering me is also flipped off with the tip of a rifle. The two men start laughing, then get serious.

"Get out!" the lead man shouts aggressively at us. *"Americanos!"*

The lead man then pokes at Manuel with the tip of his rifle and gives him a look of discontent. *"Tenerlas!"* he shouts to one of the other men.

We are unceremoniously taken from the bed of the truck. The lead man smacks the hood of Manuel's truck and tells him to go, as one of the other men aims his rifle directly at Manuel's head from the passenger side of the truck as a reminder threat. The third man grabs me by the arm and pushes me forward with the palm of his other hand on the back of my head, indicating for me to walk ahead of him. I attempt to look back to see where Brad is and am smacked across the back of my head and told to "walk" in English. My heart races with an intensity of fear I've never known until now. This is it, I thought to myself. I'm going to die here, and I don't even know where here is.

Earlier, when Brad and I were quietly waiting for the drug dealers to leave the farm, I ran over in my mind the events that led up to us being abandoned by the tour group operator. I am starting to become suspicious of the entire excursion. The way the guide was racing through the forest, the fact that of the six people in the tour group, only me and Brad were Caucasian—the others were quite likely locals pretending to be tourists. Had this been a set-up from the beginning of the tour? Was Brad as much of a victim in this scam as I am? And how could I know for sure if Brad knew Spanish so well because he once lived in Mexico?

Not knowing who to trust or what I was walking into with the armed men forcing us deeper into the jungle, I try to control my breathing, so I didn't start to hyperventilate. My deep-rooted fears are overwhelming, and my ability to stay calm and think clearly grows ever weaker.

In recent years, I'd read in the news and watched in dismay on TV the terrible stories of people who'd been abused, beaten, or killed in circumstances much like the one Brad and I are in now. I'm sweating profusely, knowing that whatever is about to happen to me is going to be horrifying. The faces of the ones I love most appear in my mind. And now, I can't stop crying.

Chapter Sixteen | No Contact

2:15 pm – Cali: “Hey. Have you heard from your mother in the last day?”

2:25 pm – Grace: “No. I’m guessing you haven’t either.”

2:27 pm – Cali: “Maybe she’s just busy and hasn’t had time. I’m sure she’s fine.”

48 hours later:

9:45 am - Cali: “Grace. Any updates?”

9: 48 am - Grace: “Nope.”

9:50 am - Cali: “That’s odd, don’t you think?”

9:52 am - Grace: “Yeah. Should we be worried?”

9:55 am - Cali: “I am! I’ve texted her twice and phoned her cell as well but I’m not getting any response. I’m definitely worried.”

9:58 am - Cali: “I’m calling her hotel, and I’ll let you know if I find out anything.”

11:20 am – Cali: “They wouldn’t tell me anything, Grace. I’m so fucking mad I could scream. They couldn’t give a flying fuck what happens to their guests. All I wanted to know is if she used her key card in the last 24 hours. Crickets. Like I was speaking Greek. WTF!”

11:28 am – Grace: OMG! What else can we do?”

11:30 am – Cali: “Hun, I don’t know. The cops down there are notoriously useless when it comes to missing tourists. They don’t like to get involved. I guess we just have to wait until she texts us. I'll let you know the second I do if she contacts me, and you do the same, please! And tell Carter that we think she may be missing. Maybe he knows how to get through to the staff at the hotel. He speaks Spanish, right?"

11:34 am – Grace: Yeah, dad speaks a bit of Spanish. I'll go get him now and let him know. BRB."

11:50 am – Carter: Cali, text me the phone number to Liv's hotel. I'll call and see if I can get some answers."

11:53 am – Cali: "I'm sending you all the hotel info and phone number by email. I've included her itinerary too. Please keep me posted. I'm losing my mind here!"

12:30 pm – Carter: "They said she booked a tour from the hotel – some inhouse thing – but that was three days ago. They don't keep track of how often a guest uses their keycard to get into their suite. I got them to connect me to her suite phone and left an urgent message on her machine. The front desk manager said if he sees her, he will tell her to phone us, but I'm not holding my breath that he'll do it."

12:35 pm – Cali: Thank you! This is really ridiculous. I told her going alone was a bad idea. JFC. So, now what? We just wait???"

12:37 pm – Cali: I'm going to call on a friend of mine. He's got contacts that might help us out. I'll keep you posted."

1:40 pm – "Daniel. It's Cali."

"Hi Cali. Sorry. I was in the middle of a meeting when you called. I was just about to ring you. What can I do for you?"

"It's about Liv. We've lost contact with her. I know you two aren't dating anymore, but I'm lost for ideas on how to reach her. She's not answering texts or calls, and she agreed to send me and Grace text updates daily while she was down there."

"How long has it been since you last heard from her?"

"This is day three without contact. I'm really worried Daniel. Carter speaks a bit of Spanish and was able to get a bit of info on when she was last seen at the hotel, but the staff have been tight lipped, as if they know something but won't say what it is. Maybe I'm overreacting."

"No, you're not overacting, Cali. But you do need to calm down. I can hear how upset you are."

"Damn straight I'm upset! Should we report her missing to the police in Panama?"

"Yes. Most definitely. Phone the Panama City Police and file a missing persons report immediately. As far as I know, any person who's been out of contact for over forty-eight hours is considered a missing person. Or would you rather I call?"

"Can you? I think they will take a man calling more serious than a distraught woman like me."

"I hate to agree, but you're right. Listen, I have a good friend who is ex-army. He might be able to connect us with someone who has investigative abilities that could be hired to search where Liv might have gone to within the Panama City area and her hotel. The sooner we get a plan in action the better."

"Thank you, Daniel."

4:20 pm – Daniel: "Cali, good news. My contact Gord got someone sorted who is in the business of going down to Central and South America to find missing people. The price for his services is high but I'm willing to pay whatever it takes to find Liv."

"Oh, my God. Thank you! I'll tell Grace and Carter. Keep me posted."

6:45 pm – Gord: "Listen Daniel, the sooner we get Roman down there, the better the chances of finding Liv are going to be."

"Yes, I'm aware of that. Let's get Roman set up as soon as possible. Give him my cell number and have him contact me directly for payment and details he may need. And thank you. I owe you one."

"You're welcome, Daniel. He's going to ask for fifty-thousand up front, and he's requested all Liv's contact information, including cellphone data, her passport number, and a recent photograph of her before he'll fly to Panama to begin his search efforts."

"We'll have that information for Roman within the hour."

Chapter Seventeen | The Outpost

The muddy and well-worn dirt driveway we've been forced down leads to a cabin at the edge of Manuel's coffee fields. This appears to be an outpost where the drug traffickers can monitor the activity of Manuel and the crop of cocaine they have growing among his rows of coffee plants. The three men are conversing in Spanish, and the man pressing me forward is pointing to the cabin where I assume Brad and I are going to be held. I don't know what their end game is and that frightens me most.

I want to fight off the scenes in my head about how I anticipate we'll be treated, but I'm gripped by my imagination, fear, and anxiety. I do what I can to familiarize myself with the surroundings of this place. I try not to move my head too much to the left or right, so I don't get smacked again. Or worse. I catalogue how long the walk from the road to the cabin is in the estimated number of steps I've been counting internally, the kind of trees surrounding the cabin, and anything else that could be of use if Brad and I ever get a chance to escape.

The air is thick with moisture and the sounds of birds chirping and monkeys chattering within the trees. It feels like another rainfall is coming soon.

Brad is still behind me being roughly handled by thug number two. Thug one, with his camo printed t-shirt, dark green khaki pants and dirty army style ankle-high boots smells like stale beer and pipe tobacco. I haven't gotten a good look at his face yet, but when I do, I plan to imprint every detail of it in my brain.

I've gone from anxiety to anger now. Brad can't help me anymore. I'm going to have to help myself or die trying.

I trip on the lip of the door's threshold and stumble a bit to get my balance back as I'm tossed inside. I take a deep breath and sweep my hair behind my ears so I can get a better look at where I am. It's dark inside as there are only two windows both covered in coffee bean sacks. There are two doors—one front and one back. Both have heavy duty locks, but I can see neither of them lock automatically. Inside the cabin is a kitchen, a satellite set-up, a rack of various automatic weapons and a seating area with television monitors. It is then when Brad and I see the set-up that we know our captors have been secretly monitoring the activity on Manuel's property and were aware that he was hiding us in his barn. We are doomed, it seems.

The most aggressive of the three men, named Juan, shoves Brad and I into the kitchen area and tells us to kneel. Another of the men, thug number two, whose name had not yet been spoken, grabs Brad's hands to tie them behind his back while Juan ties my hands. Juan leans down and licks my cheek and then begins to laugh. I shudder at the thought that this pig of a man and his disgusting companions taking their turns with me before they slit my throat.

It is everything I can do to prevent myself from crying uncontrollably. My emotions are at a peak and the only thing keeping me sane is the adrenalin fueled by intense fear. If we hadn't accepted the ride in Manuel's truck, would we have been safe from these awful men? Would we have survived walking into town without incident? These were the kind of questions I may never be able to answer.

Brad's expression is fury at the actions of the men, especially after seeing Juan lick my face. His eyes flashed with fire at Juan, telling him something in Spanish. Based on the low growl of his tone it was a threat. Juan laughed and replied in English, "Watch your mouth or I'll cut your tongue out."

The bad news is at least one of them speaks English. It will be hard to say anything to Brad without them knowing what we're saying to each other.

If this is a kidnapping with intent to extort money from our families, the disgusting and aggressive behaviour isn't necessary—

unless they have no intentions of keeping us alive even if they are paid for our safe return.

During our lengthy jungle walk, Brad told me more about his experience in Mexico living with his brother, included having to deal with a drug trafficking ring. His brother was the manager of a timeshare sales office, and the company he worked for was owned by a major drug-smuggling and money-laundering operation in Puerto Vallarta. The drug money was used to build resorts and buy up other properties to launder it. One thing Brad and I knew for sure was that in impoverished places, money talks. Brad speaks out in Spanish to ask if they wanted money.

"¿Quieres dinero?"

I know what dinero means, so for a brief moment I am following along with the conversation. Alfonso is the leader of the three-man team.

"Si, si," he replies, offering a very wide smile.

All three of the men appear to be in their late twenties or early thirties. I remind myself that in this light I can get a good long, hard look at their faces. Scars, mustaches, colour of hair, height, clothes, and any other details I gather I repeat in my head several times to lock the information into memory. Gerardo is the second in command, so I was right to call him thug number two, and he is clearly high on cocaine. He is anxious and fidgety. As the other two men move around the small cabin cleaning guns, opening packages of bullets, and making coffee, Alfonso moves Brad and I up against the wall next to the cabinets in the kitchen.

Their conversation about money begins in Spanish and Brad listens eagerly to what they were saying. The three men decided they were going to demand five hundred thousand from each of our families. They rummage through my backpack for my phone and then walk up to me and kick my legs. "Who do we call for money?" Alfonso demands.

"Cali," I blurted out without hesitation.

"Where are you from?"

"Vancouver, Canada," I say, trying not to make my voice sound shaky.

"What time is it there?" he asks.

I have to think on that for a minute, then reply, "About six o'clock," I say. "She won't be awake yet."

Alfonso scrolls through my contact list for Cali's number and writes it down on a piece of paper and then turns my phone off. He dials Cali's number on a burner phone connected to their satellite antenna and waits for her to answer.

She may have ignored the first attempt to contact her as Alfonso ends the call and redials. He has his call on speaker, and I hear Cali answer with a harsh "Hello."

"We have your friend. We want five hundred thousand in cash by Thursday, or we kill her. We will call back to tell you where to bring the money," he says, then promptly hangs up.

6:10 am – Cali: "Carter! Liv has been kidnapped. I just received a call from someone telling me they were holding her ransom for half a million dollars. They want the money in cash by Thursday! Oh my God, what are we going to do? Carter, did you hear what I just said?"

"Yes, yes, Cali! When did you get this call?"

"Just now. This is very serious, Carter. Do you have that kind of money to secure her release?"

"No, not in liquid assets. I'd have to borrow from the bank against the business to get that kind of money," he says. "It would take at least a week for any funds to be ready. What kind of money do you have? I mean, are you willing to gather some of your money with mine to get her back home safely?"

“Of course, of course. I’ll pay anything to get her back, you know that! I have to get to the bank first thing and organize how I’m going to get the money so quickly.”

“Okay, Cali. Let’s keep in contact today as we figure out how much money each of us can get and find out how we’re going to pay them. Jesus, what the hell did she get herself into? Grace is going to be beside herself when she hears this.”

“Dad, what’s going on?”

“Grace honey, we have terrible news. Your mom has been kidnapped in Panama. Give me a minute please. I’m on the phone with Cali trying to figure this out.”

“Cali, I’m going to fly down to Panama and personally deliver the money to rescue Liv. I’m going to call my dad this morning and ask him to take over the business while I’m down there looking for her. Grace, honey, I need you to be especially strong and help Grandpa out as he takes over for me. I don’t know how long I’ll be away, but hopefully it will only be for a couple of days.

“Are you sure you can do this? What about the police? Can’t they do anything?”

“I don’t trust the police down there. Just trust me, will you? We’ll get her back, Grace. We’ll get your mom back home safe, I promise. Cali, are you still there?”

“Yes. Do you really think going down there is the right thing to do, Carter?

“What choice do we have?”

6:30 am – Cali: “Daniel. I got a phone call this morning from some guy in Panama. They’re asking for half a million dollars for Liv’s safe return. I don’t have that amount of cash in liquid assets and neither does Carter. I don’t know what to do. Can you and Jason get that kind of money within twenty-four hours? We can pay you back.”

"Cali. Do we know for certain that Liv is alive, or did they only call to demand money without proof of life? I'm sorry. I don't want to scare you or be trivial about this, but I have to ask the question. I'd need to have some confirmation that she's alive before we send them half a fucking million dollars to some blackguard with your phone number."

"No. The number came up on my phone and I thought it was a robo-caller, so I ignored it. But they called again seconds later so I answered. They didn't say she was alive, and I didn't hear her voice in the background."

"Was the number a regular phone number or something weird like a V followed by random numbers?"

"Yes, it was odd. It wasn't a normal phone number. Fuck!"

"Okay. We'll have to wait until they contact you again. In the meantime, Jason and I will get the funds arranged. Have you spoken to Jason about this yet?"

"No. Just you, Grace and Carter. I'm losing my shit here, Daniel."

"I know, I know. But you have to stay focused since you are their point of contact. Do you understand me, Cali?"

"Yes, yes. I know. You're right. I'll get myself together. Just let me know the minute you have the money."

10:02 am – Daniel: "Roman, it's Daniel. Gord gave me this number. Is this your satellite phone?"

"Affirmative. Only use it as necessary. What can I do for you Daniel?"

"We've had contact. Liv's friend Cali was called this morning, and it is a kidnapping with a ransom request situation.

"Do you have the kind of money they are asking for? How much did they demand?"

“Yes. Half a million. I can wire the ransom funds to you if, and I assume, in this situation you’d be the direct contact person? But to be clear, we don’t have proof of life.”

“Affirmative. I have a bank account for the transfer, and I’ll deal directly with the ransom issue from there. I’m just landing in Colón now. I’ll send you the bank transfer information by email. Also, I’m sure they’ll want the money in US dollars. We need to know if we are doing a wire transfer or a cash handoff.”

“Listen. As mentioned, we don’t have proof of life. I’ll send you the money, but we’re not moving forward until we know that Liv is still alive.”

“Copy that.”

11:00 am – Daniel: “Cali, it’s Daniel. How are you holding up?

“I’m okay, all things considered. I’m still freaking out with worry.”

“Understandable. I hate to admit that I’m emotionally a mess about this as well, but if I stay on task, I can keep it at bay. Listen, yesterday I hired a private investigator to search for Liv after we talked, and now I’ve informed him this is a kidnapping and not just a missing persons search. He’s ex-army, so he has the skills and contacts to handle this. He’s also a specialist in this field. It’s best that we all stay home and wait for the investigator to do his work. Tell Carter it’s all in hand and we’ll keep them both posted on any new information we get.”

“Got it. Thank you, Daniel!”

Chapter Eighteen | Contact

After Alfonso had dialed Cali's number, he calls Brad's brother with the same burner phone. The identical message is relayed, asking for half a million dollars for Brad's safe release.

"Liv," Brad whispers to me, "There is no way my brother has access to that much money. Maybe your family has it for you, but I'm royally fucked here." Brad's eyes are downcast as he concedes his position. For a guy who tends to be on the glass half-full team his mood is rightfully soured by his lack of prospects. I can't blame him.

"Brad. Don't focus on the money demands. I doubt my family can get that much money in such a short span of time for me either."

I can feel Alfonso's eyes on me, and I lean back against the wall, breaking my conversation with Brad.

As we sit here with our hands tied, my belly grumbles for food, my arms are sore from being forced into the same position for several hours, and my wrists are heavily chaffed by the rough rope that binds them. Every time I notice I'm not being watched I try to wriggle one of my hands out from the rope, but I've had no luck thus far.

The three of them are standing side by side at a makeshift armory table while ensuring every weapon in the cabin is fully loaded. Alfonso pivots his head over his shoulder to look at us. The stare down he's giving us spurs more questions about what will happen next. The gun in his hand, fully loaded gets cocked with a sharp double click sound.

He furrows his thick dark brows making him appear even more vile than he already looks, then he gestures for us to stand with a curt upward jerk of his wrist firmly wrapped around the gun's grip. "Get up!"

6:05 pm – Roman: "Daniel, there are a few things I should mention. I understand you or someone in the family has filed a missing person's report with the police in Panama. Not that every police officer there is untrustworthy, and it is impossible to know which of them would be easily corrupt, so for this reason, don't expect much from them, and only give them what they ask for. Nothing more."

"Thanks. I'm well aware, but I'll pass that on to her family members."

"Additionally, the police will rarely take a missing persons report seriously if the missing individual has been out of contact for more than forty-eight hours. In most cases, it's unlikely that we'll find her at all, let alone alive. Robberies and kidnappings often end in murder. I hate to say this, but it is the most common reason for a tourist to go missing in Central America. I don't want to be an asshole here, but I want you to be clear on what we're most likely dealing with."

"I understand. I'm a practical man, Roman. I don't have any delusions of a happy ever after, but to Cali, Grace, and her ex-husband, relaying these grim statistics to them is out of the question. They need to cling to hope until we can definitively say otherwise."

"However, and bear with me here, Daniel, since the kidnappers did contact Cali this morning, it is a positive sign that Liv is quite likely still alive. They have her phone and know that Cali is a key contact. Only Liv could have told them to call Cali."

"I hear you, Roman. I'm going to remain hopeful, but I'm prepared for the worst."

"Get a proof-of-life video or photograph if you can, Daniel. It's the only way we can be certain."

7:30 pm – Cali: "Hey Daniel. I'm heading over to Liv's condo. I'm going to stay there until we know more. I um, I wonder if you'd like to stay with me there tonight. Do some brainstorming, you know?"

"Sure, Cali. I can meet you there after eight. Have you had dinner yet?"

"No. I can't eat right now."

"You have to eat, Cali. I'll pick something up on the way. See around eight."

"Thank you."

Daniel and I sat on the couch together, quietly watching a movie on Netflix to help ease our stress while we waited for the kidnappers to contact me with the ransom money drop-off location. I curled up into the corner of the couch and wrapped myself in a blanket which Daniel had draped over the back of earlier. He sat in the opposite corner with his feet resting on the top of the coffee table and a warm cup of Liv's favourite tea in his hand. There was no telling when the kidnappers were going to call. I gave everyone on my contact list a strict message to say I could not be disturbed under any circumstances due to a family emergency. This was an attempt to prevent the call we were desperately waiting for from being interrupted by someone else. Any family member looking for information was advised to call Daniel's cell instead of mine.

The waiting was killing us. After nearly two hours watching television, Daniel turned the volume off and started to ask me questions about Liv's earlier life. I knew everything that meant anything to Liv. Like identical twin sisters we were almost telepathically linked. And it had been that way since grade nine.

"She was always much shyer that I was. When I first arrived at our school, I teased her relentlessly about being so quiet. Eventually she got pissed at me and slapped my shoulder hard when I embarrassed her in front of a group of other students I'd befriended. I had respect for her that day. Nobody else ever stood up against my constant teasing like she had, and I teased everyone. It was a coping mechanism, you know? Over the balance of the school year and the following summer I taught her how to come out of her shell, and she taught me to be more respectful of my peers."

"That story doesn't surprise me," he said softly.

"Why is that?"

"It's common for lifelong friends to be quite opposite each other in spirit. They seem to thrive on each other and balance each other out. That kind of bond is a strong one."

"I guess you're right about that. I never thought of us that way, but it is so true about me and Liv. She's the one who gave me my name."

"Your real name isn't Cali?" Daniel asked, clearly surprised.

"No! My name is Catalina. I moved to Vancouver with my family from California at the beginning of grade nine and she started calling me California, then later shortened it to just Cali. It stuck all through middle school, and when we signed up for college courses I registered as Cali with my real name in brackets. I always liked it better than what everyone else used to call me, which was Cat. I think Liv knew something about me that I didn't."

"And you didn't have a nickname for her?"

I laughed. "No. You can't shorten Liv's name, but I sometimes called her dimwit. As you can tell, the dimwit thing didn't stick. I guess I suck at picking nicknames."

Daniel smiled at me. "I understood what Liv found so endearing about you. Not to make this moment odd, Cali, but surprisingly, I am feeling rather close to you now. Possibly, this terrifying situation is the reason, with Liv being the person you and I both adore so much." He paused and turned his gaze forward looking at the bedroom door. "We don't deserve her, you know. She's an angel," he added sorrowfully.

"Don't you dare lose your shit on me now, Daniel. I'm depending on you to keep *me* sane," I said, trying to hold back a flood of emotions. "You're the strong one here, not me!"

"You give me far more credit than I deserve, Cali. I may look strong, but I'm a mush pile inside. But I can be strong when I must, so if you need strong, I'll do my best to accommodate."

Just then, a text from Jason came to Daniel's cellphone, inquiring on any news. *"Nothing to report yet mate,"* Daniel replied. *"The wait is killing us."*

I laid down on the couch, covering myself in the blanket, resting my feet across Daniel's lap. He put his hand over my legs and gently rubbed the top of my shins as a sign of comfort, then turned the volume back up on the movie. But he wasn't really paying attention to what was being said in the film. After a while, he shut the TV off and we both fell asleep, waiting in painful silence for my phone to ring.

Chapter Nineteen | The Bunkhouse

The jungle is no place for a city girl to die, but I've made peace with the fact that this is my fate. After all the years I'd dreamt of seeing the deep-green foliage, the wondrous creatures and wild orchids, and feeling the dewy tropical air on my skin, it has all slipped away in these past few days of terror.

My wrists burn from the rubbing of the rough ropes around them. Brad has fallen asleep slumped over against the corner cabinet, looking as if he were already dead. My bladder aches from being filled to capacity for far too long. I look up at my captors, trying to decide whom to address with my stressed bladder issue. Just then Alfonso gives us both a command to stand. Please, make this a bathroom break. I'm dying trying not to pee my pants here.

"Get up!" he yells, and Brad startles awake. I stand with a struggle, sliding my body up the wall slowly so I don't fall over. Brad follows my move, and we chance a glance at each other.

Alfonso gesticulates with his hand for us to move forward. "Baño," he says gruffly as thug two unties my hands.

"Bathroom, Liv," Brad whispers, and I nod.

"That word I know," I whisper back. Relieved to be free of the ropes on my wrists and to have a long-awaited pee, finally, strangely brings a rush of pleasure. However, I know this brief moment of diversion will be short-lived. I rub my hands over my wrists but my attempt to soothe the pain is useless. I get shoved into the filthy bathroom. It is in this moment, looking at the cracked and peeling teal coloured paint on the interior boards across from this disgusting toilet in a crumbling cabin in the middle of the Panamanian jungle that I understand the privileges of my life that have gone so easily unappreciated.

I had recently come home from the most incredible holiday in Tahiti having spent an asinine amount of money for an overwater bungalow without a nano-second of guilt for my indulgence. Mere weeks later I am here in the most impoverished landscape I've ever witnessed. I shake my head. This blatant contrast with which I'm currently familiar with is more than humbling. If I survive this ordeal, how will it affect me?

They haven't hurt me physically or taken anything from me but my freedom and my dignity. I decide now, as I redress and wash my hands in the small metal sink, that this could be much worse. Much, much worse.

My hands are roughly gripped behind me as Brad is shoved into the bathroom after I was done. A smirk emerges on Juan's face and then he speaks to the other men in Spanish. Juan walks over to Brad after he's relieved himself and grips his hands as well. We are marched outside towards the back of the outpost cabin. The soil is damp from the recent rain. Twigs and leaves need to be navigated with caution, so I keep my head down to watch my step. Meanwhile, my heart races with yet another unknown future.

In behind, among twisted branches of trees and a heavy shroud of tropical plants, is another smaller brick building attached to makeshift horse stalls and a chicken coop. The door of the brick and stucco shelter is opened and inside were two cots, a small wood table near the door, and a toilet with a cracked seat, and a concrete sink against the back wall. Juan releases my hands and pushes me firmly inside, then does the same to Brad, keeping a handgun pointed at us all the while. Once we are thrown inside the bunkhouse, the door is slammed shut and a series of locks are secured. This is not what I expected, but then everything I thought would happen to me has thankfully been less horrific.

The kidnapper's footsteps fade as they headed back to the main cabin. While I find some form of comfort now that my hands were free from ropes, Brad wanders over to one of the cots to lay down, waiting for me to do the same.

"Aren't you tired?" He asks.

"Yes, and no. I'm so full of dread and adrenaline that I'm not sure I'd actually sleep if I did lay down."

As Brad stretches out his arms over his head on the cot, I realize he's right. Get sleep while I can. God only knows what tomorrow will bring.

"Suit yourself, Liv."

"Brad. Why are there two cots in here? Have they done this before?"

"Liv. Quit analysing this situation. But yeah, probably." He says as he covers his eyes with his forearm.

I nod reluctantly and lay down upon the cot next to his. The shoddy coil springs of the metal bedframe squeak like Brad's cot did when I sit down on the edge of the mattress.

Hunger pangs are the next issue for us. It has been several hours since Manuel had brought us the boiled eggs and coffee when we were hiding inside his barn this morning. Thankfully, half an hour later, Manuel is at the door of the bunkhouse with two plates of food and more coffee inside a thermos. My mouth waters at the sight of hojaldres served with chorizo criollos and a cup of chicken soup. Brad informs me of the correct local names of the foods are, however, I understood that no matter what they were called here, flatbread and sausages were what I was eyeballing and making my mouth water. Surprised by the quality of the food, I surmised that Manuel's wife is cooking for the kidnappers, and this was the leftovers of their earlier meal.

Standing behind Manuel is Juan, with a rifle ready in case Manuel, me or Brad make any sudden moves. Manuel is quiet and tries not to make direct eye contact with either of us as he sets the plates down on the small wooden table next to the door.

I'm not sure what to make of this. Is he scared to make eye contact, or is he in congress with the kidnappers hoping to get a piece of the pie when or if the ransom demands are met?

Manuel backs his way out of the door as he leaves, then the sound of the door locks being reapplied echoes inside our confined space while a small clay wind chime tinkled in the wind outside the door. The tiny space is filled with the scent of the food as we savour the offerings.

Between mouthfuls I say, "We should set aside a bit for later since we don't know when our next meal will come."

Brad's mind is elsewhere. "He doesn't seem like someone who'd be working with the drug guys on our kidnapping," he says confidently.

"Are you reading my mind? I was just thinking that a few minutes ago, I say as I dip my flat bread into the soup cup. "It is hard to know for sure, but I agree with you. I think he and his wife are victims of this situation the same way we are. Under constant threat of being killed for not doing what they're told."

I see Brad trying not to eat everything on his plate, contemplating what to save for later because of my suggestion.

"I couldn't imagine living somewhere where you're under the constant threat of being gunned down. I think my elevated blood pressure would kill me before the rifles do," I say. I wrap one of my sausages inside half a piece of flatbread and stick it inside my pocket.

"While I was sleeping in the cabin, did you hear anything about whether either of our families have the money they demanded?"

"No, but then I can't understand Spanish. I assumed whatever it was they were discussing was about money."

Brad nods. "I don't think it's a matter of the money, Liv, but more about the timing. Who do you know has half a million dollars just lying around in a bank account that can be put into a duffle bag and handed to drug-trafficking kidnappers within four days, from another country thousands of miles away? Not mine," Brad says, trying to hide his anger.

"My ex-husband has money, but the bulk of it is tied up in assets, not liquid. I don't think my family can save me either." I say and sigh loudly at this reality.

Brad pauses for a moment, then looks at me directly. "My name is Brad Allen Barkley. I'm thirty-two years old and my brother is a timeshare broker for the cartel in Puerta Vallarta. My dad died two years ago, and my mom lives with my sister in Toronto. I've never been married, and I've never felt so helpless in my life."

There is a deep sadness in his eyes that I never expected, since he has been so strong and heroic thus far. Brad has given up on the idea that he is going to somehow miraculously survive this ordeal.

The demands of the kidnappers are too narrow to work in our favour, and now it seems that Brad's situation is even more dire than mine. I step from my cot over to Brad's and wrap my arm around him as he continues to vent.

"My family will never know what happened to me," he says. "When these fucking bastards kill me, they won't even bother to dig a hole to stuff my body into. I'll be dumped in the jungle and left to rot or be eaten by some fucking creature out there."

My eyes well up. I can't control my emotions now. I have not imagined my demise the way he has. Until now.

"I'm sorry, Liv. I didn't mean to make you cry."

Wiping the tip of my nose with my shirt, I say, "My name is Liv Constance Nelson and I'm forty years old. I recently divorced my husband of twenty years, and I have a nineteen-year-old daughter named Grace, who is my rock. I'm in love with an investment broker in Vancouver, but I broke up with him before I left. I don't know that anyone in my family can get the money for my release, but I'm certain they will try."

My mind wanders again as I ask myself if it is likely that either me or Brad would be saved from being shot to death and dumped in the jungle as Brad had described even if our families sent the money.

I continue to hold Brad while both of our bodies heave from crying. After a few minutes, I release him from my embrace and decide to lighten the mood. I wipe the tears from my face and straightened my posture. At this juncture I am sick of crying every time the thought of never going back home enters my mind. I have to be stronger than this. "You're a real downer, Brad," I say, jokingly after a deep calming breath. "I may have to smack you around a little to smarten you up."

Brad lifts his head and offers a light laugh. He leans forward to kiss me, and I accept his warmth. He tries to get more passionate with me, but after a few more kisses I lower my head and push him gently away from me.

"This can't happen, Brad. I understand how you feel, and it would be wonderful to be intimate considering how distraught I am."

I lift my gaze to look into Brad's eyes. "I'm sorry if I led you to think otherwise."

Brad laughs in defeat and turns his head to look away from my eyes. "Can't fault a dead man for having a final wish," he says softly.

He is young, lonely, scared, and stuck in a room waiting to die with a woman who shares a unique connection with him by our circumstance.

"I get it," he says. "I got caught up in the moment. You're beautiful, Liv. Even with those bits of straw stuck in your hair and dirt smudges across your cheeks." He pulls a piece of hay from my hair. "I'm sorry. I don't know what I was thinking."

"It's okay. Honestly, I am flattered. Can I ask you a question?"

"Sure, what?"

"What are you doing down here in Panama? Were you travelling alone or was there someone with you? I mean, is there somebody here looking for you?"

"Alone, like you."

"If I have to die in the arms of a stranger, Brad, I'm glad it's you," I say, reaching to hold him again. Brad's embrace is firm and comforting, and in that moment a bond is formed between us that can never be erased. A stronger bond than I ever expected.

As I review this odd little shack with its corrugated metal roof, brick walls, and hardpacked dirt floor I try to imagine it as less dreary space. I start to redecorate it in my mind considering where I'd place a window, and what colour I'd paint the door. As I glance at what remains of what was once a lovely solid wood hand carved door securing us inside this dismal cage, and the hollowed-out gap beneath it from years of boots tracking through its dirt opening, my eyes bug out and I scramble to the corner of the bunkhouse atop Brad's bed placing my body tight against the brick wall. "Bbb..Brad," I stammer in a small voice. Brad's not sure what spooked me as he follows my moves with his eyes, conveying confusion. "What's the matter Liv?" he asks as he scans the space.

"Do you not see that snake that just slithered under the gap at the bottom of the door?"

"Shit. Fuck! Yes." Brad stands from his seated spot on the cot to examine the snake and figure out how much danger it poses, other than giving me a swift heart attack. He presses his open palmed hand toward me to indicate for me to remain still as he approaches the snake with caution and clear curiosity. "Stay back, Liv. I'm not sure what kind of snake this is or if it is venomous."

"Okay," I whisper.

Brad continues to observe the snake while I try to control my breathing.

"A chicken snake?" he asks, like I have the answer.

"Wait. A what?"

"Chicken snakes like eggs, and the coop is right beside us," he adds.

"Yeah, whatever. But is it the venomous kind?"

"No, not that I'm aware of. But I can't be a hundred-percent sure."

"Sure of the snake or the venom?"

"Either. Shush, Liv. Give me a minute here. I can't remember. Maybe it's an indigo snake. Shit. This fucker is huge."

"The only six-foot snake I know of chokes its victims."

"No, it's not a boa, Liv. Keep quiet, will you?" he says losing patience with me. He approaches the snake a little closer now as it cautiously slithers its way along the wall toward the toilet. Although it is long, it isn't a fat snake like a boa would be. My imagination is running amuck as I try to stay calm.

"I'm sure this is an indigo snake. Those reddish-orange markings on its underbelly are pretty distinctive," he says.

"But what if it bites one of us?"

"Liv. If it bites it won't…" Brad lunges forward to try to grab the snake at the head and I scream at a pitch I've never hit before.

Chapter Twenty | The Intruder

I swear my blood curdling high pitched scream has alerted every living creature and person within a country mile. The snake elevated its head in defence of Brad's close proximity – a position that means it has the intension to strike or scare an intruder, and my scream could not be contained.

As Brad lunged forward to grasp the head of the snake to subdue it, he missed and was promptly bitten. The snake went to bite him a second time, but Brad was able to retract far enough away to avert it. I grab Brad from behind and pull him up onto his mattress.

"Jesus fuck that hurts!" he says as he holds his bitten thumb and winces.

"Let me see," I urge as Brad shakes his hand hard twice before we both examine the bite marks. "Is it venomous or not?" I ask.

"No. I can tell by the bite pattern that it isn't. This motherfucker doesn't have fangs."

I can tell Brad feels like an idiot, but he was trying to catch it by the head as one is supposed to so he could wring its neck and kill it. We have no way of opening the door and there are no windows in this shack to toss it out of. The only option is to catch and kill.

God, how I hate this bunkhouse. My nerves, my patience, my dignity, my inner strength have all been tested in unimaginable ways. I had never imagined myself being at the receiving end of a military issue rifle or being held hostage in unfamiliar territory. I'm exhausted, hungry, angry, dirty, and so weak of fighting spirit that I don't know how much longer I can withstand this.

This snake is the tip of the iceberg for me. I know the jungle is full of snakes, spiders, lizards, and hundreds of other creatures that are potentially dangerous, but this was supposed to be a guided day tour, not an episode of Jungle Survivor – Destination Panama.

I tear a piece of my shirt off and soak it in the mirky coloured water from the tap at the sink. We have no medical supplies. All I can offer is to clean the wound for him. We can hope that when Alfonso decides to grace us again with his presence and a meal that they have something in the cabin to properly treat Brad's bite wound.

No sooner do I finish that thought and we hear the locks on the bunkhouse door being undone. I breathe a sigh of relief and immediately begin asking for a medical kit before Alfonso and Manuel enter. I shield my eyes a bit as the bright light from the open doorway is shocking. Even during the day very little natural light filters inside.

"Medicine? For what?" Alfonzo demands.

"A snake bite!" I say angrily. "Did you not hear me scream?" I point to the six-foot long tropical intruder wrapping itself around the base of the toilet and hold my stern face to him. "It's right fucking there!"

Alfonso laughs as he approaches the snake, takes the tip of his rifle to coax it to unravel itself and then lifts it up with the rifle barrel and carries it outside to set it free.

Meanwhile, Manuel sets our meals on the wooden table and nods to us. "Tengo medicina para la picadura," he says to Brad.

"What did he say?"

"He has medicine to treat the snake bite. Hopefully Alfonso will let him bring it to me."

"Oh. That's great!" I say standing down from my safe space on the top of the cot now that the creature from hell is gone.

When Alfonso returns to shadow the doorway Manuel repeats what he said to Brad. Alfonso nods and says, "Vamos, vamos!" sternly.

Alfonso turns to face Brad and smirks. "Tiny snake bite. You are not a man. You are a child." He then throws a fresh roll of toilet paper at Brad and laughs.

The list of obscenity laden insults I have in my head—that I know better to keep to myself—grow longer by the second. I want to lunge at Alfonso with a knife in my hand and stab him in the gut and tell him that it's just a tiny stab wound. *"Don't be a baby. You'll survive you sadistic fucking prick."*

Thankfully, Manuel returns within ten minutes with a medical kit. He applies what is likely an antiseptic and then covers the bite with a large plastic bandage. He gives Brad a pain pill and hands him a glass of water.

"Gracias," Brad says.

"Sí, sí," Manuel replies, then scurries out of the bunkhouse at Alfonso's grunting and waving of his hand to leave. The locks are reapplied, and we are back to living this hell.

"Eat something," I urge Brad.

"Yeah. Like what else is there to do?"

His mood is sullen and it's understandable. It is my turn to try to stay positive, but it becomes harder to muster any level of positivity the longer we are trapped here.

As we sit on our cots with our paper plates covered in refried beans and pita bread, I hear the frogs, birds, and other creatures settling in before sunset. These sounds have become strangely calming, marking the beginning and end of each day. It is our only way to tell what time it is. In the morning and night, the sounds are louder than during the day marking time in a way I'd not expected.

I place my hand on his thigh and say, "You were very brave to try to capture the snake. Thank you." I lean over and kiss his cheek.

"You're welcome," he says then bites into his pita bread.

"Are you going to save some of this for later?"

"I'm not big on refried beans, but if I'm starving later, I'll force them down," he says.

I catch myself looking deeper into Brad's eyes. As strangely as we met, then unceremoniously becoming protectors of each other, my emotions have gone from simple trust to admiration, to genuine affection for him. He was furious when Juan licked my face, his arms are always open when I need comfort, and now he dared to wrestle with a potentially poisonous snake to protect me. We've survived so much in such a short span of time. He catches me staring at him.

"What?"

"Nothing," I say and turn my gaze away.

"It's not nothing. What's on your mind?"

"Earlier, when you kissed me, I … I was flattered by your affections. I just want you to know that I do feel attracted to you and I don't know what to do with these emotions." I set my plate down on my cot at my side and clasp my hands together over my lap. As I raise my eyes up to look at Brad, I fully expected him to be smiling, but his return gaze was wanton. I can no longer deny our mutual feelings for each other, but I remain convicted to not getting physical. "No matter what happens I will always be thankful for you."

Chapter Twenty-One | Proof of Life

The next morning, after we were given something to eat, we hear voices outside and the locks on the bunkhouse rattle again. Our eyes flit to the door and our attempt to distract ourselves with lighthearted conversation about our favourite memories of our childhoods ceases midsentence.

The door is left open. All three men shadow the opening with rifles slung over their shoulders like malicious soldiers. I swallow hard at the sight of them and their smug faces as Brad and I sit frozen on our cots.

Alfonso is holding a local newspaper with the current date and a cellphone to video the two of us being held alive. Proof of life. This is good news as our families must be asking for it, which means they are at least trying to get the money to save us.

Alfonso tells me to go first. His instructions are clear. I'm only allowed to say my name and the amount of money requested to gain my safe release, and to hold up the newspaper to prove I am alive today.

Now that all three men have entered this tiny space, I feel the tension in my shoulders and neck tighten. I am lifted by my arm to stand and moved to sit on a small wooden chair in front of the toilet and sink. I don't bother to make myself look pretty by tousling my hair or wiping away whatever dirt and grime smudges are on my face. If they want real, I'll give them real. I look and feel like shit. I'm at my wits end with fear. The little clay wind chime begins to jingle in the jungle breeze as I nervously speak the words I've been told to say.

Alfonso has Brad do the same thing right after me, but I notice that the video is continuous, not stopped and started again between our proof of life statements. This tells both families that there are two victims—not just me, and not just Brad—being held for ransom. In a small way that makes me thankful. Grace, Cali, and Carter will learn that I have a companion in this dreadful situation which may make them feel some kind of relief knowing I'm not alone.

Cali

I gasp and cover my mouth with my hand as I watch the video the kidnappers sent to my cellphone. I'm sick to my stomach. I look up into Daniel's eyes as my tears well. Liv is such a mess that she is hardly recognizable. Her clothes and her face are filthy, and she looks terrified. It's heartbreaking to watch Liv shaking with fear, her voice cracking, trying to hold herself together.

Daniel takes my phone from me to watch the video and immediately sends the footage to his own phone to forward to Roman. Hopefully it will offer some clues as to where Liv and her companion are being held.

"She's not alone," I say as the shock of it slowly fades. But we have proof now that she's alive, Daniel!"

"Yes, Cali," Daniel says as he passes my phone back to me. "I've forwarded the video to Roman." He rakes a hand through his hair and makes a low gruff sound of frustration at seeing Liv so vulnerable. "But she's not alone, which is oddly good news. My deepest fear was that she was alone, but now we know otherwise. Surely, there has to be some comfort to her to have a companion, albeit I can well imagine how his family feels when they see the video."

Daniel sits on the couch and lets out a long, frustrated breath. "How did she get into this mess?" he asks, and I wish I knew the answer. He rubs his palms up and down over his thighs twice then looks back at me. He has to know it is impossible for me to answer.

I forward the video to Carter from my phone and tell him not to show the video to Grace. It is too upsetting. Grace doesn't need to see her mother like that. I then call Grace to let her know that we have proof of life. Carter texted back that he wholeheartedly agrees not to show Grace the video.

As much as I'd like to be in contact with whomever this Brad fellow's family is, it would be impossible to locate them.

Not ten minutes after we received the proof of life video, my cell rings again with an unknown caller. A gruff voice says, "Leave the money at this GPS location."

"Wait! I need a pen to write this down." I put my cell back on speaker, while Daniel puts his phone on record so we can get the coordinates down. "Ok, what are the coordinates?" I ask.

"91°15'30N, 79°56'11W."

The call goes dead immediately after we get the drop off location, safely recorded on Daniel's phone. Daniel is quick to forward them to Roman. Time is of the essence in both keeping everyone in the loop and getting the money in place for the drop off. His phone rings a few moments later.

"Daniel. Roman here. The video is great news. I'll be honest with you. I didn't have much hope of finding her alive past seventy-two hours. With the coordinates you sent I can narrow my search for her more effectively. I'll keep in touch with anything of importance."

"Thanks, Roman."

Daniel lets out another long breath and scrubs his chin with the back of his hand. He looks directly at me, concern written all over his handsome features, and my tears fall again.

"I'm so broken inside, Daniel. She must be so frightened."

Daniel reaches for me and holds me tight into his chest as I let out all my emotions.

"I know, Cali. I know," he whispers. "But we have to stay strong. Let it all out, then refocus for me. Can you do that, love?"

I nod with my head against his shoulder while trying to regain my composure.

"You are a rock, my friend."

He chuckles. "A crumbling rock at the moment but ta for that."

"Would you like some tea or something stronger?" I ask as I release myself and adjust my t-shirt over my sweatpants. I'm wearing Liv's clothes in a strange hope that this will bring me closer to her. I laugh at myself now, knowing I don't own a t-shirt or sweatpants. I'm just not the kind of person who has sportswear in her closet. But as far as casual clothes go, I'm quite comfortable.

"Go on, then. Tea would be brilliant, Cali," he says.

Chapter Twenty-Two | Roman – Hide and Seek

Encrypted Email Correspondence to Daniel:

I've received and secured the funds.

I've contacted Liv's hotel and gathered little information about her activities or current whereabouts. The manager was not forthcoming. I've located the tour operator Liv booked. I had to get aggressive with the staff for details of the time of the tour she attended and where or when she was last seen. When I asked why the guide abandoned two of their clients they had no answer, nor would they tell me which tour guide left Liv and Brad behind.

I'll begin my tracking efforts at 16:00 hours E.S.T., after I've done a detailed GPS mapping of the area. They may have been unknowingly looping the trail hoping another tour group would come across them before she and Brad were apprehended.

Typically, drug smuggling and human trafficking activity are carried out under cover of night.

Roman

Within two days of my arrival to the area where Liv and Brad had been last seen on the jungle tour, I have located a farmhouse with a large plantation of coffee. But the plantings are not exactly the same row on row. If my eyes don't deceive me, it appears there are coca plants within the rows of coffee plantings. As the two plants are similar enough at a quick glance, I can see why they were planted this way to disguise the illicit crop.

This location looks promising. It would be the perfect place to hold hostages since it is the only thriving settlement I've come across for miles. There are plenty of abandoned buildings in the area that I've investigated but there were no signs of recent activity at any of them.

If Liv and Brad were on foot trying to get back into the city, I'm making an educated guess that this is the direction they'd have traveled on foot. I stash my rental Jeep down the road from this active farm and cover it with branches and leaves to keep it hidden.

Based on the proof-of-life video, the style and age of the farmhouse resemble the age and materials used to construct the building where they are being held. Although this style of construction is not uncommon in rural parts of Central America, my gut tells me I'm on the right track.

I'm sorely aware that drug ops and kidnapping are not uncommon. Especially in remote regions such as this. I need to wait until it is dark enough for me to enter the property without being seen to ascertain how many people are in the farmhouse and what possible threats exist. In the meantime, I have about an hour of daylight prepare myself for what I'll need to properly investigate this location.

Now that night has blanketed this remote outpost, I can make my way through the thicket of scrub and trees next to the crops. The sky is clear of clouds, and the moon is at a waxing gibbous phase with roughly seventy-five percent fullness, giving me a bit of ambient light. At the edge of the field, I step quietly up to the side of the farmhouse and listen for voices from within. Moving closer to the rear door of the building I grip my gun and draw it from the holster. Through the window of the kitchen, I see the farmer, his wife, and two teenage children sitting at the table having a conversation over coffees. This scene seems normal enough and without suspicion of illicit activity, but that doesn't mean they aren't the kidnappers.

While I observed from a distance before approaching, I didn't see nor hear a dog which would sound off at the slightest squish of my footsteps in the wet soil. A rare saving grace. Examining the other sections of the farmhouse and barn building, I'm not seeing an underground storage space, cellar, or some other outbuilding that could be used to hold hostages. But my gut is still telling me I'm in the right place. This nice little farm family may seem innocent, but with crops of coca between the rows of coffee, I very much doubt they'd not have a hand in other nefarious dealings. Unless, of course, they are being forced by a cartel group to grow the coca for them.

I move on to inspect the outbuilding. There are two cameras on the exterior of the barn – one just above the door, and one facing north towards the farmhouse. I have stayed clear of those two cameras thus far. I need to steer clear of them while I make my way around the back of the building for a deeper inspection. I peer inside the barn through gaps in the boards and again see nothing of note. Sacks of bagged coffee, empty jute bags piled on the left, stacks of hay for the two horses, a shovel, harnesses, and a saddle hang on the adjacent wall, but nothing else. I'm perplexed. These are the only two buildings on the property.

As I turn my head back toward the coffee and coca fields, I catch a glimpse of a light in the distance between the jungle break of trees. Another farm? I sit down next to the barn and compare the distance from the GPS coordinates that the kidnappers sent Daniel, to where I am now. I estimate it is a twenty-minute drive from here to where the drop-off location is for the ransom. This has to be the right location to be holding Liv and Brad. There is absolutely nothing else in this vicinity.

I head through the crop field. Within a few minutes of trekking as stealthily as I can among the plants, I see a light source coming from the other side of the crop. Drawing nearer to this outbuilding, I hear men speaking Spanish, laughing and joking around outside the cabin next to their shiny new pickup truck. This symbol of wealth means there is a link between the coca growing in the farmer's field and these men in the cabin on the other side of the crop line. If Liv and Brad are being held anywhere near here, this is top of list.

Squatting near the edge of the field, I observe all the buildings and the three men. The weapons strapped over their shoulders are another sure sign to me. I view the surrounding area with the night-vision scope on my rifle to see if I can detect any further heat signatures around the buildings. Looking closer at the bunkhouse beside the horse stable, I cannot determine any heat signatures through the brick façade of the small brick cottage. And as I investigate from the edge of the field in the darkness, a little clay wind chime sounded out. I recognize the sound of the chime from the proof-of-life video. It was faint, and I didn't hear it the first time I watched the video, but it was evident in my second review when I bumped up the audio. This reaffirms I am right where I need to be to find Liv and Brad.

I decide it best to wait until the three men have returned to the inside of the cabin or left the property before moving in for a more detailed inspection. This rescue operation is all the more taxing, knowing there are two hostages to save. Not the original plan, nor am I being paid to rescue two people, but I cannot in good conscience leave one hostage behind.

Twenty minutes pass before the men finish their beers and cigars and retreat inside the larger cabin. It is still unclear if Liv and Brad are inside the small cottage, but now is the time to look closer. As I make my way around the property to get nearer, I'm aware that there will be cameras around the main cabin. The question is, are the cameras functioning and being monitored or not? As I walk the edge of the crops near the main cabin, I can hear the voices of the three men getting louder and more aggressive. They seem to be arguing about something, and I stop to listen to them, still crouched low near the edge of the coffee field. They are arguing about how they were going to split up the ransom money.

One of the men is telling the other two that he is the mastermind of the operation and so he deserves a larger share of the ransoms. The other men are firm about the fact that all three of them had an equal part in securing the victims and the money should be split evenly three ways. As the arguing continues, a gunshot rings out from within. It is hard to tell if one of the men has been shot or if a fired gun was a sign of power over the other two men.

I have to decide if I can get close enough to the cottage to see who is there or sit and wait for the three men to kill each other over their money dispute. Patience and keen observation of the area and the people involved is all I have to work with, but it is my specialty. I calculate the distance to the bunkhouse and look for any signs of tripwires, spotlights, or sensor mechanisms that will trigger my presence, now that I know the farmhouse is being monitored. The way seems clear. But I'll have to move slowly and quietly. Each step toward the cottage is carefully placed in case there is something hidden within the ground that would set off any sort of alarm. I have to assume I'm walking into what is essentially a mine field.

After only a few steps forward, a sensor light comes on. I duck back into the edge of the crops for cover. The tripped sensor light sends all three men outside to see what is there. Each man carries their rifle as they exit the cabin. Two of the men take either side of the cabin while the third stands ready at the front door. They yell back to each other to say it is just an ocelot looking to score a chicken for a meal and then drop their guard, lowering their weapons.

The first man walks around the back of the cabin and shoots at the ground to scare off the intruding animal. The gunshot disturbs the horses and chickens creating a cover of external noise. This was a perfect time for me to slip further toward the cottage, covering my movement noises with the sounds of the restless animals while the other two men are giving the third man shit for shooting his gun again for no reason.

Liv – Blind Fear

Why the sudden gunfire? Are they shooting at each other? Manuel? Other people? The second gunshot is so near us in the bunkhouse, I climb out of my cot and nestle into Brad's with him for security. We huddle under the blanket together and wait quietly for any further disturbances. I can't stop shaking. The dim illumination from our candle is barely enough light and the lack of understanding about what the men are doing add to my anxiety.

"With any luck they'll kill each other over money," Brad whispers. "They've been arguing for the last half hour about who should get more money."

"You understood all that shouting?"

"Yes. There is dissension in the ranks. This could be to our advantage."

"Have you ever thought about how we could escape this bunkhouse?" I ask.

"A thousand times! Haven't you?"

"Yes, but I've never been in this situation before and I really wouldn't know where to begin," I admit.

"I've looked around for weaknesses in the foundation, the walls, the door, but every time I try to inspect anything, one of those assholes is walking by or ready to come inside for something. One of the bricks is missing some mortar. If I had something to pick at it, we could pull that section apart," he says.

"This building is pretty solid, considering its location and age. I wonder if this was the farmer's original house," I say. "But I don't know for sure. I don't know anything anymore, Brad. I just want to go home."

"I know Liv. Just try to keep it together for me. I'm trying to stay positive. Can you do that with me?" he asks quietly as he firms his embrace around my shoulders.

I nod, take a deep breath, and think affirmations of positivity to myself.

Chapter Twenty-Three | Roman – The Extraction

I manage to get up next to the cottage, close enough to see through the larger cracks in the old concrete between the bricks on the back side of the building. The candle that burns near the toilet provides enough illumination to see that Liv and Brad are the two people inside as I hoped. Slipping around to the front side to the door, I see two padlocks on the outside of the bunkhouse securing them inside.

I crawl along the ground towards the back of the cabin again. The electrical cord that connects the sensor light is half buried in the mud. I cut it with my knife. I crawl back in between the cottage and the stable, positioning myself behind three stacks of hay bales for cover. I attach the silencer to my rifle and then toss a rock on top of the corrugated metal roof of the chicken coop to make the chickens squawk. I'm hoping the sound of the chickens in distress will make the three men once again go outside to chase the ocelot away. I flatten myself out upon the hay bales against the back of the cottage, peering out through my rifle's scope.

All three men emerge from the cabin with their rifles ready. The cocking sounds of their guns give me a sense of which direction they are moving. One of the men asks if the others want ocelot for dinner tomorrow night, and another asks, *"¿Por qué está apagada la luz?"*

Fuck. They've clued into the sensor light not tripping. I hope they think it is just a malfunction since anything is possible out here.

They make their way around the cabin in their standard formation with one man flanking each side of the building then circling to meet again around back, and the man whom I assume is the leader follows one of the other men instead of stationing himself at the door as he did before.

Without hesitation, I fire my first shot at the second man as he comes around the left side of the cabin, then promptly fire my second shot at the third man on the right.

The lead man aims his rifle in my general direction after my first shot dropped my target to the ground. He sweeps his rifle left to right using the equipped light which isn't enough to illuminate the open space between the cabin, the cottage, and chicken coop. And without the sensor light working, he fires repeatedly at random, blinded by the darkness.

Since the three men were arguing, I'm gambling that he's thinking one of his own men might be attempting to take him out of the picture for a larger share of the ransom money. I hadn't considered that option, but with the tension inside the cabin earlier, this could be another advantage for me.

The horses become spooked at the side of the chicken coop and begin rustling and vocalizing nervously at their stalls. The chickens are once again disturbed, clucking loudly and flapping around within their cage. The lead man runs toward the coffee field for cover. So far, it seems he has no clue of who is shooting whom.

My night vision scope easily set the runner within the crosshairs of my rifle's eyepiece. With a single shot to the back of his head as he fled, he is a confirmed kill, falling face first into the mud at the edge of the coffee field. Aiming back to where the other two men lay, I wait to see any movement and visually confirm they are also eliminated. I scan the back of the cabin again ensuring I've secured the property.

As I approach each of the kidnappers' bodies, I remove the guns laying in the mud near their hands. I toss the collected weapons into the murky darkness of the forest edge and then take each of their cellphones and stomp them with my boot to destroy them. I keep my back to the cabin as I round it to the front, peering inside through the window looking for any other men who are involved or unaccounted for.

Confirming the cabin is empty and contains no further threats, I enter to look for items that may belong to Liv and Brad. I find two backpacks, cameras and cellphones and set them on the well-worn kitchen table. I smash all the surveillance equipment with the butt-end of my rifle and the satellite set-up as well. This is quite the operation for such a remote location. At least one of them was tech savvy. I also check to see if there are recorded surveillance drives, but it appears the kidnappers are not keeping recordings from the remote cameras—it was only live-feed imagery on the television monitor. There's no internet this deep into the jungle, so I'm confident there are no cloud storage footage files to be concerned about either.

Satisfied that any possible evidence or link to Liv and Brad has been removed or destroyed, I gather up their belongings and head back up the road to where I have hidden my Jeep. I uncover the vehicle and drive slowly down the narrow roadway to the cabin with my headlights off. I park beside the cottage then pull out my bolt cutters to clear the padlocks on the bunkhouse door.

I speak firmly to Liv and Brad through the door before I open it.

"My name is Roman. I've been hired by Daniel Wesley to rescue Liv. I'm going to enter the cottage now. Do not make any sudden moves, as I am fully armed. Are you both able to walk?"

"Yes," they both reply anxiously. "Please let us out of here!" I hear Liv cry out.

I open the door with my rifle ready in my right hand. I do a quick visual sweep of the small area and then signal with my left hand for them to exit the cottage. "Get in the Jeep now!" I command.

As Liv and Brad reach the Jeep, I hear Brad call out, "Manuel!

"Who is Manuel?" I ask, aiming my rifle in the direction Brad is looking. He's appeared at the edge of the crop in the darkness – likely having watched the last few minutes of this rescue operation.

"The farmer next door. He's been helping us," Brad says.

I'm not trusting anyone in this jungle. Through my scope I see him raise a weapon, and I fire a shot at Manuel, but he's fired at us in the same instant. Liv screams as she scrambles into the back seat of the vehicle while Brad falls to the ground. He's been hit. "Fuck!"

I fire off twice more to confirm that Manuel is eliminated while Liv shouts "No!" when she realizes Brad's been hit. Brad collapses and lays motionless beside the rear tire of the Jeep. My eyes are everywhere looking for any sign of another unknown shooter. "Jesus fucking Christ," I mutter. I lunge forward to the Jeep and heft Brad to his feet to put him inside out of view.

I close the Jeep door and step back toward the cottage.

"Roman!" Liv calls out.

"Stay there," I command.

"Why was Manuel shooting at us?" she asks.

"Don't know. Don't care."

I do another full sweep of our position and decide it's clear. I hear Brad moan from inside the Jeep, and wince at the thought of him dying on my watch.

Liv is in shock, her hands shaking, as she lays his head upon her lap before I turn over the engine.

I toss my rifle into the front seat and keep my handgun within my easy reach in case we come across another unexpected situation during the escape.

While Liv is attending to Brad she says, "He's having trouble breathing."

I slam the Jeep in reverse and spin around to exit the compound. "Where is he shot?" I ask as the tires spin in the mud before finding grip within the soil. "First things first. I need to get us the hell out of here."

Liv is sobbing uncontrollably as she inspects Brad's chest. I glance over my shoulder and see her hands are covered in blood. "Keep pressure on the wound, Liv. Can you tell if it's through and through or is the bullet still inside of him?"

"I don't know. There is so much blood. I don't know!"

The adrenalin arising from the excitement of the last twenty minutes has elevated her stress and I understand what's going through her head. I hear Brad cough twice while Liv maintains pressure on his chest wound.

"He is breathing, Liv. Keep up with the pressure. We'll be out of here soon."

"Why would Manuel be shooting at us? He was helping us. He brought us food and first aid supplies when Brad got bitten by the snake." I look at Liv in the rearview mirror and it's clear she is struggling to understand any of this. As am I.

"I don't know what to tell you, Liv. He had his motive, but we'll never know what his plan was."

Liv ignores my comment as she is wholly focused on Brad.

"We're going home," she says to Brad as she uses her shirt to wipe away the blood coming from the edge of his lips. "We're going home. Stay with me, Brad."

Brad speaks weakly to Liv. "I tried to save you," he manages to say between gurgled breaths. "I saw him and thought he was going to help us, but he had a gun."

Liv tries to calm Brad and whispers, "shush."

"Why would he shoot at us?" Brad asks.

Liv continues to stroke his forehead and hold her hand tight over the bullet wound. "I don't know anything anymore. Don't talk, Brad. We're going home. You're going to be okay. You're going to be okay," she repeats.

I have to stop looking at her in the rear-view mirror and focus on getting as far away from this hell hole as possible.

"How did you find us?" she asks me as she wipes her cheeks with the back of her hand.

"Daniel and I have a mutual friend who hired me to locate you. I wasn't aware that Brad was with you at first, but after the kidnappers contacted Cali with the video, we were aware of Brad being with you. Daniel orchestrated the retrieval."

Liv's breathing is heavy and laboured as she maintains pressure on the wound in Brad's chest. In my head I'm envisioning that this whole setup with the kidnapping and the helpful farmer was a well-planned scam that they may have pulled off several times. It's the only explanation for why Manuel unexpectedly emerged from the crop's edge carrying a gun. None of us could have seen this coming.

As city lights from the nearby town become clearer, I lose hope that Brad is going to make it to the safehouse alive. He could have a collapsed lung and internal bleeding that I'll never be able to stop even if I made it to a local hospital for triage. His breathing becomes increasingly shallow the closer I get to the city limits. I stop the Jeep abruptly at the side of the road and hop out to check on Brad laying on Liv's lap.

Pulling off my t-shirt to give to Liv to help stop the bleeding, I realize we are too late. The last gurgles of air escape from Brad's lungs and he falls completely limp in Liv's arms.

"What's happening, Roman!?"

Her eyes are red, her hands still shake, and I have no words to soothe her. I lift Brad's legs and sit in the back of the Jeep with her, resting his legs over mine. I stare directly at her as I place my fingers on Brad's neck checking for a pulse.

Nothing.

My heart sinks in my chest as I reach to hold her hand over his blood-soaked shirt. "He's gone, Liv. I'm so sorry."

"No, no, no, no, no." Her head shakes back and forth at my words. "You have to do something. This isn't right. Do something!"

Liv's eyes widen as she grapples with the truth.

"No. You're wrong, Roman. He's going to be okay. Get back in the driver's seat and go to the nearest hospital." She moves her hands in a shooing motion. "Go!"

I can't make her believe what I'm telling her. I reluctantly drive to the nearest doctor just at the edge of Colón city limits to appease her. I enter the small building and drag the doctor outside to show him Brad. The doctor takes one look at Brad's limp body over Liv's lap and shakes his head while waving his finger at me. "No," is all he says as he retreats back into his ramshackle clinic.

Liv looks at me and shakes her head. "Why?" she asks. "I don't understand why."

She carefully lifts Brad's head from her lap, opens the door of the Jeep and lays Brad's head down gently on the seat as she exits. She cries, quietly at the side of the vehicle while I decide whether to try to comfort her or let her be. This extraction did not go as planned. I'm angry, frustrated and deeply saddened that I've lost someone I was trying to save.

After a few minutes Liv appears to be coming to terms with this tragedy.

"Time is of the essence. We need to go to the safe house, Liv." She reluctantly climbs inside to the front seat and buckles up the seatbelt.

"I feel sick. I feel empty. I feel lost," she says in a near whisper.

I don't reply for a few minutes as I drive onto the main road into town. I unclip my satellite phone from my hip and press redial.

"I just dialed the number to your friend Daniel. I'm sure he's waiting to hear from you." My hope is that by hearing Daniel's voice Liv will temporarily forget how upset she is about Brad's untimely passing. And Daniel has been out of the loop from my contact for far too long.

Liv grasps the phone in her hands and waits as the connection is made. She remarks to me that it is ringing before she hears Daniel's voice anxiously ask, "Is everything okay down there, Roman? Did you find Liv and Brad yet?"

Liv's body melts into the seat at hearing Daniel's voice after so long. "It's me, Daniel. I'm safe." she says.

"Liv! Oh, thank Christ! Are you okay?" he asks impatiently. "Are you hurt?"

"No, I'm not hurt. I'm shaken to my core, but I'm okay." Her breaths are still shaky from crying when she asks, "Did you know that there was another person with me when I got kidnapped?"

"No, we thought you were missing somewhere in Panama alone. That's why I sent Roman down there to find you. We didn't know anything about what happened to you until we got a call on Cali's phone from the kidnappers."

Liv wipes the tears from her cheeks and tells Daniel, "Brad died during the rescue."

This is the first time that she's acknowledged that he's gone.

The cellphone connection to Daniel crackled and she only heard part of what Daniel was saying to her. "Daniel, are you there? Can you still hear me?"

A few more broken words and static interfered with the satellite connection as Daniel continues talking, and suddenly the call is dropped.

"I lost him! Can I get him back?" Liv asks me in a state of panic.

"Don't worry about the dropped call," I say. "He knows you're safe, and that was all we needed to confirm with him. You can call him back soon. It's not the phone connection. The battery power is likely low. I have a backup battery in my bag in the hatch. When we get to your hotel, I'll change it."

"I have a charging cable for my phone in my backpack," Liv says.

She rummages through her pack for the charging cable, then connects it to the bottom of her phone before plugging it into the dashboard USB connector. She pauses for a moment and sighs loudly. "What are we going to tell Brad's mom?" Liv drops her phone onto her lap and gazes out the passenger window. I know she's trying to avoid letting me see her cry again. She turns her head to look into the back seat of the Jeep where Brad's body still lays covered in blood. "I can't call her. I just can't do it, Roman."

My hand reaches to hold hers beside me as I ease the Jeep into the parking lot of her hotel. "I'll get a blanket out of my other duffle bag and cover him while you go inside and collect your things. I'll meet you inside and pay cash for your outstanding hotel fees. It is best not to use your credit cards until you return to Vancouver."

She nods and unbuckles her seatbelt. "What happens next?"

"First, you need cover your shirt and pants before you go inside. You are soaked in blood. I exit the Jeep and search through my clothes for something that is long enough for Liv to wear to cover the clothes she's wearing. I find a raincoat and hand it to her. "Wear this until I get you to the safe house."

Liv slips the raincoat on and zips up the front. It covers her clothes enough to pass curious eyes.

After covering Brad's body with a blanket, I pay for her hotel stay and wait in the lobby for Liv to return. Although leaving a dead body inside my Jeep in such a public place is unnerving, I grit my teeth and hope that my contacts in the army base can artfully extract Brad from Panama into Canada without much explanation. My contacts know what I do here in Central America. I'm treated with kid gloves and sworn silence in my activities because my results are excellent. But not every case goes as planned and I've had to ship bodies out of Central and South America before, sadly. Sometimes I'm too late and the people I'm searching for have already died. I do the best I can with what I have available to me.

As she exits the elevator to the lobby with her luggage she asks me, "Did you check me out of the hotel?"

"Yes. You're good to go. Daniel has all the arrangements ready. I'll fill you in when we're back in the Jeep."

"Okay," she says.

"I'm taking you to my safe house while we wait to hear further instructions from Daniel. In the meantime, make whatever phone calls you need to make using my satellite phone."

Once we're back to the Jeep I tell Liv that Brad's body will be carefully handled and returned to his family with all due respect. "We have an official story about Brad being at the wrong place at the wrong time. Caught in the crossfire between two rival gangs in the city. An innocent bystander. It happens, sadly, and this will make it easier for us to get his body back to Canada," I say.

Liv nods and takes in a deep breath. "But we'll tell his mother the full story. She deserves to know the truth, Roman. If anything like this had happened to my daughter, I don't know what I'd do. I mean, I barely knew Brad, but I'll miss him like he was my brother. I can only imagine how his family will take this awful news."

Chapter Twenty-Four | The Safe House

We drive for nearly twenty miles outside of Colón, where Roman's safe house is located. He leads me inside and puts a pot of coffee on while he calls someone on his phone.

"I need access. Can I meet you in twenty minutes?" he asks.

"Where are you going? It's eight o'clock at night."

"I have to bring Brad to the base. While I'm gone, you must absolutely not leave this house under any circumstances. Have a coffee and something to eat. Rest if you can, Liv. There's food in the fridge," Roman says, pointing to the kitchen area. "I won't be long."

"Wait!"

I exit the safehouse and rush to the Jeep. I open the back door and pause to take a moment standing next to Brad's body laying lifeless on the seat. I lift the blanket off his face and my heart breaks. I tilt my head and close my eyes briefly as I place my hand on the top of his head. "I know tomorrow was never promised. You and me. Two stranded hikers in the jungle. I'd have never survived without you. We agreed that we'd either survive or die together. But not this. Not this." I lean down and kiss his forehead then recover his face with the blanket. "Rest in peace, my dear friend."

Roman stood behind me watching me say my last goodbye, his head tipped down, his cap off, and his hands clasped together in front of him. I appreciated his sign of respect. I stroked my hand down Roman's arm and squeezed his hand. "Thank you."

As Roman drove away, I locked the front door securely then looked up at the ceiling in an attempt to quell more tears. I need rest. I sit down on the couch, slumping my body deep into the cushions and set my legs up onto the coffee table. My eyes close and I drift off to sleep.

When I wake and try to move, it is then that I realize how much of Brad's blood I am wearing. My shirt and pants are crusting and sticking to my body. My heart aches as I head to the bathroom and start the shower. The trauma hits me hard as I remove each piece of clothing. I'm stunned by the shocking death of Brad.

As I climb into the tub I sit down while the warm water attempts to rinse away the dirt, the fear, the anger, the sadness, and the blood of a courageous young man who died in my arms. Suddenly my body starts to shake. Wrapping my arms around my chest, holding myself tight, I scream as loud as I can into the void of the room.

They say screaming is cathartic, but no amount of screaming, crying or showering off the stench of this ordeal is going to erase the intense fear I harboured of never seeing my family again.

Ten minutes later, the key in the door gives me a startle. "It's just me," Roman calls out as he walks inside. I scramble to my feet, wrap a towel around my wet body and head into the living room. "You're back. Thank Christ. I thought you'd be back sooner," I say.

Roman looks at me and nods. "There was a fair amount of paperwork to fill out. Did the shower help?"

"A little," I say as I adjust the towel in my grip at my chest. I'm lying. It didn't help at all. Nothing will, but Roman is doing his best to help me and I have to respect that.

"Get dressed and join me here when you're ready." As I pad my way back to the bathroom to dress, I leave the bathroom door open. I can't close doors right now. I can't handle confined spaces. Roman talks to me from down the hall.

"I spoke to Daniel while I was out. He's arranged for our flights from here to L.A., then a connecting flight for you to Vancouver. We leave tomorrow morning at eleven-fifteen sharp."

"I can't wait to be back home," I say as I sit down on the couch across from Roman. He's sitting in a wooden chair he dragged over from the kitchen. He places his phone atop the coffee table and reaches for his mug beside it then leans on his elbows over his thighs. His brows furrow as he asks. "You seemed rather on edge when I got back. Did something happen?"

"No. My nerves are completely fucked is all."

I pick up my cellphone from the coffee table to call Grace and my parents while Roman sips his fresh coffee. Our conversations go as expected – them and me being an emotional mess at hearing each other's voices and reaffirming I'm safe. I assure them as best as I can, but their concerns for my wellbeing will not be sated until I'm back home.

I then text Daniel with a graphic of a giant red heart. Within seconds my phone rings with Daniel's call. His comforting voice fills my ears.

"I eagerly await your arrival home, my love, and I won't sleep until then. Are you truly alright, Liv? Please tell me you're alright."

"I'm still trying to wrap my head around the events of today. Everything happened so fast. There is so much about the extraction that you don't know, Daniel. And losing Brad, having him die in my arms after all we'd been through together was devastating."

"Liv. I cannot imagine what you've been through. Horrifying circumstances. You know you can tell me anything. When you're ready, of course."

"I know. And I will in my own time."

"Is it not quite late there?"

"Yes, about ten PM."

"Please get a proper rest if you can. I know that's like asking a fish to stop swimming, all things considered, but it is important to try."

"I know. I will try."

"I'm very sorry for your loss, Liv."

"Thank you, Daniel."

Chapter Twenty-Five | Going Home

The morning of our flight to LA could not have arrived soon enough. I had not slept as well as I'd hoped, but I knew I'd not rest easy again until I was back home in Vancouver. Roman will be joining me on the flight arranged by Daniel to L.A., and then this search-and-rescue mission is complete.

Daniel contacted the police in Panama City where Cali filed the missing persons report to tell them I had been found safe. The story he relayed was that I got lost in the jungle and was found by another traveller four days after I was reported missing. The case was closed without further question.

While walking onto the tarmac to board the jet, I become overwhelmed by the events that had taken place in Panama. It kept coming at me in random waves that I wish would stop. I'm safe. It's done. No more reason to be afraid, I remind myself. After a few breaths of tropical scented, airline fuel tainted air of the tarmac, I decide to focus my memories on the journey that brought me to Panama on the sailing ship from Costa Rica. The smaller ports, the wonderful food, the generous ship guests who offered to keep me company and the incredible scenery of the coastline are all fond memories. I may not have found all the wild orchids I was interested to photograph, but I met Brad. I will never forget his kindness, his quick sense of humour, his bravery, or his tenderness when I needed it most.

Settling myself into my seat aboard the aircraft, I realize that for a hired gun, Roman is a surprising gentleman. He held my hand as I navigated the steps to board the plane and made sure I was comfortable once I'd sat down.

"Is Daniel just a good friend of yours, or is he more than that?" Roman asks as he finds his seat beside mine.

"We've been dating since mid-November," I say, then smile contentedly. I want to elaborate to Roman about how I dumped the *love of my life* just before my trip, but that conversation seems unnecessary now.

Roman grins politely and nods as he looks me straight in the eyes. “He’s a lucky man.”

“Oh, I think you’ve got that backwards, Roman. I am the one who’s lucky,” I say.

Roman smiles wider this time. “We’ll agree to disagree.”

The pilot starts the engines while our flight crew secure everything and do their required safety demonstration. We begin our taxi down the runway and as the wings of the aircraft lift us up toward the scattered clouds above, I feel like I too have wings. Freedom wings.

The lights of LA come into view out my window as our jet begins its descent to the tarmac of LAX. If I can’t feel safe on U.S. soil, I will never feel safe again. But home is still a few more hours away. My rising anticipation in getting back into the arms of Grace, Daniel, my parents, and Cali flood my mind. I feel as though I’ve been away from them for months rather than ten days.

I call Daniel to let him know we are safely landed in L.A., and I will be on the next flight to Vancouver within the hour. But he already knew that because my trusty saviour Roman had texted him before we landed. I elbow Roman’s arm to get his attention. “Hey, big guy. Stop stealing my thunder by texting Daniel with details of my arrival.”

Roman chuckles. “Got it. You are on your own from here on out anyway.”

When Roman and I were parting ways in the L.A. airport, I felt a huge pang of loss knowing I’d likely never see Roman again. Roman remained stoic and polite, and I needed to hug him in a way he’d never forget. And I felt the same about Brad, without whom I’d likely have never survived physically or emotionally. He was there for me without hesitation when I needed him to be. If he felt insecure at any time during our time lost in the jungle, and then being held captive, he didn't show it in a way that made me feel less safe in his presence. God, how I miss him.

I wrap my arms around Roman's thick body in a thankful hug. He reciprocates the intensity of my embrace and reminds me I'm safe. "You'll always be my favourite rescue. The sheer odds of you and Brad being alive after forty-eight hours alone in the jungle and then being kidnapped are very low in my experience. I've seen enough death in my combat forces career. My job now is to prevent that as often as possible, and on my terms. I only wish Brad had survived with you."

I nod and try not to let my emotions get the best of me again. "The words thank you will never be enough, Roman. Take care of yourself." I tip my heels up to reach Roman's cheek with my lips to give him a kiss.

"You're most welcome, Liv. Take care now." And with that, Roman turns on his heels and throws his duffle bag over his shoulder. I watch as he slips away down the long airport corridor, his figure getting more and more lost within the mix of people and their rollaway bags as he heads to the exit.

After I've lost visual of Roman in the crowd, I turn back to my luggage at my seat to check my ticket and try to figure out which way I should be walking to make my connecting flight to Vancouver. I'm almost home.

I must have sounded tired when I spoke to Daniel before my flight from L.A. to Vancouver began to taxi down the runway. Daniel's voice indicated deep concern about my state of mind the longer we talked. I'll admit my thoughts are a bit scattered and my voice anxious. I am so tired, and I've not had a chance to really sleep.

The flight attendant reminded me to end my call and so I said goodbye to Daniel and tucked my phone into my pocket.

Standing in the international arrivals lounge of Vancouver International Airport, Grace, Cali, Daniel, Carter, Jason and my parents are waiting patiently to see me clear Canadian Customs. As I pass the last exit to the arrivals lounge, I hear a loud measure of cheers from them all. I smile and quicken my pace to get to them as soon as possible. My rolling bag flips onto one set of wheels in my excited pace, but I don't care.

I am tackled in a mass hug when I reach them. My mom is crying, my dad is holding back his own emotions, and I give them both a kiss on their cheeks before reassuring them that I'm quite fine.

I kiss Grace's forehead and squeeze her again. "You look good, mom," she says, and I shake my head at her.

"Geez, my hair is a mess, my clothes are two days old, and I think I'm going to need toothpicks to keep my eyelids open long enough to get home but thank you my love."

Carter is standing directly behind Grace, and I pull him in for a three-person hug with Grace.

"I'm glad you're okay," he says softly to me.

"Thank you, Carter. And thank you for being here with everyone. You didn't have to do that."

"Shut up and hug me," he says, and I smile as I do.

Daniel turns his head to meet Carter's eyes. Carter nods approvingly at him and that was all these two men needed to not say to each other about how grateful Carter is to have me home safe. Daniel also receives a hearty pat on the back and a firm handshake from my father, Jon, in appreciation for his invaluable assistance.

Cali is absolutely itching to hold me, and I'm the same to hold her. She likely has a million questions for me and can't stop wiping away her happy tears from her cheeks.

"Stop crying, Cali. I'm okay. Honest," I say.

"Well, I'm not okay," she says as she hugs me. "I'm not okay at all. Do you have any idea how distraught everyone was?"

"I'm just so glad to be home, sweetie. I missed you so much."

"I have a few choice words for those fuckers," she says, then laughs between her tears.

"Oh, I'm sure you do," I say and laugh with her. "*Fuckers* is right. God damned fucking fuckers," I say, and we both laugh harder.

"Fuck those fucking fuckers!" she says louder, and I put my hand over her mouth and giggle at her.

"Cali! Shush. We're still in the airport."

Jason comes up to us both and pulls Cali aside. "Okay, Cali. Take a breath there, girl. She's fine."

Cali adjusts her skirt and pushes Jason aside. "I know. It all just came to a head all of a sudden. Sorry, babe."

Daniel's anxiety of waiting to kiss me is palpable. His hands were planted deep within the pockets of his jeans while he waits for my family to greet me. I become impatient to hold him, but if I know anything about Daniel, it is that he'd rather show his affections in a more private setting. Too bad for him because I'm going to leap into that man's arms and kiss his face repeatedly like a teenager in love.

Our embrace and passion-filled kiss turn many heads in the arrivals lounge. Neither of us can control the sheer joy of being within each other's arms again.

"Are you really alright, Liv?" Daniel asks, holding my face in his hands and searching my eyes.

"Yes, I'm fine, Daniel."

"Oh, thank Christ you're home and safe. I'm never letting you out of my sight again." Daniel holds my face tight to his chest while he looks around at the faces of my family. And if my family has any clue at all, they will see what true love looks like. If I could meld myself inside of Daniel while we hug so that we are as one, I would. I can't seem to get close enough to him in this moment.

"Should we head home?" he asks.

"Oh, my God. Yes, please. I can't wait to crawl into my bed again and have an actual eight hours of sleep."

Daniel chuckles and points toward the exit. "Right, then. Off with you now."

We say our goodbyes to everyone as we walk in a group to the parkade to our respective cars. I could really use those toothpicks I mentioned to Grace to keep my eyes open now. I'll probably fall asleep in the car with my head on Daniel's lap while his driver takes us home.

Just as we cross the road between the main building and the parkade someone's car backfires like rapid gunfire which echoes through the parkade. My heart leaves my chest, and I clasp my hands over my ears.

Daniel lets go of my luggage handle and hugs me.

"You're alright, love. You're home now. It was just a passing car."

Chapter Twenty-Six | In My Hero's Arms

On this first night with Daniel, all I want to do is be close to him.

I never once thought that I could adore two men at the same time until Brad and I were kidnapped. My affections for Brad were different from my love for Daniel. I understand now that it was a Florence Nightengale effect that bloomed into those emotions between Brad and me. I blink hard a few times to quell my impending tears.

After my mini nap in the car ride home I feel more refreshed and able to be a participant rather than being a sleepy zombie. I think my internal clock is as messed up as my mind.

We share a meal of grilled cheese sandwiches courtesy of Daniel and drink two glasses of wine each while he talks about anything that had no connection to my experience in Panama.

I appreciate his avoidance tactics as I'm not ready to relive the past days. And I know he wants to hear every detail but that will have to come later while I reorient myself to being safe, home, and alive. My self-confidence has taken a deep hit as my survivor's guilt eats away at me. I don't know if I'll ever appease that monster.

"Are you knackered?" he asks. "Do you need rest?"

"No. I don't feel as tired as I was at the airport," I say, forcing a polite smile. "I think I'm just going to need a few days to get back into the rhythm of my normal life again. And to mourn the loss of Brad."

"I feel like you aren't really here in the moment. If you don't want me to be here, I can go," he says cautiously, fruitlessly attempting to read my face for guidance.

"You're right, Daniel. I'm sorry," I say and sigh. "I'm not really here and I'm being rude."

"No, no. You aren't being rude at all, Liv." Daniel's eyes are filled with deep concern as he reaches to hold my chin in his hand.

"I'm concerned that you're internalizing what happened to you." He clasps my hand in his to comfort me as he searches again in my eyes for anything that will help him understand where my mind has wandered off to.

"You're right again. I'm trying not to think about it, but it just seems to be hanging there in my head like a dark cloud. I'm so sorry I put you and everyone else through this." I'm holding back another wave of emotions. My eyes glaze over, and I cover my mouth with my free hand.

He squeezes my hand tighter now. "If you cry, I'll cry, Liv. My heart can't take watching you weep, and I'm entirely too handsome and strong to be turned into a blubbering baby."

His words make me laugh. He is attempting to lighten the mood, and it is another test to see if I am actually listening to him now. He starts to laugh with me, and I begin to relax. "Up you get from that chair and into my much more comfortable lap," he insists. I realize that I have to get my head into the here and now. Nothing about what happened can be changed.

"I don't know why I let you go down there by yourself. I regretted it the moment I left your condo." He kisses my cheek tenderly, and I lean into him and close my eyes.

"Daniel, you'd never have stopped me. I had my mind made up and I was very confident that I'd be perfectly fine. We can't predict the future or change the past. But I can put the past behind me…given a little time."

I smile at Daniel and draw my fingers across my cheeks to sweep away the dampness. "We need a distraction," I announce. "I have to do something to shake these thoughts out of my head. What should we do? Watch TV? Go for a walk? Make love?"

That last option caught him by surprise. He looks at me, longingly, and I know the answer without asking. His eyes are the one thing that I can count on to calm me – his soulful, hopeful pools of deep blue win me over every time I gaze into them.

"I'm most definitely interested to show you how much I've missed you," he says, maintaining his love-infused stare.

We stand from our seat at the kitchen table and hold each other. I can feel his heart beating in his chest and the scent of his skin is also calming. Every time he embraces me, I feel like I'm in the arms of a hero, even if it is entirely cliché and he doesn't want me to think of him that way.

Daniel gently moves my hair over my ear and caresses the side of my neck with his lips. I know this move well and am hoping it will lead to the intimate bliss I missed so much while we were apart. If anything could help me now, it will be to feel the tenderness of Daniel's kisses while cocooned within his strong embrace.

I crave him now more than I'd ever craved him before. The first time we made love, it was pure attraction, and the alcohol infused desire to explore each other. This is different. We share an intimacy that bonds us in a way that is life altering. Our love may have grown fast, but it is a deeper, more mature love than I've ever known.

I rest my head on his shoulder, place my hand over his heart and smile contentedly. This hearts beats for me.

Daniel carries me into my bedroom, gently setting me down on the edge of my bed, and gives me a long, tender kiss. His eyes stay fixed on mine as he begins to unbutton his shirt, but I press his hands away from the buttons. I want to undress him. I want to remove his clothes piece by piece and run my hands over the warm skin of his chest and shoulders. He is such a beautiful man that at times I have to catch my breath at the sight of him. He is the kind of man I wouldn't typically envision to be sitting behind a desk every day, wearing an Armani suit, researching stocks and calculating financial risks. He is muscular and broad-shouldered, with luxurious dark brown hair, and strong features. He is very much *my* Mr. Magnificent.

There is nothing complicated about our affections for each other. We were easy together from the first time we were introduced at Jason's party to us making love in my bed that same night.

After what he arranged in Panama, what he was willing to sacrifice for me, for my safety, even after I'd stupidly broken it off with him, I'll never again dare to challenge how much we need each other.

Every touch of his hand, every tender meaningful kiss from his lips, every pulse from his cock deep inside of me brought my raw desires for him to a new, blissful level.

Looking up at him and smiling, I loosen the button of his jeans, lower the zipper down and ease my hands around his buttocks, slipping his jeans and underwear down to expose his impressive firm cock hiding inside.

Daniel guides my blouse up over my head, then kneels down to help me slip off my jeans and panties. As he stands, he runs his warm hands up the length of my legs, over the curves of my hips, and then cups my breasts before kissing me again. He appreciates every inch of my body with his hands in the most caring of ways. I shudder as the coolness of my room and his hands tracing my figure result in goosebumps rushing down from my shoulders to my wrists.

"Are you alright?" he asks, as he leans back to make direct eye contact. Concern shows in his narrowed eyes.

"Yes, Daniel. I'm fine. You need to stop asking me this."

He hesitates for a moment then speaks his mind. "Did they touch you, Liv. Did they take advantage of you in any way?" he asks.

"No."

"You can tell me if they did, Liv. You can tell me anything." Daniel rubs the edge of his chin with the back of his hand as he tends to do when he's perplexed. "I mean, you shuddered just now, and I'm worried that I've scared you somehow."

"No, God no! They only wanted the money. I think they assumed that Brad and I were a couple. I'd only once considered that they would try something sexual, but Alfonso, the leader of the men, put a stop to Juan when he decided to get touchy-feely. I remember Brad's fierce expression when Juan licked my face, then Juan laughed at my reaction. Juan said something derogatory, and Brad was furious. I didn't understand what Juan said, but Brad understood Spanish, and it set him off in a rage instantly. From then on there were no further inappropriate touching or advances."

Daniel holds me tight against his chest and kisses the side of my head. "Thank Christ," he whispers. I feared the worst for you, night and day."

We hold each other for the longest while. I try to erase any image of that moment and then realize how thankful and fortunate I am that it never went any further.

"Listen, Daniel. I want to live in the here and now. No more talk about Panama. I shuddered because I'm cold, not for any other reason. I could not feel safer than I do now in your hands. You must know this." I assure him.

"You're right, love. I'm sorry. Forgive me."

Daniel's soft smile makes me smile.

I press my palms against Daniel's chest to push his body back toward the edge of the bed. We fall together upon the thick duvet, me atop him. I kiss him as I run my hand through his thick hair. I love the feel of his luxurious hair in my hands. I give it a little tug and then playfully bite his lip. He tries to speak, and I shush him.

I want my lips around his cock. I want to feel the fullness of him grow firmer as I tease and lick and push him deeper into my mouth, rolling my lips and tongue in a way that will send him into a primal tension he can barely control. I begin to do this for him without hesitation.

He begs me to stop and presses my shoulders down into the soft sheets. "I need to touch you," he says. "Let me feel all of you - your breasts, your stomach, your hips. I need my face between your legs. I've missed every inch of you, Liv. Every fucking amazing inch of you."

In my head I'm yelling, *Oh, my God, yes!* But I nod and moan at the touch of Daniel's hand upon me as he trails his fingers slowly down the length of my body.

I yearned every night for his gentle touch, his lips on mine again. It was that hope that kept me strong.

"Is it possible for terror and relief to be racing through one's mind at the same time? I feared deeply for you, but I was so thankful that you were still alive."

I nod again, hoping that this is the last of any conversation about the ordeal spoken.

He places the pad of his thumb over my clit and begins to rub gently up and down. His lips and tongue taste the soft skin of my torso at the same time and I'm in the most delicious state of mind with his teasing. I want him to slow down and rush me to a climax at the same time. Such a glorious position to be in. His mouth finds my clit. He gently and repeatedly sucks on it. I can't fight the euphoria and give in to my fast crash of a climax. My gratitude laden breath sweeps through my parched lips as I place my hands in his hair again. I tug him to come up and kiss me.

"Let me inside of you," he pleads. "I can't stand to wait any longer to feel you wrapped around me in the way only you can."

"Yes."

I grip his shaft and guide him inside of me without hesitation. The afterglow throbbing emulated the pulses of my heartbeat and his deep penetrations. This trifecta is exhilarating. I had to catch my breath at how beautiful it felt to have him inside of me again, giving me everything he had with his own personal brand of emotional and physical passion.

He takes my mouth with abandon, devouring me in intense desire as he thrust his hips forward and back, in a trance-like state from the powerful sensation of me enveloping him. And while he normally watches my face when we make love, his eyes remained closed.

As his release draws nearer our kissing slows to an eventual stop. With laboured breaths he whispers, “My world is nothing without you, Liv.” A moment after those words are uttered from deep within his soul he comes blissfully. When he opens his eyes, I understand why he had closed them this time. He was holding back the urge to weep at the poignant emotion of having me safely with him again. I’m sure hiding his tears is an attempt to not look weak in my eyes, but in truth, it only makes him look stronger. He could have any woman, but it is me that brings him the most pleasure in mind, body and soul.

I stroke his cheek, feeling the bit of dampness around his eyes with my fingertips, and it chokes me up inside. But these are tears of elation, not sorrow.

“Liv?” he says in a hushed voice.

“Yes,” I murmur.

He caresses my shoulder with his thumb, then says, “It was everything I had to not completely crumble at the thought of losing you.”

Holding my face warmly in his hands, he looks intently in my eyes before pressing his forehead against mine.

“No more tears, no more fears. You are adored more than you’ll ever know,” he adds.

I nod and smile. And with my nod, he begins to leave a trail of kisses over my body once more.

Chapter Twenty-Seven | Misplaced Guilt

I've heard it said a hundred times that after a frightful event everything seems more precious, more valuable, more important than it had before. It is undeniably true. But all is not perfect.

It's a new day. The sun is shining through the partly open drapes in my bedroom, and my handsome Mr. Magnificent is asleep next to me. I should be in my glory.

Although I want desperately to forget the events of the week earlier, they fill my mind no matter how hard I try to push them away. I wonder why I'm suddenly so concerned over the deaths of the three men holding Brad and I hostage. Could Roman have taken another route, or was violence the only option he had at the time? And if Roman had not killed them, would they have done the same thing again with other stray travellers? And why did Manuel shoot Brad? Or was he trying to shoot Roman and missed?

My mind is rarely resting. It's filled with questions I have no answers for, and now I'm approaching a state of overload. The longer I bandy the options around in my head, the more convinced I become that Roman had no choice but to kill Alfonso, Juan, Gerardo and Manuel.

As Daniel lay sleeping with his back to me, I run my fingers along the edges of his shoulders, over to the nape of his neck then down the length of his spine. I hope the gentle touch of my hand will wake him. I need to talk. I have to say what is on my mind and ask him the questions I don't have answers to. Daniel exhales deeply and turns over to see me sitting upright beside him.

"It's very early," he says.

"I know, but I can't sleep any longer. I woke up every two hours last night, and my mind won't rest."

"What's bothering you, love?" he asks worriedly.

I laugh gingerly and say, "Everything is bothering me. It's not about my safety or your concerns for me. In that respect *I am* okay. What isn't okay are the questions that are racing through my exhausted brain. And it's why I couldn't get back to sleep most of the night."

"Right, so let's talk then. What kind of questions do you have?" he asks as he sits upright next to me and reaches to hold my hand.

"Do you think it was really necessary for Roman to kill the men that had Brad and me held hostage? Could he have gotten us out of there without violence? Am I as responsible for their deaths as Roman?"

"Roman's a professional. He saved you, but so many things could have gone wrong. And something did go wrong with Brad being a casualty of the rescue. I'm sure his decision process was accurate for the circumstances."

"But how does that absolve me of some level of responsibility for their deaths?" I ask with my brows deeply furrowed.

Daniel adjusts his position beside me. He's holding both my hands over his lap.

"Had those men not told us, or you and Brad, that they were going to kill you, then perhaps it would have been dealt with differently. But we all know they would have killed you both without question had we not met their demands. Our biggest fear was that they would take the ransom and kill you both anyway."

Daniel stops for a moment to gauge how I'm feeling. "Listen, love. Roman told me as much and I believe him. This is what he does. He rescues people all over the world from the very same situation as you and Brad were in, and if he has to use lethal force, he will without hesitation or regrets. You saw their faces. You knew where they were stationed, and you also knew they were likely members of a drug cartel. They were not good people, Liv. They threatened your lives. They held you captive in squalor for ransom."

I sigh and tip my head up to meet Daniel's eyes with mine. "You're right. I just feel like the weight of their deaths is on my shoulders and I'm having a tough time reconciling it. For the life of me, I don't know why."

"It isn't your weight to bear, Liv. It cannot be, and it never will be. This isn't on you. If anything, it's on me. I'm the one who hired Roman. And when I hired him, it was to track you and find you—before we were informed of your kidnapping. Once it went from a missing persons search to a rescue mission, the stakes grew higher, and I gave Roman the okay to get the job done at any cost."

The room falls silent for a moment as Daniel searches my eyes again for confirmation that what he's said helps to answer my concerns.

"How does your friend know Roman?" I ask.

"They had done a few tours of duty with each other, and once Roman returned from duty, he left the military to become a private gun for hire."

"How much did you have to pay Roman?"

"It doesn't matter what it cost," he replies as he presses his forehead against mine. "Money is replaceable. You are absolutely not. Cali feels the same too. She tried desperately to get the money together on her own. When she and Carter were short on liquid assets to use for the ransom, she contacted me for financial assistance, and Jason and I put the funds into transfer to Roman within twelve hours. You really must stop questioning what transpired, Liv. It was either you or them. You must remember that is the world *they* live in. They knew the risks."

"So, you think I'm being stupid for worrying about the deaths?"

"No, of course not! I understand your rationale. But rest your mind. It isn't stupid at all to have these afterthoughts. The simple facts are that you were in imminent danger and Roman took the appropriate measures. End of story, love," he adds firmly.

"Okay. You're right. I guess I just needed to say these random thoughts out loud to someone sane who would understand me."

I'm pulled in close to him and hugged. "And if we're smart, we won't talk of it to anyone. Do you feel assured now that you don't need to feel guilty or worried about what happened?" he asks, while running his palm gently up and down the length of my arm. I lay my head upon his shoulder and close my eyes.

"Yes. And I can't thank you and Cali enough for being my heroes. The entire time we were locked up inside that disgusting bunkhouse, all Brad and I could talk about was seeing our family again. Well, we talked a bit about ourselves as well. I mean, we had no idea how long we were going to be there and so there was great comfort in getting to know about each other's lives.

I lay the side of my head down on Daniel's lap and he gently strokes my hair. "I was terrified of being killed and dumped in the jungle and that none of my family would ever know what had happened to me. If you never let me out of your arms again, I'll be a happy woman."

"As you wish," he says. "I don't know that I'm a hero, but I'm sure Cali would wear that badge with honour if you told her that." He smirks, trying to give me something to smile about. "She and I became very good friends while we waited to hear of your release. There is a lot of depth beneath that party girl exterior, and now I understand why you and Cali are so close."

Daniel continued to stroke my head, then begins to run his warm hands down the centre of my back. "I also finally understand why she's been Jason's muse for so many years," he said through another cheeky grin.

I laugh, then roll onto my back to look up at Daniel's face, now aglow in the morning light through the drapes. "I don't know how much Jason has told you about Cali, if anything at all. She and Jason dated for many years, but they agreed that marriage would ruin them, so they kept it casual. They travelled the world together and I saw little of her for nearly five years. When she met and married her second husband Garret, I think Jason's nose was very much out of joint, but he managed to get over it. Then, just three years later, Cali caught Garret in bed with his first wife, and Cali filed for divorce the next day. Within a month, she and Jason were back together doing their friends-with-benefits thing again. They get each other in a way most of us will never understand."

"Yes, I see that now," he says while he brushes his fingers across my brow and then down the bridge of my nose. When his fingers begin to tickle around the edges of my lips, I gently bite his finger and grin up at him.

"Why is my head markedly higher on your lap than it was a second ago?"

"Right, yeah, I have no control over that when I'm with you," he admits. His gaze is still fixed on me as he breaks into a bashful smile and a chuckle. How can I resist those beautiful dark-blue eyes and that wonderful laugh of his?

As my bedroom grows brighter, I find the glow comforting. There were no windows in the bunkhouse, and I cherish the sun pouring into the room now. And it reminds me that it is how I think of Daniel. He is my warm glow. And in this light, he looks so incredibly sexy. The messed-up hair somehow makes him even more attractive, if that is possible. His smile, his laugh, his gentle touch and manner of speaking are all so genuine.

I rise up to my knees facing him while an *I know what you want* grin emerges on my face. Removing the covers over Daniel's lap, I expose Mr. Magnificent standing at full attention. It's so rigid and remarkably straight that I feel like I need to salute it before commencing in coitus. Crawling atop him and straddling his thighs, I say smiling, "Do you have a name for him?"

A loud outburst of laughter follows my question. A little shocked, his eyebrows peak high on his forehead. "No, I've never named my penis. Should I have?"

"I have a pet name for him, and that is my little secret. But for fun I think we should refer to him as *Randy* because that's how I feel every time I see him." I laugh heartily at myself for my comment as Daniel continues his surprised expression at my admission. In his thickest English accent, he says, "Randy? Are we feeling a bit randy now, love?"

"Ahh, that's too funny. We'll figure that one out later," I say.

I let Daniel slide down on his back in the sheets as I held Mr. Magnificent in my eager hands. I stroked him slowly at first, feeling the amazing strength of his cock at full mass. His eyes are soft on mine as I continue my stroking and rolling my open palm gently over his tip on the stroke up. The precum glistens and I know he's ready to receive me. I slide my hips forward and gently ease him inside of me without losing eye contact. I move my hips in slow motion to control how deep my penetrations of him are. He is loving every second of this connection, this quiet pleasure, and the visual of me riding him.

"You feel amazing, my love," he says and sighs.

My lips part and my eyes close while I savour the sensation of him inside of me. After a while I pull him almost completely out of me and then plunge down deep. A good couple of repeats of this move makes him breathe audibly and I love hearing him react this way. Holding his shaft with my left hand I begin firmly rubbing the head of Mr. Magnificent over my clit, back and forth at first, then in tiny circular movements multiple times. My gratification mounts quickly. My eyelids flutter and my body flushes with heat but I can't stop now. I jut my chin up just before I come over him.

A grin tugs at the corner of Daniel's mouth as he realizes that I have masturbated for him using his cock as my toy.

"That may have been the sexiest thing I've ever witnessed," he tells me, and I grin like the cat that caught the canary. He's probably lying, but I don't care. I lower my breasts over his face and let him suck and roll my nipples in his mouth. They are as hard and erect as his cock and I'm loving the sensation of his teasing. I need him inside of me again now. I literally yearn to have him slam into me, deep and hard while he tells me how delicious I am to him.

Daniel flips me over to my back on the sheets. We are still riding this slow, passionate wave of heightened sensuality. I moan, feeling him slowly pressing Mr. Magnificent deep inside of me. My eyes close enjoying the rhythm of his breaths and the sound of his dark chocolate gravel of a voice telling me how turned on he is. After a few minutes of his slow hunger-filled pulsing, I beg him to go deep and hard. He doesn't hesitate to accommodate my request, and I'm in my absolute glory.

"God, you are amazing," I say to him. "You're turning me into a nymphomaniac. It's crazy how much I love what you do to me."

His brilliant release gave me a shiver of satisfaction. Spent, and blissfully, unbelievably satisfied, he kisses my mouth tenderly now, dipping his tongue between my lips to tangle with mine. I swear we are made for each other.

He slowly releases me from his lips and lays back down beside me, reaching for my hand beneath the sheets. My body shudders again in the afterglow.

Rolling over to lie on my side, I place a kiss on his shoulder. Daniel turns to his side to meet my gaze. He moves my hair away from my eyes and he looks content.

I slip in closer to his chest, tucking my head under his chin, weaving my legs in between his and draping my arm around his waist.

"You are my warm glow, Daniel. I don't deserve you. Promise me we will love each other like this always."

Kissing the top of my head, he whispers back to me, "I promise."

After a few quiet moments of our comforting embrace under the sheets, I ask, "Are you hungry? Can I make you some breakfast?"

"Yes. Let me have a quick shower and I'll join you in the kitchen. I have a lunch meeting with Jason and a new prospective client today at eleven-thirty, so I'll need to go back to my condo to change. Oh, and I wanted to tell you that Jason and I have secured a third partner so I can spend more of my time with you instead of at the office," he adds, glancing up at me to see how I'll react.

"That's wonderful, Daniel. Are you sure that's what you want? I told you I didn't want you to choose me over your work."

"If it's important to you then it's important to me," he says, affirmatively. "You'd like Michael. Jason and I are chuffed to have him partner with us. We've registered our company as JDM Investments and it's in full swing, my love. Are you good to be on your own for a few hours today, or shall I ring someone to stay with you?"

"I'll be fine," I say, mustering a polite smile. I feel guilty for making him adjust his business plan with Jason in order to appease me. "I'm meeting with Cali later this morning, so I won't be alone."

Since my return home it became clear to me that being a strong independent woman comes with a price tag I had not anticipated. I have doubts about my ability to be who I thought I could be. Now the only thing that matters is being beside Daniel. I no longer yearn to travel alone, to live alone. And as much as I realize my terrifying ordeal has damaged my original vision of an independent life, it is in the warm glow of Daniel's arms where I belong. And I know he will help me reacquire that kind of independence that was lost.

Cali enters my place like she owns it, but then she does that everywhere she goes. After exchanging long hugs, she follows me into the kitchen for some conversation and tea.

Cali wants to talk about my experience and offer me the emotional support she thinks I need. For me, there is nothing more to say except a massive thank-you to Cali for her efforts to get the ransom money arranged in time. But her efforts don't surprise me, as I'd have done the same for her without hesitation. And now that I have all my lingering questions answered by Daniel, I'm on the path to healing.

"Okay, change of subject then?" Cali says. "How is the romance between you and Daniel going?" She pours herself a fresh cup of tea at the kitchen table.

"Are we kissing and telling again?" I ask, glancing sideways at Cali from the edge of the open door of the refrigerator. I grab the container of cream and close the fridge door. Cali plops two cubes of sugar into her cup and stirs gently before looking back up at me.

"Yes, I want you to kiss and tell, Liv. I live vicariously through you and Daniel. It's all I have now that Jason and I are so busy with our work." She offers me a cheeky grin.

"All I can say is that his cock is rather impressive, and I can't seem to get enough of it," I blurt out and then promptly flush with my cheeks turning raspberry-coloured.

"Ooh, tell me more, you little sexpot! Can you take a picture of it for me, now that you've piqued my interest?" Cali laughs so hard at herself, then almost chokes on her next sip of tea.

"I will not under any circumstances take a photograph of Daniel's Mr. Magnificent for your viewing pleasure, Cali," I say, rolling my eyes into my head at her request after setting myself down at the kitchen table across from her.

"Oh, and we have a name for it, too! How exciting," Cali says with widened eyes. "You didn't need to tell me it was impressive when all you had to do was say what you've named it. *Mr. Magnificent* kind of says it all, Liv." Cali takes another sip of her tea and raises her eyes to meet mine across the kitchen table, waiting for my reaction.

I smile bashfully, and my cheeks flush again with a hint of embarrassment. I nervously reach to touch the petals of one of my orchids blooming on the tabletop container. It isn't like me and Cali haven't been frank with each other over the years with sex talk, but I want to keep my amazing sex encounters with Daniel my own little secret, even from Cali. "Don't you have a name for Jason's cock?" I counter, staring her directly eye to eye now.

"Depending on my mood," she says, smiling. "Sometimes I just call it *Bad Boy* and other times," she says as her voice rises to a higher octave she adds, "I just call it *Monsieur Cock*, depending on how much wine or mixed cocktails I've consumed before we turn the sheets inside out."

I break out into a full belly laugh at her, like only Cali can make me do. When she said the word *Monsieur,* pretending to be very French and holding her teacup elegantly with two fingers, she winked at me.

"Good God Cali, you kill me sometimes," I say, continuing to giggle at her.

"Last week we stripped naked in my closet, and I wrapped a hot pink feather boa around his neck, and then we fucked like rabbits against my shoe rack," Cali says, as if that were just another day at the office.

I wave my hand in front of my face. "Oh, erase, erase! I do not need that visual in my head, Cali!"

"Hey," Cali giggles at herself. "He only had five minutes before a dinner meeting, so we did what we could in the time we had! Fun, fun, fun."

Chapter Twenty-Eight | More Harvey, Less Wallbanger

To keep myself occupied, I focus my energy on the redecorating of the lake house. Grace and I went shopping for furniture pieces, paint samples and tile to coordinate with my new white kitchen cabinets and granite countertops earlier in the week and I'm quite happy with our choices. I need the space inside to be bright and airy to reflect my new perspective on life. The original plan to go with a tropical theme has lost its charm.

It will still be a few months before I'd be back up in lake country, tending to the contractors and suppliers for the renovation work, but it is best to be prepared and keep myself busy in the meantime. June and Karl are there to let the contractors in and out of the house when I can't be there.

My relationship with Daniel grows stronger by the day. Our devotion to each other is also beneficial to my healing process. The more Daniel and I talked about the lake house, the happier he is for me. I'm driven to complete the work before July so we can enjoy the fruits of my labour in August. I know that is the hottest month of the year at the lake, but that is also when the lake is at its warmest.

At last night's dinner, Daniel proposed the idea of going up to the lake with me and Cali for two weeks in early August. He is ready for a mental break from his work and thinks some summer sun at my vacation property will be a perfect way to unwind. Cali and I love the idea of Daniel coming up with us. I'm excited to show off my renovation work after so many months of preparation. I also know that Daniel enjoys a good glass of wine, and a visit to lake country will give him a chance to visit the area's award-winning wineries.

By mid-June, most of the construction work I had arranged has been completed. The new hardwood plank flooring and the exterior painting were the only two projects left before the big reveal.

Cali takes it upon herself to plan our excursions and activities while also allotting a few days of alone time for me and Daniel.

Daniel is set on driving up there in his Jag, but I firmly disagree. “We have to take the Jeep, Daniel,” I insist. “For one, where the hell is Cali going to sit? The back seat in your Jag is way too small for an adult to sit in for a four-hour drive. And with all our bags, it just doesn’t make sense to not take my SUV. In fact, it is one of the reasons I have the Jeep because it has enough seats and hatch space for all the supplies and luggage.”

“But I love driving my Jag on the highway.”

“Well, you can drive up there on your own, because I’m taking the Jeep, with or without you in it.”

“Fine, the Jeep it is. But our next trip will be just you and me and my Jag.”

I can’t help but smile at him. When it came to cars and suits, Daniel is quite pretentious. It makes me laugh a little but being a bit of a glamour puss is just his style.

The drive up from Vancouver to Vernon is as pretty as I said it would be. Cali had forgotten how beautiful the Fraser Canyon is, as it has been years since she last went up to the lake with me, Carter and Grace. Daniel is surprised to hear that the area where we’re heading is considered desert and that there other pseudo deserts in Canada. But as I remind him, it is because of the uniquely dry summers and milder winters of the Okanagan that the area does so well in wine growing, along with stone fruits like cherries, peaches and apples.

“I’m so used to seeing wine grown in France, Italy and Spain, even California. I would never have thought it could be done so well here,” he remarks.

As we approach the lake, Daniel is shocked at the incredible colour of the water. "This looks like the Bahamas!"

"I know!" I say excitedly. "But it's only this colour in summer." Daniel is puzzled by my comment.

"What do you mean?"

"The dissolved mineral rich carbonate minerals crystallize in the water when the temperature gets above a certain point, which makes the water go from a darker blue to light teal blue. In the cooler months, the water is like any other lake water. They're called marl lakes. In fact, the white cliffs of Dover contain the same material—marl."

"I think it rather sexy when you get all science-y on me," he says and winks.

"Well," I say as I flip my hair off my shoulder playfully, "It's a little more involved than that, but that is the short answer."

"And is the lake good to swim in?"

"Oh, my God, yes. It's warm, as in seventy degrees this time of year. How can you call yourself a Canadian and not know this stuff, Daniel?" I say, frowning at him.

"I was born here, but we moved to London when I was ten. I have dual citizenship with Canada and the UK."

"Oh, okay. You're forgiven. I'm very good with geography so if you have any questions, fire away."

"One day I will give you a tour of the UK and then we shall see how good your geography is."

I look back over my shoulder from the front seat. "Cali, you are awfully quiet back there. What are you thinking?" I ask.

"I'm thinking that my high school education has eluded me and you two are boring me to death. And my one-litre Harvey Wallbanger thermos premix is nearly empty," she responds dryly.

"Well, hold on to your panties because we're almost there," I say, giggling at our drunk passenger.

Daniel shakes his head and looks back at Cali in the rearview mirror. "Perhaps next time you could put a little more Harvey and a little less Wallbanger into your premix? And I hope you have a backup liver, Cali, because I'm certain the one you've been pickling for the last twenty years is on its last breath."

"Oh, don't you worry about my liver. We have an agreement, my liver and me. It puts up with my drinking as long as I give it a full cleanse once a month," she says, winking back very slowly at Daniel in the car mirror.

"Doctor-prescribed, I'm sure." He shakes his head again and chuckles.

After climbing out of the Jeep and unloading the bags on the driveway, Daniel takes a second to review his surroundings. The air is dry and hot, reminding him that he is indeed in a desert. It all makes sense now. The constant talking about my precious lake house is understandable.

I'm excited to open the front door and reveal the changes I'd made to the interior over the spring. And even though Daniel hadn't seen the house before the renovations, I'm sure he'll be impressed.

"Okay, Cali. Are you ready to see what I've done inside?" I ask with excitement.

"Yup. And the first room I want to see is the bathroom," she says with a bit of a slur.

"You know where it is. First door on your right." I furrow my brow at her.

"Wow. This is impressive, Liv," Daniel says as his eyes glance over the fresh, clean-lined appeal of my decorating choices. "I don't know what it used to look like, but I like the way it is now!"

"Thank you," I say, smiling ear to ear. "Go out onto the deck. You won't believe how pretty the lake looks from the front of the house."

June and Karl must have heard my Jeep pull up into the driveway. They were here seconds after we arrived, knocking three times on the open door and then calling out, "Liv? It's just us. How was the drive up?"

"June! Karl! Come in, come in! The drive was awesome, as usual. I'd love for you to meet Daniel."

They wander inside and approach us. "Pleasure," Karl says, shaking Daniel's hand firmly.

"Karl and June are my wonderful neighbours," I add, smiling up at Daniel.

Daniel smiles back at them both, as June darts me a look of "Oh my, he's a keeper." Daniel offers to put on a pot of coffee for everyone.

June waves her hand in the air. "Coffee was so two hours ago. It's margarita time. Liv? Where's your liquor cabinet? I think we can all agree that margaritas are in order to toast to your new renovation completion."

I giggle at June as she sets herself down at the bar stool of the kitchen island. "All the ingredients you'll need for drinks are in the end cabinet on the left."

Just then Cali emerges from the bathroom to hug June and Karl. She hasn't seen them in several years but always remembered how much fun they are to have around.

"Did I hear the word margarita?" she says, grinning, after releasing Karl from her hug. "I think I just may be sober enough to enjoy one, or two, or five." She winks at me, and I roll my eyes.

"You never change, Cali," Karl says.

"Consistency is the key to my success, Karl," Cali says, kissing his cheek. Cali does a little dance on the spot where she stands then realizes the party is missing something. "We need music," Cali states boisterously. "Liv! Where is the music?"

I sashay my way over to the credenza next to the fireplace and put the stereo system on to the local radio station while June happily mixes up five margaritas. Karl wanders around the living room, inspecting the tile on the new fireplace façade and the shiny new hardwood floors.

I grab Daniel's hand and lead him back out to the deck. He turns to hold me in his arms and plants a very quick kiss on my lips. "I love this place, Liv. It's so you. And you know how much I love *you*."

"Mm," I whisper. "I'm so glad you love it as much as I do." I hug Daniel a little tighter and reply, "Back at ya on the love thing."

When June and Karl arrived, they'd brought a bag with them, which I assumed was filled with alcohol. June calls out to me from the kitchen to tell me that she and Karl had bought a housewarming present.

"You shouldn't have brought anything, June," I say as I stroll back into the house from the deck and open the gift bag. "You guys already do so much for me—this is silly." Inside the gift bag is a beautiful, handmade glazed-ceramic wind chime created by a local artist. When I realize what the gift is, I'm overcome with emotions.

"Come now, Liv, the gift is not that special that it requires tears," June says.

"It's lovely. Thank you," I say and nod.

Daniel's eyes narrow as he scans my expression. I take a deep breath and set the chime aside on the counter. "Let's just get back to mixing up some drinks."

Daniel pulls me aside and says, "You know Liv, if not for that wind chime sounding off in the video, I'm not sure Roman would have so easily found you. To him, it was confirmation that he had the right location."

I nod and force a smile. "Daniel, the chime sound sent me right back there. I get what you're saying, but I can't have anything that reminds me of that bunkhouse in my house. But I don't want to upset June and Karl, so I'll set aside for now."

"Okay, love. No worries."

The five of us drink, dance and talk excitedly with each other until the hands of the kitchen clock near midnight. Karl and June tell me they need to head back home, or they'd mess up their daily routine of a five-kilometre walk after breakfast at eight. I wave goodnight to them from the couch, cuddled up into Daniel's arms. Cali has been asleep out on the deck in the lawn chair since eleven, and I place a blanket over her before we head to bed. I know that sometime around three in the morning Cali will wake up and find her way to the guest bedroom to sleep off the balance of her massive wallbanger of a hangover.

Chapter Twenty-Nine | One More Makes Four

Considering how much drinking Cali had done the day before, she was up bright and early with the singing birds, messing around in the kitchen, looking for something to make breakfast for everyone. Daniel slips out of bed, and I follow suit due to the noise Cali is making in my kitchen. Donning a pair of sweatpants, he yawns, rubs his tired eyes and heads downstairs to see what she is up to.

"You're up bright and early, sunshine," he says.

"I'm always up early when I'm on vacation. Not sure why, but I'm like this no matter where I am on the planet," she says. Cali checks the coffee machine and grabs two more coffee mugs out of the cabinet above her head for us as I descend to the last step on the staircase. "Do you want cream and sugar, or do you take it black?" she asks Daniel.

"Double, double," he says, mustering a half smile after a long yawn.

Daniel whispers to Cali, but I hear every word. "Liv had a few nightmares last night and woke us both up twice because of it."

"Crap, I'm sorry to hear that. She never mentioned having nightmares to me. Is there anything we can do?"

"I can hear you two chatting about me," I say as I reset the cushions on the sofa and pick up our empty cocktail glasses off the coffee table. "My therapist says I'm doing very well, but I'll have the occasional trigger that will set me back from time to time. Last night was one of those nights."

"I'm sorry, Babe," Cali says. "We worry about you. That's all."

"I know," I say as I place the dirty glasses inside the dishwasher. "I don't have as many restless nights as I used to, but I guess that chime set me off. I know they meant well with the gift, and they don't know the whole story either." I force a grin. "I'll be fine tonight. I promise."

Daniel decides to change the subject. "On another note, do you think we should call Jason and ask him to join us up here for the weekend?"

"I've asked him up here before and he's declined. Maybe you'll have better luck than I do," I say as Cali pours coffee into three mugs.

"Tosser," Daniel says. "He could fly up to join us. I'm sure he will if I ask." Daniel picks up his cell from the counter and calls Jason. He sets his phone on the counter and places the call on speaker.

"Hey mate. Book a flight up to Vernon Friday afternoon and we'll pick you up at the airport. You can fly back to Vancouver Sunday night and be back in the office Monday."

"Is that a question or a request?" Jason asks.

"It's a request, and don't be a wanker about it. We need you here to make sure Cali behaves herself," Daniel replies back, winking at Cali across the island counter.

"Okay. Sure, why not?"

"Brilliant." Daniel gives Cali the thumbs-up. "Text me when you know what time your flight is landing, and we'll see you then." The call ends and Daniel is all smiles.

"Well, that was easy," Cali states with a look of minor shock on her face.

"Glad to be of service."

With Cali's schedule of events for the two weeks posted on the refrigerator door, the first item on the list is to get my boat out of the garage and into the water. Cali is dying to go for a boat ride on the lake, and she knows I'd be up for doing the same. It will also give

Daniel a way to see the entire lake from a different perspective. It took a little help from Karl next door to get the boat motor running smoothly after sitting for an entire year unused. He's hands down the best neighbour ever. All it takes is a case of his favourite beer to make him a happy clam.

We hook up the boat to the Jeep and drive down to the boat launch within two hours of finishing breakfast, hitting the water just before lunchtime. I packed a few sandwiches plus two bottles of white wine. Under the hot summer sun, we're off for the afternoon out on the crystal clear, teal-coloured water of Kalamalka Lake.

Cali finds herself the perfect spot on the stern of the boat to lay out and sunbathe while Daniel takes on the role of pilot. I worried that Daniel didn't have the experience of navigating a boat. It turns out his father had a river boat that they often spent weekends on when he was a teenager. My speedboat is quite different, and entirely more fun to use. When we find the perfect spot to drop anchor and sit for a while enjoying the wine and the sandwiches I'd packed, Cali drops her bathing suit top and bottom and dives into the water for a swim.

"Right then. That was unexpected," Daniel says as he raises his eyebrows. "I'm not immune to nudity, but surely she'd have given us a wink or something as warning."

"Get used to it, Daniel. The more often Cali can take her clothes off, the happier she is. She is a happy little nudist," I say, toasting Cali's unabashed style of living with my wine glass raised in the air.

"When is Jason arriving?" I ask.

"Today at four o'clock. I'll pick him up while you and Cali organize the cocktails and something to eat for supper, if that's alright with you."

"Yes, that's perfect." I set my wine glass down in the cup holder and start to pull all my clothes off to join Cali skinny-dipping.

"Bloody hell. Not you too!" Daniel says, looking a little left out and not quite sure if he should drop his swim trunks to join us ladies. "Are you not concerned to be breaking any exposure laws?"

Jumping off the stern of the boat, I dive in with precision and pop up seconds later to shake my head to indicate no to him. I then beg Daniel to join us.

Daniel pretends to be shy as he states, "Only if Cali closes her eyes."

"What's the matter?" I tease. "Is Danny Boy embarrassed to go naked in public?"

"I'm chuffed to partake," he says puffing up his chest. "And I'll have you know the last person who called me Danny Boy was my Gran, and I'm certain she wouldn't approve of public nudity," he says, then promptly drops his swim trunks down in one straight draw. "Sorry, Gran."

I have always found jumping naked into water, be it the lake or an ocean, to be invigorating and freeing.

"You're right, Liv. I don't know why I hesitated. It's not like I've never gone naked on beaches in Europe before," he admits.

"This is my favourite thing to do in the lake—swim naked off my dock at dusk."

Daniel laughs and replies, "Don't mind if I do."

Cali swims up to me to whisper in my ear as Daniel swims nearby. "You're right to call it Mr. Magnificent. That is indeed impressive!" she laughs heartily as my face turns red.

"Shush, Cali. You are such a brat." I splash water in her face, and she sticks her tongue out at me then laughs again.

Chapter Thirty | Wine Tour

Jason's arrival to Vernon is as scheduled. Daniel is glad to have his partner and good friend here with us, if only for the weekend, so he didn't feel like a third wheel to me and Cali. As they enter the lake house, Jason's response to the beauty of the water and the hot dry weather is just as Daniel's had been—shocked. "Did you know this lake was here?" Jason asks Daniel.

"Nope, not a clue. Hidden treasure, just like our girls."

"So, what are the big plans for the weekend?"

"One step at a time there, mate. Cali has the entire weekend organized on a chart on the fridge."

Cali greets Jason and Daniel at the front door as they arrive. Jason looks at Cali and says, "You are a sight for sore eyes."

Cali purses her lips and presses her cheek toward Jason for him to kiss her, and he does as non-verbally instructed. "How many times have I asked you to come up here and you declined?" she asks sternly, not looking up at his face, but smiling to herself.

"Just once, if I recall. And I wasn't even in town when you asked me."

"Fine, you're forgiven. I'm just glad you're here now. Nobody here knows how to mix a proper martini but you, my *Prince of Playfulness,"* she says, turning around to wink at him. "The glasses and booze are in the end cabinet. Go on, get to work, Jason," she demands, slapping him on the ass.

Jason looks at Daniel and mouths, "God, I love that woman." I turn my head and snicker to myself.

The dinner, martinis and conversation are amazing. Jason is relaxed, and he can see Daniel is equally comfortable in their surroundings. I fill their minds with stories about the lake, how long I've been coming here, and the best parts that I hope they have time to see.

After all the entertaining is over, Cali and Jason head to the guest bedroom, as expected, to – and I quote - test out the mattress springs. Daniel and I sit out on the deck with the last of our martinis, and I notice that Daniel's mind seems to be elsewhere. "Are you thinking about something?" I ask. "You seem to be staring blankly out into the lake."

"I was just mulling over something Jason said to me earlier tonight," he replies, turning his head to look at me.

"Business?"

"No, not technically. I asked him what he thought about me renting out my condo and buying a house. What do you think?"

"Cali is the one to talk to about real estate. But I think that's a great idea. I wish I had a house. Why Carter bought the penthouse in Vancouver baffles me, especially when he's the head of a landscape-supply empire," I say, furrowing my brow.

"Investment value, I'm assuming," Daniel replies. "There's often a higher return on downtown property than there is on residential houses. It's the same all over the world."

"I've always wanted to have a greenhouse for my orchids in my own yard," I say and sigh, "but I had to settle for putting one up on the lot at the main branch because there was nowhere else to grow them."

"Okay, so we know one thing that I must have for this new house: a greenhouse for my green thumb girlfriend." He smiles while reaching for my hand.

"You don't have to do that for me, Daniel, but I appreciate you thinking of me."

A brief moment of pause and contemplation between us follows my last words.

"If I bought a house, would you move in with me?" he asks.

I'm taken by surprise at his offer. I stall to wrap my head around the seriousness of his question. "Since we pretty much live together at my place as it is, I say yes. I will move in with you if you buy a house."

I continue to be surprised by Daniel's thoughts. It is a big deal deciding to officially move in together, and into a house no less, not just into one or the other's condo.

"It's settled then," he says, smiling broadly, clearly happy with my positive response. "We'll start looking for a house with Cali when we get back home."

Daniel leans over from his lawn chair to give me a quick kiss to seal the deal, but that one sweet kiss led to several more passion-filled kisses. Before we know it, we are standing in front of each other attempting to remove each other's clothes on the deck.

"Upstairs. Now," I whisper between breaths and feverish kisses.

Cali's calendar of events on the fridge noted that today is the day of the self-guided wine tour. It starts at noon, and we'll be home by dinner time. I'll stay sober so I can drive my wine-soaked friends home.

She and Jason awoke early as usual but must have decided to lay in bed for a while to cuddle and talk. They often had their serious conversations in bed in the mornings before coffee, discussing everything from portfolio investments to what to wear to their next dinner party at Jason's penthouse. Their bedroom door is open, and me and Daniel can hear every word they are saying.

"Why are you so cuddly this morning?"

"Am I?" he responds.

"It must be the air at the lake house. Or perhaps you're still a little drunk from last night," she says. "Okay, bunk buddy. Are you going to shower first before coffee or after?" Cali asks.

"Is the shower big enough for two?"

"Honey, you wore me out last night. If you just want to shower, yes, I will join you, but not if you plan on playing hide the wet weasel. My vagina needs a five-minute break before she agrees to another workout with Bad Boy," she says dryly.

Daniel and I crack up with loud laughter from upstairs.

Jason, not wanting to miss an opportunity to add fodder to our intrusion on their conversation says, "Listen, Bad Boy. We've been turned down, buddy. At ease. You're dismissed."

Cali's giggles from within the shower added to the moment and now we are all cackling with laughter.

Later, as Daniel and I arose from the bedroom we hear them making a fair amount of noise in the kitchen. Cali is in the mood for pancakes, and only my pancakes would do apparently.

"What's on the agenda today, *my muse*?" Jason asks.

"Wine tour," she says. "Liv is our designated tour guide. She's going to stay sober while we sample numerous local wines."

"Then I imagine she will have loads of catching up to do by the time we're back here."

While the two of them chatted, Daniel stood at the top of the stairs listening in while I had stepped into my ensuite bathroom.

"Why don't we run upstairs and jump on their bed before they get out of it?" he says, snickering like a teenager at camp.

"How about a spray bottle full of water?" Cali suggests as she rummages through the cabinet under the kitchen sink.

"I love the way you think!"

Jason jumps up from the couch and helps Cali find a water bottle to spray us with. He finds one in the main bathroom and fills it up with water from the tap.

Before they could get upstairs, Daniel steps back inside our bedroom and presses his pointer finger over his lips to make sure I stay quiet.

Slinking their way upstairs, the two pranksters ease their way to the top of the staircase, giggling to themselves. But Daniel heard them plotting and stood at the top of the stairs waiting. Just after Cali reaches the landing of the second floor, Daniel jumps out from around the corner and yells "Boo!" in Cali's face, making her scream and jump.

Jason and Daniel break out into a fit of laughter as I peek around the corner of the open bedroom door. Cali is as pissed as a swatted hornet.

"Are you trying to give us both a heart attack?" I say disapprovingly.

"No. Shit. Sorry, love. I didn't mean to fuck up. I could hear them coming upstairs and, well, I don't know what I was thinking. Daniel holds out his arms to give Cali a hug. "I'm sorry, Cali. I didn't think I'd scare you that badly." He turns to face me and tries to gauge my reaction.

"I'm fine. But please don't do that again," I say.

"You're a jackass, Daniel." Cali gives him a one-two jab in the ribs with her fists.

"Oh, I deserved that."

While still within Daniel's embrace, Cali looks at me over his shoulder and says, "All I wanted was some pancakes!" She pouts like a child for effect while I laughed at her silly face.

"Yes, Cali. I'll make you pancakes. Just as soon as my heart rate recovers."

Cali sprays Daniel in the face with the water and turns to go back downstairs. "We're even now."

It is going to be another hot, clear day. The light wind that picked up just after we'd finished lunch was appreciated, but it too was very warm. The four of us loaded ourselves into my Jeep and drove off with the winery map Cali had downloaded off the internet. I knew where to go, but Cali liked to be in command and wanted to tell me where to turn and how fast to drive from her perch in the back seat next to Jason.

"This is exactly why I only drive a two-seater car," Jason said. "Cali can't backseat-drive from the passenger seat," he chuckles while Cali furrows her brow at him and mutters something under her breath. "Oh, and I'm taking Cali out for dinner at the Range Lounge and Grill tonight," he adds, "so you two will have to fend for yourselves."

The day was brilliant. We visited six different wineries, toured their facilities, and enjoyed the amazing landscapes that surround their tasting rooms and gift shops. We came home with no less than a dozen cases of various whites and reds and it made me wonder where all our luggage was going to go on the trip home. I guess Cali will have to share the back seat with boxes of wines which she'll surly sample along the way. I'll save a few of the boxes to stash at the lake house for the next season up.

While Cali and Jason prepared to head out for their dinner date, me and Daniel happily opened a case of the red wine Daniel decided was the best of the day. It was another beautiful evening out on the deck, watching the boats pass by on the water and enjoying the superb weather. I ponder what we are going to make for dinner before Daniel interrupted my thoughts. "Do you want to go for a late-night swim sometime after dinner, Liv?"

I couldn't agree more with his pattern of thinking. "Why, yes, I would, Mr. Wesley. We should also bring down the portable stereo for some music on the dock. Are you in the mood for barbequed prawns, scallops and peppers with rice? That's what I was going to cook for everyone for dinner tonight."

"Yes, of course. Let me pop two more bottles of white into the fridge to chill and set up the barbecue," he replies.

Daniel and I are happily enjoying our wine and the music on the dock when I remind him that we were supposed to go for a swim. "I'm going in for a dip now. Are you coming?" I ask as I set my wine glass down on the deck beside my chair.

"Let me finish this glass," he says, "then I'll join you."

I place two towels on the edge of the dock and pull off my summer dress and bathing suit before diving into the water. As I pop my head up out of the water, I give him a devilish grin. I float around on my back to expose my breasts above the water line as a gentle tease, hoping he will join me. Daniel smiles bashfully at me being so brazen, as the sun has not yet set behind the hill and I'm clearly visible to anyone looking out into the lake from their decks or passing boats. Shaking his head at me, he set his glass down on the dock, quickly peels off his swim trunks and jumps right in after me. He swims up, and I wrap my arms and legs around his body and kiss him.

"Your fascination with skinny-dipping is amusing, Liv," he says, holding me tight.

I whisper into his ear, "Swim over there beside the kayak where we can't be seen. It's shallower there and you can stand."

Daniel agrees to my suggestion, regardless of him not knowing what I have in mind. He is prepared to participate in my sexy romantic plans. In the shallows by the shore, I grab Mr. Magnificent with my hand under the water to see how ready he is for me. I wrap my legs around his hips again for an impromptu moment of sexual bliss, and Daniel is ready and willing to oblige my advances.

The idea of making love in the water as we hid behind a kayak by the dock of my home in broad daylight is invigorating, a bit cheeky and so arousing. And once I begin to kiss him and slip Mr. Magnificent inside of me, slowly pressing my hips into him repeatedly in the water, Daniel was like putty in my hands. After a few fulfilling pumps I pull away, plug my nose and then drop myself under the water to orally pleasure him for as many seconds as I can hold my breath. After ten seconds, I guess he couldn't believe that I was still holding my breath and hoisted me out of the water.

"You are quite mad, Liv Nelson!" he says, gazing very contentedly into my eyes.

"I've never tried that before. It worked out surprisingly well! Shall I go down a second time?"

"No, oh my God, no," he says, laughing. "Just stay up here in my arms and stick to conventional measures, shall we?"

"Oh, I thought you'd enjoy that."

"Yes, yes, it was brilliant, but I can read the headlines in tomorrow's newspaper now: *Beautiful local resident Drowns Giving Head to Boyfriend Underwater*," he says, shaking his head at me.

“Party pooper,” I say and then proceeded to get on with underwater “conventional” sex methods.

While we enjoy a slow ride in the shallow water he says, “I have to admit that this is fucking amazing. I get the naked swimming thing now.”

Daniel drops his body down into the water to mouth my breasts and tease my nipples. I hold on to the side of my kayak for support as Daniel slips his fingers inside of me, hoping to make me feel as good as I’d made him feel moments before. I exhale deeply and try not to vocalize by biting on my lower lip, almost losing my grip on the kayak as he played with my body under the warm water. He surfaces to watch me as he continues to pleasure me with his magic hands, and the expression on my face did not disappoint him. I squeeze my thighs together when I reach climax and he smiles broadly at me.

“I love you, Daniel Wesley. I love you so much it makes me wonder if I’m crazy,” I say after letting go of the kayak. I grip him tighter with my arms and legs and he sweeps my wet hair away from my face. I nibble on the lobe of his ear, and then slowly lay back into the water to float on the surface, my legs still wrapped around his hips, allowing my arms to float freely at my sides.

Aside from our temporary split when I broke it off after New Year’s then traveled to Panama, we have been inseparable over the past several months. Now, more than ever I can’t imagine being without him in my life. We are pure bliss together.

By the time me and Daniel had collected ourselves, got back into our bathing suits and gathered up all the things we had brought down to the dock, Cali and Jason were arriving back home in their taxi. We all entered the house at the same time—Cali and Jason from the front doors and me and Daniel from the deck, all sporting huge smiles.

Cali is clearly bursting to tell me about their dinner, but for whatever reason she kept tight-lipped.

"How was the dinner tonight?" I ask, doing an extra towel-off on my legs and feet.

"Very nice," Cali says. "We both truly enjoyed our meals. We talked business and he suggested another great investment opportunity for me, which I thought was impossible to say no to," she adds, cheekily smiling at Jason.

"Well, trust you two to talk business on a date," Daniel says, looking at Jason with a furrowed brow. "Jason, mate, would it hurt to not constantly talk business on your weekend off?"

"Oh, well," he says to Daniel, "this business couldn't wait. And Cali never minds when I bring up good investment ideas." He gestures subtly with his thumb towards Cali's hand and the giant ring seemingly weighing her hand down. Looking at Daniel, he put his finger up to his mouth to let him know that he wasn't to say a word, but I was all eyes on them both during their non-verbal communication. Daniel nods in understanding, widening his eyes at Jason and smiling broadly now.

"Does anybody need a glass of wine?" Jason asks casually.

"Yes, I'd love a glass of wine," says Cali, sliding her left hand through her hair hoping I'll notice the giant glaring rock on her ring finger. I take a moment to pretend I don't see it because I know she's absolutely dying inside for me to say something.

Cali wanders into the kitchen area and calls out to me as I remove my bathing suit and put my clothes back on in the bathroom, "How is it possible that your bodies and hair are wet, but your bathing suits are dry?"

I laugh loudly from the bathroom. "You are a super sleuth, Cali. You of all people should know how we performed that magic trick."

"You are going to get a reputation for being the lake slut if you keep swimming without your clothes on," Cali calls back, giggling to herself.

"Pot – kettle – black!" I yell back. Cali brakes out laughing at herself as I enter the kitchen, reaching to Jason for my wine glass. "I'll toast to skinny-dipping!" I say, smiling from ear to ear.

Cali holds her wine glass in her right hand and then steps up in front of me as if she was going to say something.

I smile at her and say, "You are glowing. What did you have for dinner besides an abundance of alcohol?"

Cali doesn't answer but instead casually pulls her left hand out of her pants pocket and shifts her wine glass from her right hand to her left, exposing the massive diamond ring.

I didn't want to spoil the fun since I'd already clued into what the *business opportunity that Cali couldn't turn down* was. My comment is as sincere as if I'd not already figured it out.

"Oh, my fucking God!" I say loudly, looking up at Cali's face then back down to the ring, then over to Jason and then back at Cali. "You finally asked her to marry you?"

"Yes! I said yes!" Cali exclaims, emulating my true excitement for them both.

"I'm so fucking happy for you two," I say, as I reach to hug Cali and kiss her on the cheek. "Jason, I only have one question for you. What the fuck took you so long?"

He shrugs. "I'm an asshole—what more can I say? I should have done this years ago, but I was so afraid she'd turn me down," he says honestly. "When she started dating Garret, I found myself incredibly jealous, which I'd never been before. And then when they divorced, I thought it would be a perfect time to express my long-standing feelings for her. But you know Cali. She needed to be free for a while."

He shrugs again but follows that with a wide smile. "Anyway, enough was enough. I couldn't take another day without knowing if she'd agree to finally marry me."

"Do you know how many years of drunk nights Cali and I spent together talking about how much she wanted you to ask her to marry her?" I ask Jason while shaking my finger at him. "I told her time after time to just propose to you, but she said she was too afraid of *you* turning *her* down. I swear you two are the dumbest lovers I've ever known," I say while replenishing my wine.

Daniel goes to Cali to hug her in congratulations and then steps over to Jason to shake his hand. "Nicely done, mate. This is the most impressive engagement ring I've ever seen."

"You know, I bought that ring five years ago, but she and Garret were so swiftly swept up in love, so I just put it back into my drawer and forgot about it. When you invited me up to the lake Thursday afternoon, I pulled it out of the drawer, had a jeweler polish it up, and decided that it was now or never."

Daniel pats Jason on the shoulder and in a very rare moment we see Jason blush. That has to be the sweetest thing I've ever seen.

Cali lightly slaps Jason across the shoulder with the back of her hand while her jaw dropped open. "Five years you've had this in your penthouse for me! You *are* an asshole!" she says, laughing quite heartily at him.

Jason grins back and replies, "I'm sorry, Kitten. I have all the balls in the world for finance and law, but I'm a complete wimp when it comes to matters of the heart. You forgive me, don't you?"

"Yes Jason, and there is nothing to forgive," she says, kissing him quite sweetly on his lips.

"Well, this calls for a celebration. Turn the music on and let's party!" I say as I raise my wine glass in the air. "These two crazy kids are gettin' married!"

Chapter Thirty-One | The House Hunt

Everyone is thrilled Cali is finally marrying to the man she'd been dating on and off for nearly twenty years. I swear the two of them emailed or texted every person in their cell phone contact lists to share their exciting news. The lake house is abuzz with joy.

Early Sunday morning, Daniel dropped Jason off at the airport to fly back to Vancouver. Cali was dying to fly home with him, understandably, but Jason insisted that he is swamped with work, and they'd hardly see each other until Daniel was back in the office too. Once she took a moment to breathe and accept this minor blip in her plans, we had something else for Cali to focus on. Daniel broached Cali on the subject of buying a house for us to move into together.

While I listened in on their conversation, Daniel wasn't clear on exactly what he was looking for. Cali would have to show him a few properties that were markedly different from each other to narrow down what it was that really sparked his interest on both an investment level and personal taste. He liked the idea of being close to his office downtown, but if the perfect house was farther away it wasn't a deal-breaker. He was also willing to buy a property where the house was no longer viable and rebuild, but that would be a last-ditch option. Cali was certain that with her experience she'd be able to find the right multi-million-dollar investment property for her favourite couple to enjoy.

I mixed a few mocktails for us to share since the last week was one long string of hangovers strung together. I get a frown from Cali when she realizes her drink is sans alcohol, but after a few sips she didn't even notice and soon after is asking for a refill.

The balance of our stay at the lake house was far more relaxing. We hiked to Rattlesnake Point, saw lots of wildlife, some deer, and even a young black bear scoping out berries and bugs along the trail, swam off the dock, read books in the shade when the sun was too much, and toured the lake twice more in the speedboat.

Another lake house season has passed. I'll be sure to come back at the end of September to lock it up properly for the winter and stay a few days on my own or with Grace.

Once we'd returned to our routine lives in the city, the first house Cali toured with Daniel and me was built in 1929. The property is beautifully landscaped; however, the privacy level is low, which didn't appeal to him. The second home we viewed has a small lot. Though the inside has been completely renovated in a style Daniel appreciates, he wants a larger lot, so that one is out. The third property has great street appeal and a large lot size, but the amount of work needed to renovate it won't be worth his time. Although none of these properties fit the bill, he remains eager to buy a home as soon as possible.

After three strikes, the only thing Cali could ascertain from Daniel is that he wants privacy and a move-in-ready home. Some renovations would be fine, but it has to be livable now. Cali believes that the Shaughnessy area of Vancouver will suit Daniel's taste, boasting spacious lots with grand homes new and old. A cul-de-sac just off Granville Street called The Crescent is renowned for its opulent homes close to downtown Vancouver. Rarely do properties on this coveted street come available for purchase, but timing is in Daniel's favour. The lot is over twenty-two-thousand square feet and very private, including an outdoor pool and space for a greenhouse for my orchids. Inside, the home has been well maintained and recently renovated but those updates do not suit his style. Asking price: $18,900,000.

Daniel says, "Cali, this is very close to what I'm looking for, but at over eighteen million it has to be perfect. I'm sorry, but this isn't quite right." I look at Daniel and remark that I wouldn't feel comfortable living in a house this large. He agrees.

Cali thought otherwise. "Oh, come on, Daniel. It's perfect! And you boys probably made that much money last week," Cali says, trying to be glib.

"You're a funny one, Cali, and your financial projections of what we accomplish in a week are a touch off," he says. "I know the Vancouver real estate market is pricey, but I'd like to stay closer to ten million. We'll keep looking, yeah?"

"Yes, we will keep looking, Daniel," Cali agrees.

Since the house hunting was taking longer than either Cali or Daniel anticipated, she would have to put her nose to the grindstone and possibly knock on the doors of some properties that were not currently listed for sale but would fit the description of what Daniel and I need. In these situations, she liked to hand-deliver a slick brochure from her real estate office to try to pique the interest of the current owners. Cali knew that people often don't consider moving until an agent lets them know they have an exclusive buyer for their home.

In the meantime, I receive a text from Daniel:

"I'm going to visit a client in London next week. Can I convince you to join me?"

"Yes! I'd love to see London with you."

"Perfect. Start packing. We leave Tuesday morning at nine AM."

I quickly text Cali to let her know me and Daniel were heading to England and would be gone a week. Should she have any properties come available for Daniel to view, she'd have the week while we are overseas to organize the private viewings.

Daniel never travels anything but first class, so he books with British Airways on their 787-9 Dreamliner, offering one of the most prestigious ways to travel by air. He wants me to have the best experience possible on our trip together and decides to cover the forty-thousand-dollar return airfare for the two of us personally, even though it is officially a business trip.

As much as Daniel enjoys living in Vancouver, he misses his family. It has been nearly a year since he uprooted himself from his base there.

Boarding the flight to the UK, I am delighted to travel in such spacious seating. As I settle into my designated seat, I scold Daniel about the expense.

"Why on earth would you spend so much money? I know you can, but I still think it's crazy."

"Crazy, am I? Spoiled, I think, is the word, and I've earned every penny, Liv," he reminds me, kissing me before he sits himself down across from me.

"I know you've earned it, Daniel. I didn't mean it that way. I'm only saying that there are equally comfortable seats at a more reasonable price. I'm sorry, but I'm hardwired to be fiscally responsible after managing Carter's landscaping business for so many years."

"I want this trip to be special to you. That's all that matters, yeah?" Daniel winks at me as he sips his whiskey on the rocks and pulls out some business paperwork to review. We've reached cruising altitude, and I gaze out my window at the expansive aerial view for a few minutes before I start to read a travel book I'd purchased at the gift shop.

Upon landing at Heathrow Airport, Daniel arranged a car for hire and then retrieved our two suitcases at the turnstiles. Within an hour of landing in London, we are on our way to the Rosewood London Hotel to settle in. In keeping with Daniel's penchant for the finer things, he booked the Grand Suite, offering over nine hundred square feet of luxury for us to enjoy for our one-week stay. The historical appeal of the exterior makes my eyes widen, as they did once again when the suite doors are opened when we are escorted to the room.

"You're kidding me, right?" I say, staring at Daniel. "You're making me feel like royalty!" I wander around the inside of the suite, filling my eyes with the rich details of these new surroundings. "You can't keep doing this, Daniel. You'll turn me into a spoiled brat. Something far less opulent would have been just fine."

"I didn't work this hard for 'just fine,' Liv. The fruits of my labours are these finer things. I like fine things—you should know that of me by now," he says, looking surprised at me for questioning his extravagant ways. Daniel quickly hands the bellboy a hundred Euros and closes the suite door.

"Well, just so we're clear, I have no idea what the second fork is for on the dining room table," I say jokingly.

"Oh, I'm quite sure you do. No matter what you say, Liv, you cannot make me feel embarrassed for being extravagant. I'm not one to boast, but my net worth is over sixty million, even after my divorce settlement." Daniel tilts his head up and appears to be a bit offended that I'm teasing him for his high-end taste.

"You're right," I say. "I guess I haven't seen anything yet, then? Do you mind me asking what the settlement was in your divorce?"

"No. I suppose it doesn't much matter now. Including the property assets and the prenuptial agreement she walked away with nearly thirty million," he says casually.

I turn my head away from Daniel's gaze and whisper, "Oh my fucking God" to myself, then turn back and smile politely at him. "Well, I guess she's pretty comfortable then?"

Daniel laughs surprisingly heartily at me. "Yes, my love. She is quite comfortable. You may be surprised to know that once one masters the numbers game, the assets jump by leaps and bounds. I estimate I will recoup my divorce losses in about a year's time—assuming my projections are on track. My goal is to reach one hundred million, and then I will officially retire."

"This sounds like a game of foot-itis," I say.

"What's that now?"

"You know. A guy buys a boat, then a year later he trades it up for a bigger boat, and a year later he buys an even bigger boat. Foot-itis." I say and throw him a cheeky grin.

"Are you saying the amount of money I earn will never be enough and that I'll never retire because I'm hooked in the game?"

"Maybe. You do love what you do, and I can't see you hitting a plateau and then being satisfied. You'll just add another goal and try to hit that one."

"One day at a time now, love. I will retire. The future could change in any direction. I'd rather be prepared than not."

"Okay then," I say, still shocked at his first confession over his current net worth. "How about we unpack our suitcases and have a few glasses of wine before dinner?"

"Now you are talking my language," he says, approaching me for a hug. "In all honesty, Liv, you mean more to me than my financial assets, although it would take me *at least* a week to get over myself if I lost it all tomorrow," he says, laughing again.

"Liar," I say, poking him in the ribs, then begin kissing him in a way that let him know I want him to show me the bedroom. He picks me up and I wrap my legs around his waist. As he walks towards the bedroom he whispers, "I believe this is the room you are looking for?"

Chapter Thirty-Two | London

The pampering continues the following morning as Daniel orders breakfast up to our suite, so that I don't have to shower and dress before nine o'clock.

"What's on the agenda today?" I ask while sipping a bit of tea from an elegant bone China cup and setting it gently down on the ornate matching gold rimmed saucer. I feel like everything in this suite is untouchable, and I'm careful to be less clumsy than I tend to be in my own home.

"First things first. I've had a credit card arranged for you. The limit is one hundred thousand, so don't spend it all in one place," he teases, handing me the platinum card.

I blink twice and examine the card for a second. "What the hell do you think I'm going to spend that much money on, Daniel?" I ask, flipping the card around in my hand. "You do know I still have some money left and don't need you to look after me."

"Of course, but since I've invited you here, the least I can do is pay for whatever it is that you may want or need." He pauses to gauge me and realizes I'm uncomfortable. "I'm sorry, Liv. It wasn't meant as an insult," he says and frowns at himself.

"It's alright, I get it. But I'm here because I love you, not because you are going to lavish me with a massive limit credit card."

His frown continues to sully his previous chipper mood. "It's my nature to be generous with the ones I love," he admits.

I hand the platinum credit card back to Daniel and squeeze his hand. You show your love for me in so many ways. That's enough for me. You know me. I get what I need when I need it and not before."

His smile returns and he swiftly changes the subject. "I'm planning for us to have dinner with my family on Thursday night. Are you good with Thursday?"

"Yes, of course. You make all the schedules, and I'll tag along," I say, grinning, knowing the money issue has been put aside.

"Brilliant. Today my meeting with Roger Davis is set for one this afternoon. You are welcome to join me, or you can take advantage of the guest services offered. Get a massage, or a facial—whatever you want."

"I'd like to join you for lunch," I say. "I think it would be interesting to see what it is that you do. I mean, I'm curious."

"I can't guarantee that you'll be entertained by our business conversations, but I'm quite sure you will enjoy the restaurant. But for now, why don't we take a stroll down at Trafalgar Square before the lunch meeting? There are four very large lions I'd like to introduce you to," he says, grinning like a child. Daniel is taking his tour guide position quite seriously, and I find it as charming as it is amusing. "There are several classic tourist attractions such as Westminster Abbey, The London Eye, Abbey Road, The Shard, Tower of London and of course, London Bridge. I'm not sure we'll get to them all, but you can choose whichever appeal to you."

As advertised by Daniel, the restaurant for his business meeting is quite beautiful and the food delicious. I listen quietly as he and Roger discuss what it was that Daniel and his partners have to offer. Daniel never mentioned a word about Roger and so I went into this meeting blind of details. I had expected Roger Davis to be the same age as Daniel, but he was much older. He had elegant mannerisms, was shorter than I expected and a little overweight, but a very pleasant man regardless of my preconceived notions. His accent is much thicker than Daniel's, and the longer they talk, the more Daniel's

English accent is revived. When in Rome, I suppose. I found this a bit amusing, and a tad sexy as well. I'll have to remind him that he didn't need to tone down his accent on anyone's account simply because he'd moved to Canada.

As the two men talk about investment options, it's clear that Daniel has a very powerful position in this realm. When Daniel talks, others listen. And when the lunch meeting is over, Roger gives me a kiss on the hand and Daniel an affirmation that he is ready to invest with the Vancouver operation once Daniel returns to his office.

On our way back to the hotel I ask Daniel, "What is it that gets you up in the morning to go to work? What is it about investments that excites you? To me the two of you may as well have been speaking in Greek."

"It's not the investments," he says. "I may have an affinity for finance and investments, but my entire purpose is to put a smile on my clients' faces. If they smile, I smile," he says, reaching to hold my hand. "I don't make money unless they do, so when I see a smile, I know I also lined my own pocket."

"Ah, I see." I squeeze his hand and nod at him. "Okay. Go ahead and speak Greek all you want."

The Thursday dinner with Daniel's family went exceptionally well. They seemed like lovely people and very happy to meet me. Once I'd met his parents, sisters, and brother, it made sense where Daniel got his sense of humour. His father is as charming as he is and has those same beautiful eyes.

I didn't know much about his family before I met them. He speaks of them rarely but then I don't talk much about my family either. Perhaps the fact that I'm an only child and that my parents spend most of the year traveling it never occurred to me to discuss them with Daniel. Half the time I have no idea where on earth they have decided to explore and I only get notification when they send me a postcard, which ironically arrives to me just days before they come back home.

Come Saturday morning, I suggest we cram in as many attractions as we can from my list—make Daniel a tourist in his hometown and my personal guide. I find Westminster Abbey quite fascinating, and I very much enjoyed the view from The Shard. Abbey Road is a visit simply for nostalgic reasons, and as tradition would have it, I made Daniel snap a shot of me crossing the road like on the cover of the Beatles' album from 1969. I'll bet the locals are quite tired of the crosswalk being such a busy attraction even after all these years.

By the end of the day, we are spent and ready to relax in our massive suite at the hotel. Daniel has arranged for chilled wine to be sent up to the suite just before our return, along with some traditional English sweets.

I sit down on his lap and trace my finger around his ear. "You are by far the sexiest tour guide I've ever had the pleasure of being guided by. Not just showing me around but also giving me history lessons," I add as I decide to pop a red jelly baby into my mouth from the silver dish on the side table.

"I offer valuable tips as well," he says, chuckling at me.

"And what kind of tips are we talking about, Mr. Tour Guide Extraordinaire?" I ask while chewing on my candy.

"Hmm, that is a good question," he says, pretending to be thinking hard and tapping his finger against his chin. "I do know that sex is far more enjoyable if you first remove your clothing. Does that count as a good tourist tip?"

"Oh, Danny boy … you must have something more original than that," I tease, tipping my head back dramatically and closing my eyes. I let both of my shoes drop to the floor while Daniel rubs his hand over the top of my thigh.

Daniel clears his throat and replies in a slow, deep voice, "You didn't say I had to be original."

"I'll tell you what I want. I want you to talk dirty to me in your thickest English accent."

"Really? This is what turns you on?" He tips his head back and laughs, a bit shocked at my request.

"You have nooo idea," I say before nibbling on the lobe of his left ear.

"Ooh, kinky," he smiles. "We Brits do like a bit of kink."

On Sunday, Daniel wanted to go for a stroll around the local area. The weather was inclement, with periods of light rain after the early-morning fog had dissipated, but it didn't put a damper on our walk. I had so many questions about London, particularly what Daniel loved most about it.

"As a former Londoner what is your favourite place to visit?"

"Mm. So many things are fascinating here. I love the history, the old lichen encrusted remains of castles, the progressive music scene. Union Chapel in Canonbury is both historically relevant and a brilliant music venue. A Grade I-listed Gothic chapel, built in the late 1800s. I'm certain you'd love it."

I nod and feel excited to see such a grand place. As we approach a crosswalk, Daniel pauses to ensure the city bus has stopped as we ready to cross the street. Holding my hand, he leads me in front of the bus, but he is suddenly and violently struck by a taxi. The screeching tires at the driver's millisecond realization that the crosswalk was in use is a sound that will live in me for eternity.

Daniel loses grip of my hand in the impact. I am jolted forward while I watch in horror as he's thrown over the hood of the taxi, then falls with a deadening thud to the ground in front of it. The taxi has halted mere inch from his body.

"Daniel!"

Chapter Thirty-Three | Aftershock

Rushing to his side as he lay unconscious on the wet asphalt, several people attend to us on the ground, while many others gasp and watch. A nurse who had witnessed the accident from inside the bus clamours down the stairs and kneels at Daniel's side.

I feel my heart pound, not knowing what injuries Daniel may have sustained. I can't even tell if he's breathing. The surrealness, the shock, the panic, and the noise of the cars passing driven by those unknowing of the accident makes me want to scream. "STOP!"

The nurse pushes bystanders out of her way to properly check Daniel's condition and then urges the gentleman standing next to her to call for an ambulance. This can't be happening. In a split second our beautiful perfect world has come to a shocking halt.

Within minutes, the distinctive sound of a London ambulance siren can be heard drawing closer. The crowd disperses to allow the paramedics to address Daniel. The nurse responds to them with her basic assessment. All I hear is noise rather than her words. He is unconscious, listless, and seeing him this way makes me feel lightheaded. One of the paramedics support Daniel's head as they lift him onto a gurney and move him inside the ambulance for delivery to the local hospital. The nurse from the bus takes my arm and leads me to the ambulance, helping me into the back.

I'm not sure what to think, what to expect. I'm in a country where I don't know anything but that the locals like tea and crumpets and have double-decker buses. Suddenly, I feel alone and out of control. I'm holding Daniel's hand in the back of the ambulance while the paramedic tells me that Daniel is likely going to remain unconscious for a while.

And then the battery of questions arises. I'm not prepared to answer as adrenalin still courses through my veins like a runaway train with no destination.

"Miss? Does he take prescription medication?" one of the paramedics asks. I notice his tousled bleach blond hair and rich brown eyes as I stutter as I reply. Where is my mind? What does this paramedic's appearance have to do with this situation. I shake my head and try to stay calm.

"No," I say, wiping the tears from my face.

"And alcohol? Has he had any alcoholic beverages or recreational drugs today? Allergies?"

"No, nothing. And he doesn't do drugs," I confirm, "and I'm not aware of any allergies."

"Okay. I'm going to give him something for pain in case he wakes up, as I'm sure it'll be full on when he does."

"Is he going to be alright?" I ask, still too distraught at the thought of losing Daniel. I squeeze Daniel's hand and feel the warmth of his skin reassure me he's alive.

"We have no way of telling what the full scope of his injuries are until he's been assessed by a physician. You will be the most help to him if you remain calm. Can you do that for me?" he asks.

"Yes. Yes, of course," I say, nodding. "My name is Liv, and this is Daniel Wesley."

"I'm Nigel. We're nearly there now, Liv."

It is two hours later before I'm able to see Daniel in his hospital bed. The emergency ward physicians had given him x-rays to assess his internal injuries, and the nurses had given him a heavy dose of pain medications to help keep him as comfortable as possible. The good news is that he is no longer unconscious, albeit groggy from the meds and the head trauma. He appears to be resting peacefully when I sit beside his bed in the chair. He is pale and has numerous scratches and bruises on his face and arms. I try to be strong, but I still have little information on his condition, and it takes everything I have not to break down and cry like a baby. This uncertainty is too much to bear.

After another long wait, the attending doctor comes back into Daniel's room.

Pulling up his chart from under his arm he says, "Daniel has a broken left femur, a fracture in his pelvis and a dislocated shoulder. The femur is a good clean break and should heal quite nicely. The fracture in his pelvis will take much longer to heal. He'll have to be here under our care for a while."

"How long," I ask.

"Four to five weeks, typically for these types of injuries. At that time, we can reassess and see if light physiotherapy can help him with a full recovery. He appears to be a healthy man, based on blood tests and his physical shape, and that will help him heal quicker," the doctor added. "Do you have next-of-kin information we can add to our records?"

I nod and scroll through Daniel's cellphone for the phone number of his mother and father. I offer the number to the nurse assisting the doctor, and then she promptly dials it from the nurse's station outside of Daniels room. His family arrive within an hour of her phone call to be by his side with me.

Daniel continued to go in and out of stages of grogginess from the pain medications as the days passed. The nurses insisted that it was best he be sedated continuously for the first week because of the fractured pelvis, which is an exceptionally painful injury. The broken femur had been set and cast, and his shoulder had been realigned and taped.

The nurses are quite enamoured with him, as even with the bruises and the scrapes, it is obvious he is extraordinarily handsome. I hear one of them often refer to Daniel as “the movie star in Room 212.”

It is now the third day of his full-time bed rest. I am witnessing a nurse come in to change Daniel’s catheter. Her eyes widen when she pulls his hospital gown aside. I can’t help myself and break out into a fit of giggles as the nurse became embarrassed after letting her eyes say the words she was thinking. She quickly regains her composure and smiles at me.

“Is this your husband?”

“No, but we’ve been dating for a year now,” I reply, smiling broadly.

“Lucky girl,” she says quietly. “Sorry, that was highly unprofessional,” she adds.

“It’s okay,” I say. “I know how lucky I am.”

While Daniel is laid up in his hospital bed, I stay with him during the day for as long as I can keep my eyes open, going back to the hotel at night for a quick rest and a shower. After our initial reservations for our room at the Rosewood had passed, I moved accommodations to a hotel closer to the hospital, so I didn’t have to travel so far to visit with him. And the last thing I wanted was to be rambling around that massive suite by myself at a daily rate that made my head spin. The platinum credit card Daniel arranged for me is still on the table where he left it. It is the perfect tool I needed to pay for a more reasonably priced room for myself until Daniel was well enough to travel home.

I decide to take a little stroll at four o’clock this afternoon to get some fresh air for myself and find a park nearby the hospital to enjoy the greenery and a beautiful flower garden around the edge of the park entrance. As I sit down on a bench, I notice some young boys running around being typical twelve-year-olds. I shake my head and mutter, "Boys will be boys," under my breath.

As I open my novel to the bookmarked page, one of the boys set off a ladyfinger firecracker just steps from where I'm seated. The loud bang rattles me down to my core. Panic rushes through my body and my shrill scream gathers looks from others around me. With my heart racing and a look of deep fear on my face, I have caught the attention of a stranger. She stops and asks if I am alright. My eyes are stone cold as I gaze up to the strange woman's face and my breaths short and fast. I drop the book, and my eyes fill with tears. The stranger sits down beside me, reaching for my hand.

"Are you alright, miss? Are you in distress? Is there someone I can ring for you?"

I squeeze the woman's hand and take as deep a breath as I can muster to stop myself from hyperventilating. After collecting myself for a minute I say, "I'm sorry I reacted so abruptly. I thought it was gunfire. Thank you so much for your concern and kindness," I say softly. I muster a light smile while the woman reaches to the ground to retrieve my fallen book.

"Are you sure you'll be alright?" the woman asks again.

"Yes, yes. Thank you so much. I should be just fine in a few minutes."

As the woman walks away, I start to cry uncontrollably, my chest heaving regardless of how hard I tried to control my breaths and my sudden burst of emotions. Between the unceremonious recall of my terror at the sound of the firecracker and my concerns over Daniel's injuries I'm having a breakdown, in the middle of a public park in a foreign country, alone.

Then, a second emotion steps in, and now I'm angry. I'm angry with myself for letting the past eat me alive at any sudden loud sound.

It takes me nearly ten minutes to fully regain my composure before I head back to the hospital to see Daniel. He doesn't need to see me this weak; I have to be strong for both of us now.

Throughout the following weeks of Daniel's hospitalization, I spoke almost every day to either Cali or Jason about Daniel's condition. They wanted to fly out to London for Daniel, but I told them it was unnecessary. He knows they worry for him and that is enough. His family visited regularly, bringing food, magazines, and well wishes for a speedy recovery. He appears to be doing much better with the pain after the first week but is still spending most of his days and nights sleeping.

On the third week in the hospital, Daniel is moved to a private room. It is quieter and far more comfortable than a shared room, and he appreciated the privacy now that he was spending more time awake than asleep.

He appears to be healing well, according to the doctor, who ordered a new set of x-rays of his pelvis to check his progress.

"Daniel should be able to start physiotherapy in the next day or so," Dr. Bannon says. "The fracture has begun fusing together better than we expected, and I don't want him stuck in this bed any longer than he has to be."

This information is such good news to everyone. Once he is able to sit upright, get out of bed, and use the bathroom on his own, he'll be safe to fly home and work with private nurses and therapists from his condo in Vancouver.

I came into his room with his favourite sandwich only to find him highly agitated.

"I don't want a bloody sandwich, Liv."

"It's your favourite. You hate the food here, so take the sandwich and enjoy it," I counter.

"You don't understand." He throws off the sheets that cover him and attempts to get out of bed without assistance. I drop my purse and the sandwich on the chair behind me and try to assist him.

"Stop! I'm not a fucking child."

I'm taken aback by his sharp tone and words. "I beg to differ since you are acting like one." His stare at me held daggers. Something isn't right here. "I'm sorry. Talk to me," I urge.

He shakes his head. "Talk. Really, Liv. What the fuck is talking going to do? I'm weak as a fucking kitten after lying in this hospital bed for weeks. Do you not understand how maddening this is?"

As he struggles to get to his feet, holding on to the end of the bed frame for support, I spot the walker provided at the side of his bed but knew better than to suggest it.

"What do you want from me, Daniel? What am I supposed to do to make you stronger? I'm just as frustrated as you are."

He chuckles at me incredulously and shakes his head. "Nothing, I suppose. Nobody can do anything. That is what is so bloody maddening." He rests his hip against the bed for stability and scratches his fingers through his hair. "You know what would be fucking nice? A shower. A bath. A way to make me feel like I'm part of the living world and not the half-dead world."

"I can help you with that. All you had to do was ask."

"I'm asking now. Please help me to the bathroom so I can clean myself."

I nod and offer my arm to him. He eases himself one step at a time and I'm surprised at his increased level of stability over the past few days. "You're doing great. See how much better you are now?"

He sniffs at my comment then acquiesces to it. “I know. I am stronger day by day, but for the love of God, why is this taking so long?”

His question is rhetorical. Even the doctors can’t answer it because healing is an individual thing. But he is a strong man. As long as he keeps trying, he’ll come out of this sooner than later.

Speaking of his return to normalcy, Daniel also has a deep concern of how his fractured pelvis would affect our sex life and hesitated to bring up the subject with his doctor while I am in the room, but he needed an answer.

Dr. Bannon enters the room once I’ve helped Daniel dress after his shower.

“Dr. Bannon,” Daniel starts, “how soon will I be able to have sex again? I know nothing about how this injury affects that aspect.”

“Mr. Wesley, once you’re fully recovered, I’m confident everything will be fine. But I don’t recommend jumping into that kind of activity until you are certain you’ve recovered completely. You don’t want any setbacks. Your physiotherapist will tell you which activities to attempt and to avoid during your recovery at home.”

“And how long do you think that would be?” Daniel prodded with his brow furrowed in concern.

“You live in Canada – is that correct?”

“Yes.”

“I will get your physiotherapist here to give you a list of suggested treatment exercises that I hope you will continue with once you return home. Also, I will send all the information regarding your hospital stay here to your physician in Vancouver for follow-up visits.” Dr. Bannon places his hand on Daniel’s shoulder as he continues, “Your recovery has been stellar, and so I hope that you can return to regular physical activity, including intercourse, within a few weeks of your return home. But nothing too strenuous to begin with,” Dr. Bannon said, smiling confidently.

I had not realized how intensely concerned Daniel was about how long it would be before he and I could have sex again. Eventually he decided to talk to me about how I felt. After we finished watching the local news on the small television Daniel broached the subject. "Liv, does it bother you that we haven't been able to be intimate for so long?"

"I know you, Daniel Wesley. I know that you are bursting inside to make love, and I am too. I feel like you've been ripped from me, and I have no control over what is happening to us," I confide. I bring my chair closer to his bedside and lay my head upon his ribs. He drapes his arm over my shoulder and gently strokes my hair.

"Yes, bursting is putting it lightly," he laughs, then makes a groaning sound. I try not to laugh, but I can't control myself. "I'm pleading with you not to laugh, Liv," he says. "I can't even fucking laugh without being in pain, so you must stop."

"I'm sorry. But you have to admit that this is a huge snag in our regular 'routine,'" I say, using air quotes and smiling at him.

"Ah, so that's what we're calling it now, are we?" he says, smiling back and trying not to laugh again. "I'm also dying for a nice stiff drink, but I can't have any of that nonsense either. Bloody hell this is torture. I think my last dose of meds have worn off." He says and sighs, trying to adjust his hips within the sheets without wincing. "Tell me, love. Have you been able to entertain yourself in our suite?"

"I moved to a less expensive hotel near here," I admit.

"Please tell me it isn't something shoddy. I hate to think of you in a poorly appointed hotel."

"It's perfect, Daniel. They even accept platinum credit cards with one-hundred thousand-dollar limits, so you can stop worrying about my accommodations."

"You're rather cheeky today. So, no mirrored ceilings and gaudy red velvet drapes?"

I giggle. "No, Daniel. I'll have you know that the silverware and porcelain dishes are all in matching sets. The staff are lovely, and my view is of a greenspace across the street."

"Mm, quite alright then. But you've not answered my question. Have you been "entertaining" yourself in my absence?"

I quirk a brow and shake my head at him. "Really? This is what you want to know. You want me to tell you how many times I've masturbated since you landed in this hospital?"

"Come on, Liv. Give a bedridden bloke something to be happy about. What was it that made you randy?" he asks and tries not to laugh at himself. "Was it my boxers next to your skimpy pink knickers side by side in the luggage?" He sits up and winces a little in pain then continues. "Wait, no. Don't tell me what turned you on. Just tell me how you moved your hands over that luscious body of yours, yeah?" He follows that question with a wink, and I roll my eyes at him.

"Right. Like I'd tell you what I do to pleasure myself, which I have not done in your absence, by the way, in a hospital room where at any moment a nurse or doctor could walk in on that conversation."

"You? The woman who will take her clothes off at a moment's notice and show the world her beautiful body before diving into a lake, and you are worried about being overheard? You are entirely no fun, Liv. Here I am all banged up asking for a simple favour, and you have refused me." He pretends to be wounded and I'm not falling for it. The good news is that his sense of humour is intact and I'm loving every minute of his banter.

I try to keep him mentally engaged and bring him newspapers and magazine articles that interest him, and he is receiving reports through Jason by email, so he won't feel completely useless in these next few days of his "incarceration" as he puts it. His mind is working overtime, since he is unable to get up and walk around freely except for a few minutes with the physiotherapy practitioners twice a day. He could walk further, but they'd rather he adheres to their protocols than let him up and about at his leisure. Progress is positive, but too slow for Daniel's liking. He also hates that the pain meds make him so sleepy.

"I'm sorry, Liv. Obviously, we didn't plan to spend an extra three weeks in London trapped in this insipid hospital."

"It's alright, Daniel. I don't mind if I know you're healing. I'm happy to see you getting better," I say, touching his hand. He squeezes my hand quite tightly in return. I can see in his eyes that he just wants to punch something to get his anger out.

"You should go out and see London," he says. "Go visit the places we didn't think we'd have time for instead of staring at my depressing face all day. You've been stuck here with me for weeks, yeah? Surely, you're ready to explode from boredom."

"Mr. Wesley, how could I possibly be bored next to you," I say. I wonder if I should mention the firecracker incident in the park, but I didn't want to stress him out any more than he already is with his own issues. "Besides, I've read four books, made some good friends in the cafeteria, had long chats with your mum and dad, and have had to beat the nurses off you because they think you're so handsome," I say.

"Really? How charming!" he replies, being facetious.

"Yes, Daniel. My work here is very rewarding," I tease back. "Now stop your complaining and go back to working on your computer. The time will pass quicker if you keep yourself occupied. Or you can tell me more about the house you want to buy for us when we get home."

"Yes, the house," he says, his expression softening. "I want some level of privacy. I'm not much for others gazing into my home at their whim."

"I'm sure Cali can find that for us. She mentioned that she has people interested in selling to you."

"I guess we'll see when we return," he says and lets out a long breath.

As week four approaches, Daniel is dead set on getting up on his feet as often as he can. He needs a walker to assist as his leg still aches. His progress makes him feel much happier, knowing he will be released within the next few days to go home to Vancouver. The positive side of his extended hospital stay is being able to see his family and friends who pop in and out regularly to check on his progress. His stepson Ian also managed to visit, and Daniel was delighted to see him and have a face-to-face report on the headway of his tech company.

He was able to walk confidently with a cane by the time he was released from the hospital at the beginning of week five. His dedication to getting out of there as soon as possible had driven him to prove to the doctor that he was well enough. The smile on his face could not have been broader when he was given the okay to head home. I booked the flight. Within the next twelve hours we will be on our way back to Vancouver.

Daniel was confined to a wheelchair until me and the flight attendant could assist him into his seat. He didn't like the wheelchair, but it is a long trek through the airport to board the plane.

It is interesting how similar the weather in England is to Vancouver. Strangely, that made me feel connected to London without ever having been there before.

Our flight home is uneventful, thankfully. The last thing either of us needed was more drama.

Over the next two weeks, while he worked from his home office and did his daily physiotherapy treatments, his mental health had also improved substantially. I doted on him every second of my waking day. I never complained when Daniel was frustrated or in a bit of a mood over his lengthy recovery period, his lingering pain or his inability to make love to me yet. He had also lost nearly twenty pounds since the accident and didn't like feeling so thin and weak.

I realize after looking at the calendar on the wall that this is week eight of his recovery. He walks with confidence. I'm delighted for him. Movement is no longer the issue, but his chronic pain emanating from his left side has yet to subside. He hates that he can't just "muddle through" the pain like a real man should. Daniel is no wimp, but he feels like one having to rely on pain medications to get through the day.

Out of seemingly nowhere he gets frustrated with me. "Go home and do something for yourself, Liv," he says. "You need to get out. Visit Cali for lunch. Walk in the park. Go shopping. You must be quite sick of me." He raises his voice as he continues, "I'm not a bloody invalid. I can cook my own meals, make tea, wipe my own fucking arse."

I drop my tea towel into the sink and turn around to look at him feeling shocked at this behaviour. "Glad to hear it. And if you're done yelling at me, I'll happily leave you alone to sulk and carry on with my life since you're so sick of me." I reach for my purse beside the microwave on the kitchen counter and toss it over my shoulder. "And you can have your keys back too since I won't be needing them anymore." I toss the keys on top of the counter and head to the front door to leave. I don't know which of us is being the bigger baby here, but I won't let him talk to me like that.

Daniel rises from the kitchen chair and chases after me to the front door. "Stop, Liv. I'm sorry for the outburst. You've been so accommodating, and you have no idea how guilty this makes me feel. For two months you've done nothing but care for me."

I stop at the door but don't turn around. He's right. I've been ignoring my life, my condo, the joy that was lost when we didn't continue to search for a house to buy, that we haven't been as intimate as we thought we would once we'd returned home. Everything seems wrong and out of alignment. Perhaps we've reached a tipping point, and this outburst was his way of expressing it.

Then he clears the air.

"Liv. How are your counselling sessions coming along? We talk about me at nauseum, but we don't ever discuss your healing process."

"My sessions are fine. I'm making progress."

"But you are still angry. I know you are. Yet, I never see you angry," he says with deep concern in his voice.

"Yes! I'm angry, but do you really want me throwing dishes and to scream like a child in a tantrum?"

"Why not? Get it out of your system. Let loose. Let it go. Good God, you've survived something most people couldn't imagine living through and yet seem perfectly fine to ignore it," he says.

The hairs on the back of my neck stand up as my temper begins to finally rear its head. "Fine! What should I break first?" I ask pointedly with fire in my eyes as I stare down Daniel.

I march into the kitchen and throw my purse on the counter. "How about those beautiful new wine glasses in the China cabinet? Those would make a *great* cracking sound smashing against the tile floor, don't you think?"

I plant my palms down firmly on the kitchen island, my arms straight and rigid as I claw my fingers repeatedly over the granite surface. "Or what about grabbing a slab of meat out of the fridge and stabbing it repeatedly with your biggest butcher knife while I scream out the names of my captors?" I shout back at him. "Is that what you want me to do? Would that satisfy your vision of me getting it *out of my system*?"

Slightly shocked at finally seeing me lose my cool, Daniel replies without hesitation, "I don't mean to sound condescending, but I like this angry Liv. I want to see some fight come out of you. You are too nice, too accommodating, and you're making me feel like such an arse for not letting you release your inner frustrations the way I have to you since my accident."

I turn my head to look at him over my shoulder and then start to laugh. “So, this is a guilt trip of yours, then? You feel bad for me because I’ve put up with your whining and not complained to you in return?”

“No! You’re missing my point. I’m simply telling you that after all the shit you put up with for me while in hospital, you’ve never given me a single indication that you’ve vented properly over your kidnapping or even looking after my sorry as shite arse. It isn’t healthy, Liv. You must let some part of you lash out. Break the glasses, stab a steak. For the love of God, scream at the top of your lungs if you must, but dammit woman, let the monster I know is hiding inside of you out!”

As I listen to him state his concerns over my inability to give myself permission to express how I feel inside, even after so much time has passed since my safe return, my only reaction now is to laugh. I laugh louder than I’d ever laughed before, nearing hysterics. And after a minute of Daniel listening to my strange fit of hearty laughter, he sees something that I don’t. I’m breaking down again. He approaches me slowly. Just as he reaches for my arm, I go from hysterical laughter into a wave of tears, ending in a deep, loud sobbing. I slap at his arms as he approaches to hold me close then acquiesce to his comfort. My body heaves within his embrace.

“They killed Brad,” I manage to say. “Why him and not me? The guilt is gutting me.”

“What have I done? I’m so sorry, Liv,” he whispers. He kisses the top of my head, still encompassing me in his arms while I let my emotions overflow like a river bursting its banks. I make a weak attempt at pounding my clinched fists into Daniel’s chest, but I no longer have the strength to be physically aggressive. I am spent, and limp from holding back for far too long. I thought I’d gotten all of this out of me in the park in London, and even through my therapist, but now I see it isn't as easy to let go as one simple solid public cry or talking it out.

Daniel is right. I needed to get angry, truly angry. Daniel has forced that anger out of me. As I regain control after my outburst, I wipe my cheeks and continue to rest my head on Daniel's chest. He strokes my head with his hand while we stand holding each other for a while longer.

When I speak again, my voice is shaky. A wave of relief washes over me. Daniel's prodding brought out the deep emotions I was still harbouring.

When he releases me from his arms, he places his palms on either side of my face, holding it there to be eye to eye with him.

"Are you okay, love?" he asks softly.

"No," I reply, closing my eyes and taking a deep breath. "I'm never going to be okay with Brad dying in my arms. It happened so fast. I tried to save him, and while he took his last breath, he told me that he was trying to save me. Before he was shot, we were so elated to have been rescued. All we had to do was jump into the Jeep and drive off into the sunset. But no. Life doesn't work like that. It's unfair, grossly unfair. I miss Brad with all my heart."

I feel foolish and relieved at the same time for my fit of rage. I change the subject because there will never be an answer for what happened. Any of it.

"I hate losing control, which is why I started laughing. I know that doesn't make any sense but that's what I do when I'm embarrassed. And then I was also reminded of what I lost of myself out there in the jungle."

"What was it that you lost?"

"I lost the Liv that was strong, independent, a bit ballsy and sure of herself. I've lost that part of me, and I don't know if I'll ever get it back."

"You will," he assures me. "That part of you is still there—perhaps on hiatus while you found a way to fight back."

Chapter Thirty-Four | Big Boy and Kitten

Although Daniel has returned to a relatively normal daily routine he is assured by his physician and physiotherapist that his intermittent pain issues will subside soon.

I am managing to increase Daniel's weight with hearty meals that are far more delicious than the food he'd been offered in the hospital. He's happier and ready to go back into his office.

Daniel thrives on routine, scheduling, and analyzing information. He did plenty of it from his condo since we've come back to Vancouver, but it isn't the same as dressing in his three-piece suits sitting behind his desk in the downtown skyscraper or doing business meetings with clients face to face. He is a creature of habit who needs his natural habitat to thrive.

The first day back to the office, Jason had arranged for a celebratory lunch gathering for Daniel and a few of their favourite clients. Cali and I joined in on the lavish lunch and drank a few too many glasses of the Okanagan wines Jason had brought back from the lake house.

In this late fall season, it grows chillier by the day. I mark these chronic cloudy and rain filled late November days with red X-marks on my wall calendar. Green check marks for sunny days and red X-marks for rainy ones. I loathe this time of year, but even the dreary outdoors can't douse my giddy mood at the upcoming wedding for Cali and Jason.

Their wedding ceremony is a private affair on the rooftop deck of Jason's penthouse apartment. Daniel and I are witness' to a Justice of the Peace service followed by a catered champagne lunch for the four of us. Cali and Jason wanted the service to be simple – a shocking reversal of how they would normally have celebrated such an incredible day. We are honoured to be the only two people who witness their exchange of vows.

Five patio heaters warm the rooftop as the wedding planner dotes on the finishing touches of the archway flowers, the two massive column floral displays set up behind where the JP will stand during the ceremony, and the black runner carpet leading up to the alter.

Cali and I sit on the edge of Jason's bed and share a glass of wine before it is time for her to say *I do*. The dress Cali chose is a form fitting design made of the palest of pinks in open lace fabric with a deep V plunging neckline, and a three-foot long two-tiered train. Her coat is a satin lined white feathered shrug to keep her shoulders warm and is clasped together with a rhinestone broach that her mother bequeathed to her before her passing several years ago. She is a vision to behold.

As the moment for them to exchange their vows arrived, Daniel and I watched Cali walk through the open deck doors with the most beautiful smile on her face. Jason looked at her as though the world had stood still, and this made me quite emotional for both of them.

After the ceremony and the photographs a few more close friends and family joined us inside Jason's condo for celebratory drinks. Cali decided it was time to toss her bouquet, which she did with gusto and as she turned around to see where it landed, the photographer's assistant stood there wide-eyed at having caught it. She then bowed to Cali and giggled. Very sweet moment.

As lowkey as this wedding was, I loved every minute of it. It felt intimate and loving and made me want the same for myself should that time ever come for me again to tie the knot.

Cali and Jason will honeymoon for a week in the French Riviera, which had been one of their favourite places to visit when they were travelling together many years ago.

It was well past one in the morning when we had returned to Daniel's apartment after the wedding service and party. In his drunken state he was feeling rather confident that he would finally be able to make love to me in the way that he used to.

"Daniel, are you sure you're up for this?" I ask softly as he make moves to see if I'm up for the challenge.

"I'm always up for this with you," he murmurs into my ear. He tries rather clumsily to climb atop me on the bed, but as he raises his hips to insert himself into me, he is suddenly stabbed by a sharp pain in his left side and groans loudly. He squeezes his eyes tight and blurts out, "Fuck!" then collapses on the sheets beside me.

"What's the matter?"

"I'm so fucking sick of this, Liv. I'm never going to be the same again," he says, infuriated and embarrassed.

I attempt to soothe him with my words, but he is well beyond that now.

"Nothing you can say is going to make the pain and my frustrations subside," he barks. "I shouldn't have these pains anymore. It's been too bloody long."

I nestle up close to him and drape my arm over his chest.

"Nothing can be said to make me less frustrated," he chides. "You'll only make matters worse."

"Is this really what you want? For us to fight tonight?"

Daniel takes a deep breath and exhales slowly. "No. I'm sorry, Liv. I'm drunk and randy as fuck and I can't do anything about it." He rubs his face vigorously with his palms in frustration.

"Relax and we can try again in a few minutes," I urge. "Maybe I can go on top?"

"Liv, I don't think the pain will be any less regardless of how we approach it."

I do my best to help him calm down. "Perhaps our first time shouldn't be when we're drunk. I'd rather it be a beautiful moment together. Not like this."

"You're right, my love. I just feel so useless."

"You've been on your feet all day. That can't have been good and I'm not surprised you are uncomfortable." He lets out a long breath then kisses me tenderly.

"Agreed." Minutes later he is sound asleep at my side.

On Sunday morning after the wedding, Daniel got back on track on finding the perfect home for us. It would be another week before Cali and Jason return from their honeymoon. Daniel had waited this long, and another seven days before the house search started again was not going to make any difference now. Still, he scoured the local listings in the areas Cali suggested months ago in hopes of having a few listings to show her. Like a dog with a bone, he won't let up until he's satisfied.

I have seen a side of him that he admits he isn't proud of—the brooding, anger and frustration. All quite understandable given his circumstances. Yet, atop all his personal issues he also bears the burden of mine. I've come to love him more than I did before *because* he allowed me to see him at his worst, something I think he had hidden from me for a long time. I'm not perfect, and I'd not expect him to be either. If we can survive our struggles without losing track of who we are to each other, that is a true test of a loving relationship.

I do sometimes laugh to myself about his unbelievable libido though. The man is a machine of lovemaking, the complete opposite of Carter. I should have been more careful of what I wished for as once Daniel is no longer in pain, he's going to be a sex force to be reckoned with. I'm now picturing myself walking bow-legged as I fold my laundry, and mimic that walk as I carry the folded clothes to my dresser.

Daniel walks into the bedroom as I waddle my way across the floor. "What in the Devil are you doing? Have you shat yourself?" he teases and smirks.

"No! I'm just being silly. Is it okay to be silly?"

"Well, alright then." Daniel grabs one of his socks from the basket and high step prances toward me, flips the sock across my cheek then prances backwards, then does it again mimicking Monty Python's fish dance routine.

"Very funny, Daniel."

"Yes, quite. You asked for silly, and I gave you my best silly. You are quite impressed, are you not?"

"I'm impressed you were able to do that fancy walk and not complain once about pain in your hip," I say reaching forward to snatch the sock from his hand.

"What?"

"What?"

"Oh, fucking yes!" His eyes bulge out of their sockets and then a devilish grin forms on his face. "Upon thy bed now, wench!" he says. He throws all the folded clothes and the laundry basket off the bed without a care where any of it lands and scoops me into his arms. My mouth is devoured by his passionate kisses as we fall atop the mattress.

Upon Cali and Jason's return from their honeymoon, Cali went straight to task house-hunting, as promised. In our absence, Cali had managed to find two property owners who agreed to allow Daniel to view their home and negotiate a sale price. Neither of the two homeowners was in any hurry to sell their homes, so the wait for Daniel to recover and return to Vancouver didn't become an issue for the interested parties.

The first property was a Tudor-style home built in the 1930s, with beautifully maintained gardens and a private setting. Tall trees surrounded the back half of the property, and on the other side of the outdoor pool was a guest cottage perfect for resident staff or out-of-town guests to use. Daniel fell in love with the exterior of the home and the grounds, because it looked very much like a traditional English estate and had ample room to put a greenhouse in for my orchids. The interior had loads of authentic details relevant to the age and style of the home which had been carefully maintained. Cali had tentatively agreed with the owners to put the value of the home in the eleven-million-dollar range. She didn't think Daniel would be too upset about it, based on their last conversation about what he was willing to spend. Overall, this was a very promising property. The only thing Daniel and I agreed we didn't like was the kitchen, but if he had to rip it out and replace it to his and my taste that was perfectly fine. Daniel thanked the owners very kindly for allowing him to see their home, and then we moved on to the second property on the same street to compare our options.

House number two was a recent rebuild after an extensive fire consumed the original ranch-style home in late 2023. Daniel was torn between his love of the old-world-style homes and ultra-modern homes in the area. The exterior of the second home offered interesting slate stonework combined with vertical wood detail and a black-lined reflecting pond filled with water lilies and koi. It had a clean and tranquil appeal that pleased him. The interior offered extra-high ceilings, glass railings along the staircases, a wine room, a good-sized dedicated office space, and a bright open floor plan that gave the lower level the feeling it was much larger than its actual footprint. The rear yard was not quite as private as the Tudor home's, especially on one side, but a few strategically placed trees and the addition of a greenhouse would properly solve the problem.

The landscaping was minimalistic and would require almost no effort to maintain. A large concrete in-ground swimming pool, a covered outdoor kitchen and entertainment area completed the landscape design. Inside the house, nothing was missing or in need of change in Daniel's mind. The current owners had been in the property for just over a year and half and hoped to retire to their estate on Maui, Hawaii in the coming year. With Daniel's possible interest in their home in Vancouver, they could retire to Maui earlier than expected. It seemed like a win-win for both parties. They agreed to sell the home to Daniel for eleven-and-a-half million and would need a few weeks to arrange for their move before Daniel could take possession. He told them he'd confirm within twenty-four hours.

His heart was already set on the modern home. As much as the Tudor property appealed to his English upbringing, it reminded him too much of the estate he gave to his ex-wife, and somehow buying a similar property in Vancouver didn't quite fit his new lifestyle. The modern home appealed to me as well, and so it was a done deal. Cali called the owners to say their home was sold for the agreed-upon price. The timing couldn't be more perfect, as we'd have a new home for ourselves before Christmas.

As moving day approaches, I put a call in to Carter with respect to our joint ownership of my condo. We agreed that instead of selling the condo to a stranger and splitting the profits, it would be best if we put it into a trust for Grace. This would allow her to have some freedom from living under her father's wing but still be close enough to him if she needed anything. The new home Daniel and I are moving into is only a ten-minute drive away from my condo as well. It is a great solution for everyone involved, and Grace is ecstatic to know she had her own place to live.

The last bit of business is to sell Daniel's downtown condo. Once again Cali comes to the rescue. Daniel's original plan to rent it out and keep the property as an investment was sidetracked when he read the updated bylaws from the strata council, which indicated his building no longer allowed rentals. Cali listed the condo right away, as Daniel just wanted it off his books.

Cali sent Daniel a text to let him know that the conveyancing paperwork for the purchase of the house are ready to be notarized. We can move into the house in just under a week. I am so excited I can hardly contain myself.

We took our time moving into the new house. Daniel wanted his home office sorted first, then each room was organized by how we'd both use those various spaces. We have also purchased new furnishings to go along with the pieces we had already amassed on our own. I left most of my furniture in my condo for Grace, but a few select pieces were handpicked by me on my travels that Grace would not appreciate the way I do. Many of those items are artwork, and of course my lovely orchids that did so well in the natural light of the condo's kitchen and dining room windows.

I like that we took our time to move in rather than rushing everything in at one time. Our combined decisions on what should go where was achieved organically and was without the usual stress moving house can be.

Now that Daniel's pain issues have been sorted, he is trying to make up for lost time. As we prepare chopped vegetables in the new kitchen, he stands behind me and drops his chin on top of my head. Slowly, he raises his hands to cup my breasts. "You feel so good, and I'm so hard I'm going to blow a seam in my trousers."

"I'm surprised you don't blow seams in all your pants," I say, laughing. "You do know you have an enormous cock, right?"

"You think you're quite funny, do you?" He spins me around and stares me straight in my eyes. "I was hoping you could do something about my enormous *cock* who is always ever so delighted to see you."

"Well, when you ask so politely, how can I refuse? Are we going to solve your problem right here in the kitchen, or shall we find somewhere more comfortable?"

"If I could do to you what I want to do to you, we'd be clearing off the kitchen island this minute, but I think the bedroom is the better choice."

"What are we waiting for, then?" I ask, dropping my utensils and grabbing his hand.

Pleasuring each other orally offered at least some level of satisfaction while he was injured, but Daniel never felt complete without feeling himself moving inside of me. He was apologetic about asking me to satisfy him with fellatio or to stroke him in the shower to quell his urges. And because of his deep desires for me, his urges were frequent. He pleased me with his hands and his mouth in any way he could to make up for his sexual demands on me, and I appreciate how much he wants me to be satisfied in return.

It seems crazy to us how quickly time is passing. Between being swamped at work, Cali and Jason's wedding, and buying and selling properties, the demands of our time as of late seem to be endless. I'd love a vacation, even a simple quiet weekend away up the coast, but there are still many things to take care of first.

Daniel's plan to step back officially and work only two or three days a week in the office is slated for January. This will give us all the extra time I wanted to have with him. The accident in London had delayed his initial plan to be done full-time work by late August or early September, but I understood and waited patiently for him to resolve his business obligations to Jason and Michael's satisfaction.

Daniel was also on track to recoup his thirty-million-dollar loss in his divorce to Jane with two high-risk long-term investments he'd initiated three years earlier. The high-risk investment paid off, and his net worth is now nearing seventy-eight million. I have no idea what Jason's net worth is, but I assume it is in the same ballpark. I had always felt that Carter and I were quite well off after twenty years of hard work, but the money Daniel and Jason are amassing is mind-boggling.

I notice an email on his laptop about a cleaning service contract while I was using it to look for a cake recipe. I look over my shoulder at him sitting on the couch with a glass of whisky being swirled around gently within the glass in his hand and ask, "What am I supposed to do with my time if I don't have to clean anything? It's going to make me feel like a kept woman, Daniel. I'm going to be bored out of my mind."

"Come," he said while rising from the couch. "Let's have dinner first and we can talk about what you can do with your time."

After dinner, Daniel gave me a proposition he thought I'd like. "Can I interest you in heading a philanthropic fund for Jason and me?"

"What is the fund for?"

"We've decided to donate two million dollars each to help Roman with his search-and-rescue efforts in Central and South America. What he does is important to us all after what happened to you down there, and we realized that there are many people like Brad and his family who don't have the money required to properly help locate missing loved ones. What do you think about that?" he asks, reaching to hold my hand across the dining room table.

"Wow!" I say, shocked. "That's amazing! Yes, of course I'll manage the books for your fund. Will there be other people donating money to this cause, or is it just something you and Jason are doing?"

"We'll let some of our philanthropic clients know about it, and if they're interested there might be a few more dollars infused from outside sources. We have the account set up and Roman is very happy to have our financial support. We won't set it up as an official charity because we will be privately funding it, but it will be open-ended based on what Roman's clients' needs are. You would be working directly with Roman on the monies used and the records keeping."

"I love it, Daniel. Can I give the fund a name?" I ask excitedly.

"Yes. What should we call it?"

"How about The Barkley Rescue Fund, after Brad's last name?"

"Perfect," Daniel agrees.

"Oh, and one last thing, Liv," Daniel says as he rises and walks over to put the stereo on in the living room. "Will you dance with me? I haven't been able to dance since the accident that I just feel like I need to spin my heels around the floor with my favourite lady."

Daniel saunters over to me to hold my hand as I rise from my dining room chair. "You are such an old soul, Daniel," I say, grinning up at him.

"Let's wait for the next song to begin," he suggests. "It's a new favourite of mine."

Daniel moves the coffee table out of the way, so we have more room for him to "spin his heels." He gently wraps his arms around my waist, and I look up to his face as he smiles and kisses my forehead. "What's the name of the next song?"

"You've likely never heard this one before. It's a slow song, so I'll not be whipping you 'round the floor per se," he says and laughs.

As the first notes play, I don't recognize it but listen intently to the words. He hums along with the words while we slow-dance together.

"That is such a pretty song," I say, smiling up at him. "Who is the artist?"

"My brother," he replies and grins contentedly. Although Daniel has many talents, singing isn't one of them, but his brother's voice is wonderful.

"I thought you'd like it," he murmurs.

As we hold each other slow-dancing, and I absorbed that warm glow of Daniel's that I love so much, he tips his head down and kisses me. The sheer romance of this moment is "brilliant," as Daniel would say.

"Could anything about this moment be more perfect?" I ask still basking in his tenderness.

"That all depends on your answer to my next question," he says. He moves my hair to tuck it behind my ear and caresses his lips in light kisses upon my neck. Speaking tenderly to me he asks, "Will you marry me, Liv?"

I am speechless as I lean back to search his eyes for any reason to not believe the words I've just heard from the shock of them. The answer is clearly yes, but I'm not quite ready to say yes without giving him a most passionate kiss. My heart aches with joy and my eyes water. I can't get close enough to him even though our bodies are cinched tight to each other. He receives me and my fervent kiss with all the love in his heart. I can hardly breathe with the excitement thrumming through my body. Our lips part and we both smile.

"Is that a yes?"

"Yes, yes, yes. A thousand times yes!"

"A thousand times yes, indeed," he says, smiling and laughing at me. He squeezes me firmly, holding my head against his chest and rocking me back and forth. "I love that you said yes," he replies softly. "I am the happiest man alive. Oh, and I have this little bobble I bought for you that hopefully fits your finger… just in case you said yes."

Daniel smiles like a little kid, quickly digging inside his pants pocket then placing the black velvet box into my palm. "Is it too late for me to get upon my knees?" he asks. "No. Yes? Gaah, just let me open the box!" I say anxiously prying it open. Sparkling back at me is a vintage-inspired three-carat marquise-cut diamond set atop a platinum band encrusted with a row of smaller diamonds on either side of the center setting.

"Daniel, this is ridiculously beautiful! It's perfect, and I love it! Okay, not as much as I love you, but it's a solid second place," I say and laugh nervously. "I'm getting a hot flush on my face." Daniel chuckles as helps me slip the lavish engagement ring onto my finger.

"Only the best for the most amazing woman I've ever known. And I like it when you're hot!" he says, continuing to laugh at me blushing over the engagement ring. "Also, I have the perfect wedding gift already on order for you."

"Really? What could that possibly be?"

"A motorized retractable dome pool roof, so we can have some privacy when you want to go skinny-dipping in the backyard with me!"

I break out into a full belly laugh. "Daniel, that *is* the perfect wedding gift! But what the hell am I supposed to give a man who literally has *everything*?"

"My love, I didn't have everything until two minutes ago when you agreed to marry me. Wait, that didn't come out right. You're not my possession," he laughs nervously while he tries to correct his words. "I mean to say that I didn't feel like my life was in a perfect place until you said yes."

"Oh, nicely done on the backpedalling there, Danny boy," I say cheekily. "Well done indeed." I start clapping slowly with my hands and giggling at him as my stunning ring catches the light and reflects a prism across the room.

"I'm sure you'll think of something that I will appreciate. Maybe a new Jag, or a condo somewhere hot and beautiful in Greece that we can escape to whenever we want?"

"How about I get you both. I've never gone into a car dealership to buy a new car, and if you don't mind me picking the colour, you've got a deal."

"You can pick any colour you want," he says, sliding the back of his finger across my forehead and down the flesh of my cheek endearingly. "As long as it's metallic blue to match my pretty eyes," he adds, chuckling at being so full of himself and fluttering his eyelashes at me.

"Cheeky. You are very cheeky, Danny Boy."

Chapter Thirty-Five | Portofino Blue

The next morning Daniel and I couldn't wait for the dealership to open its doors. We waltzed inside the showroom well dressed, slowly roaming around the gleaming cars on display. Another couple were there to view the cars and smile politely at us when our eyes met theirs. One of the sales reps approached Daniel and introduces himself as Randall. "What can I do for you today?" he asks.

"We'd like to purchase a car today. An F-Type convertible like this one," Daniel says as we stand next to the showroom model.

"It is a showstopper," Randall says. "A favourite of mine as well. Let me get you the brochure on the F-Type," he adds as he steps over to the reception desk and fetches a slick ten-page booklet for us to peruse.

Daniel looks up from inspecting the detailed stitching on the seat of the model in front of us. He asks, "Does this F-Type convertible model come in a metallic blue?" as he takes the booklet from Randall's hand.

"Yes," Randall says, "it's available in our Portofino Blue. A fabulous rich tone. Very eye catching. If you'll come with me, I'll show you the one we have in stock."

We follow Randall out into the dealership's display lot as he locates the vehicle he thinks Daniel will be interested in seeing. "Is this the colour you were thinking of?" he asks, smiling and opening the driver-side door for Daniel to seat himself inside.

Daniel slides with ease into the driver's seat and sweeps his palms over the steering wheel. "What do you think, love?" Daniel calls out. "Is this the one that matches the colour of my eyes?" Randall smiles and looks over to me, waiting for my reaction.

"Yes, baby. If that's the one you want, have them wrap it up and I'll buy it for you," I say, jokingly, but it sends a minor shockwave through Randall who automatically assumed Daniel has the money. I mean, he's not wrong, but since I'm supposed to be buying this car for Daniel as his engagement gift, I may as well own the character role I've inadvertently thrown myself into. I switch my handbag from one arm to the other and then inspect my new manicured fingernails in the bright sun watching the opalescent pearl flecks in the polish glint back at me.

Redirecting Randall from staring slack-jawed at me Daniel asks, "Is this F-Type convertible fully loaded, or do I have to custom-order one with all the bells and whistles?"

"This one has every possible option available for this model. The brochure will list all available options should you have any questions.

"Hm, I see," Daniel says as he goes about inspecting every switch, gadget, compartment, and finishing detail of the car. He presses the button to open and close the convertible top and waits patiently while it closes and locks in place automatically. He presses the button again to open the top, and Randall slides a quick glance at me and smiles tight lipped.

"Do you have any other questions? Would you care to go for a test drive?" Randall asks.

"No. A test drive is unnecessary. I've owned Jaguars for years. I know how well they handle."

Randall nods then opened the driver's door for Daniel to exit. "Should I draw up the paperwork?" he asks as he looks over to me again for approval.

"Oh sure, why not," I drawl and wave my hand in the air like it doesn't matter. "If that's what my baby wants, who am I to say no?" I grin sweetly at Randall and then wink at Daniel.

This is the most fun I've had in a long time. I've never been shopping with an unlimited budget, and the accidental "who's got the money" role reversal turned out to be a private joke that Daniel and I will laugh at later.

After I let Randall charge my new platinum credit card for nearly as much as Carter and I paid for our first house, Daniel walks over to me, kisses me on the lips and says, "Thank you for the new toy, love."

Randall smiles politely and says, "Just a few documents for you to sign, and you can be on your way. I'll have her detailed and ready for pickup tomorrow at eleven a.m. Does that work for you?"

"Yes, brilliant." He says shaking Randall's hand firmly.

As we leave, I say to Daniel, "I feel like such a bitch now. I mean, I know the guy assumed you were the man with the money, but when you flipped that narrative on him, I couldn't help but play along."

"You played that role so well, Liv. You had the poor sod quite confused."

"Well, it makes me recall a friend of Carter's who walked into a car dealership after work wearing his construction clothes. He had eighty-thousand dollars to burn on a new car, and the sales rep on the showroom floor ignored him. Finally, after fifteen minutes, Flynn was heading out the door to leave when another sales rep introduced himself to Flynn and that salesman made the sale on the exotic car he wanted. All cash sale. He drove it off the lot an hour later. I'll never forget that story. People are so easily judged by their clothes, and in our case, my gender. Anyway, I'm happy you love your new car, and I can't wait to ride in it with you."

"You can take it for the first spin," he says.

"Aw, thanks, buddy," I say and smile sweetly.

"Liv, it was your money that bought the car, not mine."

"Um, no. The last time I checked my bank account it did not have enough left to buy a bus ticket to Calgary, let alone a new Jaguar."

"Well, you see, I put you down as the sole beneficiary to everything in my name six months ago and set up an investment portfolio for you that has been doing rather well, if I do say so myself."

"What!?"

"Jason drafted all the paperwork, including my revised will. Did I forget to inform you?"

A blank stare covers my face as I try to figure out if my ears have deceived me. "Tell me you're joking. You did no such thing, Daniel."

"I've already given my family in London loads of money to secure their futures. The only person I feel deserves to have my fortune in their name, whether you are married to me or not, is you," he says firmly.

I swallow hard and almost choke on my words. "I swear you've lost your mind, Daniel Wesley," I say, staring at him and frowning. "That is just crazy talk."

"You missed using my middle name, like my mum does when she's angry with me. Daniel *Alexander* Wesley," he says, laughing at me.

"You are certifiable. Tell Jason to fix that immediately. I couldn't possibly know how to manage that amount of money should you die before me."

As we round the corner off Granville to our street he says, "I'll go over the details with you later. Trust me, I've given explicit details of how the money is to be managed by you. I'm sorry if this shocks you, Liv. That wasn't my intention," he says calmly. "Jason has done virtually the same for Cali."

After a minute of trying to comprehend what he'd just told me, I resign myself to dealing with it later. "Okay, okay, I trust you, but I still think you need have your head examined." I take a deep breath and try to think of something else. "So, where in Greece is this hot, beautiful location where you want to buy a condo? My big-ass investment portfolio isn't going to spend itself."

"Ha! I knew you'd come 'round." Daniel rolls his car into the driveway of our new home and parks in front of the garage. He kisses my cheek and says, "This afternoon we should sit down and hammer out some of the wedding details, yeah?"

"Yes. I'll make a pot of tea once we're inside."

I bring my laptop out to the kitchen table to make notes while the kettle boiled.

"The first thing we need to decide on is how many people we're going to include in the guest list," I say.

"We'll have to fly in my family from England," he says, "and so I think with the nieces and nephews there will be nine. I also have about twelve clients and their significant others who would be interested in attending, or at the very least would be insulted if I didn't send them an invitation."

"Right," I say and nod. "On my side I only have five people, since my grandparents are no longer alive. It would just be my mom, dad, Grace, Cali and Jason."

"Do you not have friends you'd like to ask to attend?" Daniel asks curiously.

"No," I say. "Oh wait. How about inviting Roman? Do you think he'd come?"

"Roman's attendance would be anyone's guess, depending on his work at the time of the service."

"And Jason? I'm guessing he'll be your best man, and Cali my matron of honour?"

"Yes, brilliant. No question there, love."

Daniel and I type out our list of invites on my laptop. "Wow, this is going to be very easy to arrange. I think that makes close to thirty guests at most. Small wedding, which is just fine with me," I say and grin contently.

"I love it when you're easy," he jokes as he pours two cups of tea for us.

"Behave yourself. Next decision," I say, typing away at the keyboard, "where to host the ceremony and reception. I'm going to do an online search for some local places and see what comes up."

"Oh, look at this! How about the Shaughnessy Golf Club? It's perfect for an outdoor summer wedding. And I never thought to ask you this, but did you want a church service, Daniel?"

"No, love. Have it wherever or however you want," he says, adding a bit of milk to his cup. "We can do the Justice of the Peace thing like Jason and Cali did, if you'd prefer."

"Planning this wedding is going to be easier than picking out a dress," I say, grinning.

"Is it possible to marry you tomorrow?" he asks half joking.

"What do you mean? Have a private ceremony like Jason and Cali instead of a traditional wedding?"

Daniel put his teacup down and leaned forward in his chair. "Yes, but with a twist. How about we invite Jason and Cali over for dinner next weekend. We'll have the service right here in the house with just the two of them, then do a proper wedding service and reception whenever we can set a date at the golf club for family," he says. Daniel's eyes focus directly on me, and a half grin emerges on his lips. "Liv, I've wanted you to be my wife since the end of our second date. Do we really have to wait several more months to make me the happiest man on earth?"

I stammer briefly as I think about what he has suggested. Like Daniel, I'm eager to tie the knot. No question in my mind. "Yes," I blurt out, finally. "Yes, let's do it!" I jump up out of my chair to hug him.

"All settled then?" Daniel looks very content as he picks up his cellphone to call Jason, while my mind races over the details of what to wear, where in the house we'd get married, or even if we could get a JP by next weekend. I also have to decide whether to call my mom and dad and Grace to tell them or just wait until we have a full service for family and friends later on in the year. I decide I can't not have the service in the house without Grace present.

After only three hours of discussing the more minute details, all that is left to do is buy a wedding dress and the rings. Daniel has already decided where we'll honeymoon and is keeping that information secret as a surprise for me. I'm sure whatever he has planned will be spectacular.

The materials for the custom retractable pool dome arrive the following Wednesday afternoon, and tomorrow a crew from the manufacturer are supposed to arrive to build it on site starting first thing in the morning. I turned the pool heater on and hope that by Friday afternoon the pool temperature would be perfect, and the retractable dome installation would be complete.

I'm afraid to ask Daniel what something like this cost and decide I really didn't want to know because if feels like money is flying out the door at a speed I can't control. Hopefully it wasn't as expensive as Daniel's new convertible Jag. And God only knows what we'll spend on the wedding rings and my dress.

No matter how hard I try to understand, the thought of having the insane amount of money Daniel has amassed at my disposal continues to baffle me. We could never spend that much money in our lifetimes, although I do know a large portion of it is slated for philanthropic purposes.

Sandra A. Sigfusson

Chapter Thirty-Six | The Pool Party

When Daniel arrives home from his meeting with Jason and Michael at four-fifteen, he notices me lying naked on a pool float with my eyes closed, enjoying my wedding gift pool dome exactly as it was intended. I hear him enter and I open my eyes.

"Well, isn't this a brilliant surprise," he says as he pours two glasses of wine for us to enjoy. He stands at the edge of the pool, inspects the erection of the dome and nods in agreement. "Great investment," he utters and smiles.

He removes his clothes and stands at the edge of the pool admiring me with nothing but two glasses of wine in his hands.

Daniel sits himself down at the edge of the pool on the stairs and clears his throat to get my attention. He always has my attention, but that's my little secret. I float over to him and take one of the wine glasses from his hand.

"What's the verdict, Daniel?"

"Impressive. You have the most brilliant ideas. How long have you been in here by yourself?" he asks.

"Your healthy libido never ceases to amaze me," I tease as his erection—big as life itself—dictates his mood without the need for conversation. "I've only been here a few minutes. I called your office to see what time you left so I'd be ready for you when you arrived."

"You sexy minx. I love it. You can greet me home this way every day," he says and wriggles his eyebrows at me. "How was your day, love?"

I roll off my floating lounger and take my glass of wine from his hand. A quick kiss is in order before I answer him. "Peaceful, yet I got a lot of little things accomplished around the house, I say as I set my glass on the edge of the pool. It is kind of funny that once you move into a new place you put things in spaces you think will be perfect then realize that there is a better place for them elsewhere. I must have puttered around here for four hours doing just that. I also looked at wedding gowns online and talked with Grace for about twenty minutes at lunch. How was your day?"

"Good. Mike has two new clients and so we were doing a collaborated overview of what they'd invested in prior, and where they might be best to invest to grow their net worth a little faster. It's a bit of a temperamental market at the moment. We came up with a game plan that I think his clients will like."

I climb onto Daniel's lap and rest my arms on his shoulders while he sits halfway down the pool stairs, submerged up to his chest in the warm water.

"I got my first phone call from Roman today," I say sombrely. "He's looking for a newlywed couple who haven't been seen since the day they arrived at their hotel in Roatán. He said it's been twenty-four hours since they were last at the hotel, so he's hoping he can find them before anything terrible happens. Assuming they might be in danger, of course."

"Are you upset? I'm sorry, Liv," he says, now angry with himself. "I didn't think about how the stories of who he'd be looking for would affect you. I'm so bloody stupid."

"No, Daniel. It's fine. It upset me at first, but I'm okay. Us helping people is healing to me. I'm just praying that he finds them quickly. He promised to keep me posted on his progress."

"All we can do is hope," he agrees. "And if Roman can't find them, nobody can." He pauses to look me in my eyes. "Can I get you something?" he asks, tenderly kissing my shoulder. "Are you sure you're okay?"

"Yes, I'm good. I'm just glad to see you here with me enjoying this amazing pool and the new dome. I mean, how fucking cool is this!" I exclaim. "Put your wine glass down and swim with me."

We swim together back and forth along the length of the pool three times. He tries to keep up with me, but my expert swimming skills outmatched his. I know that swimming will be an excellent exercise for Daniel's pelvis and hope I can convince him to use the pool regularly as part of his ongoing physiotherapy.

We return for a rest to the shallow end by the stairs. As he stands in the water waist deep, I reach down to hold Mr. Magnificent in my hand and stroke him in the warm water, hoping I can satisfy him like I did up at the lake.

Daniel gently eases my hand from his fullness and drapes my hand over his shoulder. "Lay back in the water," he urges. I nod and lay back, floating on the surface with my legs loosely encircling his waist. Gradually, he eases his fingers across my thighs, stroking the soft skin between my legs.

I've been waiting for him to come home so we could make love in the pool. The thought has aroused me for the past hour. Tugging my floating body closer to him, he teases my aching clit with the pad of his thumb rubbing gently in a circular motion. All my senses are heightened and my arousal reaching its pique before he guides his fingers deep inside of me. Teasing me as he watches my face express the deep pleasure of his movements within me. I close my eyes because I cannot focus on anything but this delicious sensation. Then he begins plunging his fingers into me faster and faster knowing that what I crave is coming to fruition. My lips mouth the word yes over and over at his expert fingering. I don't know whether to let go or demand that he fills me with Mr. Magnificent before I lose all control.

"I want you inside of me."

Daniel smiles. "Do you, now? How badly, Liv? Tell me you want my hard as fuck cock in your wet pussy."

My reply is barely audible. "Let me come with you inside of me. You have one second to decide."

He pulls his fingers out to massage my clit again just as I was about to come. He's edging me. "Damn you," I whisper.

"All you have to do is tell me how much you need me to fuck you and then I'll let you come." He lifts my legs up over his shoulders and presses his lips over my clit, sucking and flicking his tongue repeatedly until my legs go rigid from getting so close to coming again.

"Hm," he moans.

I can feel his voice vibrate my tender flesh against his lips as he asks me, "Are you ready for me, Liv?"

I nod with my head half submerged in the water. Daniel guides my floating body in a smooth motion so that I can hold on to the handrail that runs down the middle of the pool stairs. He grips himself firmly then presses his rigid cock into me while gripping my thighs in his strong hands. Each press is a little deeper, a little firmer, a little more satisfying for both of us. The water splashes gently around us in a rhythm emulating the waves lapping at the shoreline. My heart beats at the same measure of his cock moving in and out of me. I feel a sense of euphoria flow through my body from this amazing moment. Desire, fulfillment and pure love saturate the air we breathe, and I feel intoxicated by his need for me. I am primed and ready to let go and just seconds later I release around him.

He continues to fuck me, staring deep into my eyes and then says, "Do you have any idea how much I love fucking you? Every time I think I've died and gone to Heaven."

His words, crass and unabashed, fill me with joy. He holds my thighs tight as he releases and I let go of the handrail to float freely while he's still inside of me. He pulls out slowly and leans forward to lift me up. His hand caresses my cheek before his lips show me how much he loves me. "You intoxicate me. You just feel so fucking good. This should be illegal."

"I don't ever want to miss a second of the pleasure of Mr. Magnificent inside of me," I say, slipping my fingers through his wet hair and locking my eyes his on his.

He holds me firm and close, giving me love bites on the base of my neck and shoulder. "You are glorious," he whispers. A few moments later he says, "Wait a second … is that your secret name for my cock? Mr. Magnificent?" He widens his eyes at me and sports a curious grin.

I burst out laughing as my cheeks heat with embarrassment. "Yes, yes, it is. That's what I call the monster between your legs," I reply, now covering my mouth with my hand in disbelief that the words slipped from my lips.

"Brilliant," he manages to say between hearty chuckles.

"I can't believe I let that slip out. I was going to keep that secret forever," I mumble.

"I love it," he says. "And you are very soon to be my Mrs. Magnificent. From now on we will refer to each other privately as Mr. and Mrs. M.," he adds, continuing to chuckle. "And I'll be damned if you didn't just give me another reason for a hard-on, woman." Daniel spins me around in his arms and then dunks us both under the water as he kisses me.

We surface with a splash to come up for air. "You're a crazy man." I stroke my fingers through my soaked hair and then cup my hand around the stubbled edge of his chin. "Have a sip of wine, Danny boy. I have a question for you."

"Do you now? And what would that be?"

"Does it bother you that you've never had your own children?"

He ponders that question with all seriousness. "Honestly, Liv, yes. But I fear that ship has sailed, and I've come to accept it. Why do you ask?"

"You talk fondly about Ian, but you mentioned that he never resolved to calling you his dad. It seems to me that it was a bit of a sting to you."

He thinks on that for a few seconds too and nods. "Perhaps. But I was by far more of a father to him than anyone else in his life. I earned that title but never suggested that he address me as such. That was his decision to make."

"Ah, well. I might be able to change that for you."

"You've spoken to Ian? When did he call? Does he need my help?"

"No, no. I'm not talking about Ian. I'm saying that one day very soon there will be someone who *will* call you Dad."

Daniel shakes his head, smirks, and asks, "What the devil are you playing at, Liv?"

"We're pregnant!"

"No. Really? Are you sure?"

"Yes! I say smiling brightly at him. His shock at the news hangs in him even as I kiss him. His expression conveys uncertainty as he wraps his head around the fact that his dream of being a father is now a reality.

I slowly lean back separating our lips and search his eyes. "Are you ok? Talk to me, Daniel."

"Fu-cking hell. I'm going to be a father. I'm-going-to-be-a-father!"

My face lights up again. "Yes! You are going to be a father!"

"You didn't drink any wine, did you?"

"No. I put it on the edge of the pool deck."

"Okay. Brilliant. No more drinking for either of us. We're in this together. How far along are we?"

I giggle. "We are four weeks. I only found out yesterday. And I think you can have at least one glass to celebrate the news. I can have a glass of sparkling water."

“Right. He reaches for his glass, has a quick sip and then swims back up to me. “There’s no time limit on how long we stay here making sweet love to each other, is there?”

“Nope,” I say and laugh with a heart full of joy. “But there is one favour I have to ask of you.”

“What’s that love?”

“Let’s have the wedding here at the house with all our family and friends next month. Then we can announce our baby news after we’re married.

I get the most beautiful smile and kiss from the man with the warm glow.

“Anything for you, Mrs. M.”

The End.

Please visit my website at https://www.sandrasigfusson.com

for more information about my novels, and where to connect with me on social media.

Your reviews are greatly appreciated!

About the Author:

Sandra was born in Vancouver, British Columbia, Canada. Her artistic nature led to an avid interest in art and photography from an early age, and that passion continues today. Her foray into the realm of writing romance novels started as a personal challenge to write a romantic made-for-television movie script in her spare time, but instead it became her first full-length novel. Sandra was nominated for a Society of Voice Arts and Sciences award (SOVAS) in 2024 for her audiobook production of The Irishman's Promise for which she wrote, cast, directed, and engineered. Sandra is also a proud member of The Writers' Union of Canada.

www.ingramcontent.com/pod-product-compliance
Lightning Source LLC
LaVergne TN
LVHW010644110826
845149LV00014B/2941

9781989829257